PRAISE FOR *WITNESS*

'It is no secret that I love anything this lady writes. I find that her style carries me along beautifully. From the very first moment I felt Rebecca's tension I did not breathe properly until I read the very last word. As ever I was entranced by the sharp characterisations that convinced me I knew these people personally. This book was thrilling, tense, exciting, dark and twisted in the best possible way. It is only now, the following day, that I am able to breathe normally again.'

—Angela Marsons

'A dark yet compelling domestic drama that had me hooked straight off. The tension built up and up, the fear and sense of dread layered throughout, and the ending had me breathless. I devoured every page.'

—Mel Sherratt

WITNESS

ALSO BY
CAROLINE MITCHELL

DC Jennifer Knight

WITNESS

CAROLINE MITCHELL

THOMAS & MERCER

Published by Thomas & Mercer, Seattle

www.apub.com

Amazon, the Amazon logo, and Thomas & Mercer are trademarks of Amazon.com, Inc., or its affiliates.

ISBN-13: 9781503941502
ISBN-10: 1503941507

Cover design © blacksheep-uk.com

Printed in the United States of America

'Beware the fury of a patient man'

John Dryden

For Neil

PROLOGUE

12th September 2005

'Stay away from me,' I cried, shielding my face with a bloodied hand as the beam of a torch found me. A strong female voice responded, lowering the streak of light to the floor.

'It's the police. You're safe now.' The officer spoke in a Jamaican accent. The late September night was making her sweat in her fluorescent jacket, her eyes wide as she took in the scene.

'Where's the light switch?' a male officer said, his flash lamp strobing through the darkness of my home. I blinked against the sudden glare as the light flicked on overhead. My Tiffany lamp lay smashed on its side, and had plunged us into blackness. The policewoman was still speaking to me, but her words were muffled, as if she were talking underwater. My head spun. I was drowning in confusion. It wasn't until her fingers dug into my shoulder that I could distinguish her words.

'Why don't you come over here and let the paramedics do their job?'

Paramedics . . . It felt like forever since I had made the call. I cradled Jake's head in my lap, the tips of my fingers making blood-stained patterns on his greying skin. Glassy-eyed, he stared unblinking at the ceiling.

'No,' I said, as the woman took my elbow to pull me up. 'I've got to stay with him.' But his skin was cold. So very cold, and something sticky and damp had soaked into my linen trousers. My boyfriend had bought them for me, on a rare trip to London. *You can tell a lot about a woman by the clothes she wears*, he had said. I pulled my cardigan closed as his presence infiltrated my brain. But not quick enough to hide the yellowing bruises on my collarbone. *I should have worn my polo neck, but I wasn't expecting visitors . . .* My thoughts were interrupted by a calming voice, and I stared numbly at the bearded man crouching down beside me. His green uniform was grubby, but his eyes were kind. Eyes that had witnessed this sort of thing too many times before.

'C'mon, love, let's get you onto the sofa.'

Gloved hands gently moved Jake's head to one side and a puff of air left his lungs, escaping through his parted lips in a deadened moan. Faltering, I leaned gratefully against the paramedic helping me to my feet. My legs fizzed angrily with pins and needles, and I limped to the couch. The paramedic joined his colleagues, who were kneeling around Jake's body, one urgently plugging the stab wound as another unpacked a defibrillator. The female officer and two male officers gathered around me, their radios buzzing like a nest of angry wasps. The sound penetrated my brain, and I allowed myself to fall deep into a distant fog.

'Did you make the call?' the female officer asked, her voice sounding very far away as she crouched down beside me. 'Are you Rebecca?'

I nodded numbly, my eyes on the casualty on the other side of the room. The CPR that was being administered expelled even more blood. It pooled on the mat and seeped through the cracks in my varnished floorboards. The third paramedic, balding and in his fifties, attached the pads from the defibrillator. A button was pressed, and a mechanical voice repeated the command, *stand clear*. My television flashed in the background, as a news commentator reported a pile-up on the M25.

His report was cut short by one of the officers, who jabbed at the mute button on the remote control.

I shivered, then realised why I felt so cold. The sticky crimson substance coating my trousers had lost its heat. A wave of nausea swept over me as I imagined Jake's blood soaking into my pores. Inhaling a shuddering breath, I rose, only to be grabbed by both arms.

'Where are you off to?' a gruff police officer said. He towered over me, and his glare expressed little sympathy.

I turned to the female officer. 'Changed,' I blurted, my words disjointed, my eyes welling with tears. 'Got to get . . . changed. Got to get . . .' I was powerless to stop the repetition of words. 'Changed. Got to . . .'

In the corner the machine blared *life extinct* in a cold mechanical voice. Tears and snot ran unbidden down my face as the meaning became clear. I wasn't thinking. Shock had hit me hard and I didn't know what I was doing. My knees gave way, and I fell back on the leather sofa, crying for the life lost. 'He's dead, oh God, he's dead,' I whimpered. All I could hear was the machine declaring *life extinct*, and the police officer squeezing my arm, asking me over and over, 'Who did this? Tell me, who did this?'

The cavity that housed my brain felt stuffed with cotton wool, and I forced the words out of my lips. 'Please don't ask me. I can't. I just can't.'

The gruff officer bowed heads with the paramedic and it seemed they came to the same conclusion. Jake Barrows, aged twenty-two, had been murdered. I was only two years older, and now a key witness.

The next twenty minutes passed in a blur of police updates, photographs and crime-scene investigators invading my home. Surely this wasn't really happening? This scene was more suited to a movie set in Beverly Hills, instead of my cosy Clacton house. But this wasn't my home anymore. It was a crime scene, and the female officer, now known to me as PC Clarke, stressed the importance of my testimony. Questions were fired like bullets, the police officers' observations scribbled into black-leather pocket notebooks. I was told CID were on their way. That was how the police worked. Now was not the time for sympathy. Now was the time for action, and they had to act fast if they had any hope of catching Jake's killer. And still the questions came. *Where is the murder weapon? Was there anyone else involved?* I scrunched my fists. Jake's blood had dried into my skin, making it feel like tight red leather. I pushed a long string of hair from my cheek; from the corner of my eye I could see that the blond strand was tainted with red. My breathing accelerated, and the urge to strip and shower returned with overwhelming force. The alien red substance was everywhere, crawling on my skin and hair like angry red fire ants.

'Please,' I cried, gripping PC Clarke's fingers, making her wince. 'I need to get clean. Please let me change. It's in my hair.'

The woman pulled a hair band from her braids and handed it over. 'Here, use this to tie it back. Forensics won't take long. Then we'll get you out of here. Now how about you tell me what happened?'

I bit my lip. I had learned to stay quiet. But my mouth seemed to take on a life of its own as the words tumbled out.

'Jake's a colleague. We teach at the same school,' I said, unable to place him in the past tense. 'My boyfriend . . . he thought we were having an affair. He came home from work early . . .' A sob caught in my throat and I wiped my face with the back of my sleeve. 'Oh God, Jake's dead, isn't he? He's really dead?'

'What's your boyfriend's name, Rebecca?' the woman said. 'Where is he now?'

I shook my head, slowly returning to reality as self-preservation kicked in. 'I've said too much.' Fresh tears began to fall, and I patted my pockets for something to wipe my eyes.

PC Clarke handed me a tissue. 'We'll keep you safe. Just tell us who he is, and we'll have him arrested. He won't hurt you anymore.'

An image of Solomon flashed in my mind, standing over me, his face hard and cold. I could see him clearly, his steel-grey eyes shooting me a warning look. Was I strong enough to give evidence against him? A sudden rush of cold fear enveloped me. I shuddered. 'I'm as good as dead,' I sobbed, my voice low. 'He's going to kill me.'

'In which case he needs to be stopped,' PC Clarke replied.

'But you don't understand,' I said, my red-painted fingernails imprinting half-moon crescents in my palms. 'He's . . . he's one of yours. His father's a superintendent in the police.' The room fell silent, and the officers stiffened in response. My heart lurched in my chest. What if they didn't believe what I had to say? I put my hand to my mouth, wishing I could suck the words back in.

PC Clarke took my hands in hers, her brown eyes locking on to mine. The vibrancy of her Jamaican accent made her words seem all the more genuine. 'Now you listen to me, girl. I don't care if his father's the damned prime minister, we'll keep you safe.'

Safe. The word hung tantalisingly in the air, and I tried to imagine a fresh start. Not having to account for my time or whereabouts. Being able to make my own decisions, choose my own clothes. An escape route from the mental torture Solomon inflicted on a daily basis. PC Clarke was offering me sanctuary, but was I strong enough? There was no way I could tell anyone where I was going; I would have to do it alone. I wrapped my hands around my stomach and leaned forward, contemplating two parallel futures. The argument flew back and forth in my brain like a ping-pong ball. I could stay with Solomon, get married as planned, have a family. Perhaps then he would change. Or I could speak to the police, have him put away, and just disappear. Leave him to rot and start again. It was all he deserved. He was a murderer, after all. I found my lips parting, the words tumbling out in a sigh of relief.

'He's my fiancé . . . His name is Solomon Kemp.'

CHAPTER ONE
SOLOMON

2016

The computer monitor reflected in Solomon's designer glasses as he settled behind his workstation. It felt good to be back in his old swivel chair, although technology had advanced considerably, and it had taken him a while to get the hang of the new programs in place. The smell of his mother's cooking wafted up the stairs and in through the crack in the door. He rolled his chair over the wooden floor, slamming it shut with his foot. It was roast chicken, which was marginally better than the prison muck he had consumed over the last ten years. He flicked on the monitor to his left, and watched as the vision of his mother stirring the bubbling pots came into view.

At least he had been able to pay his respects at his father's grave. He grinned at the memory. He had stood with legs spread, his steaming hot piss catching the sunlight as it splattered on the withered cemetery flowers. And now here he was, the prodigal son, taking his place at the table.

He had learned of his father's death from a letter, after his second year inside. *It was the stress,* his mother had written, *the shame of having a son in prison that caused it.* Nothing new there. His father had been ashamed of him for most of his natural life. Tempting as it was, he had turned down the opportunity of day release for the burial. A police funeral was the last thing Solomon needed. Rows of men in uniform, giving him the eye, acting as if they were better than him. Being in public would have been too much to bear. Especially without Rebecca by his side. Solomon's jaw clenched. He had given up the last ten years of his life because of her, and she had repaid him in the most despicable way. At first, he was unable to comprehend it. Gradually his disbelief turned to hatred that burned white-hot from the confines of his prison cell. Prison was not kind to the son of a police superintendent, particularly one that had been privately educated. Ironically, it was his experience of boarding school that got him through it. He was no stranger to bullying, beatings and sexual abuse. It was his quiet anger and his ability to dissociate himself that kept him alive. Solomon didn't scream or plead when his fellow inmates inflicted their brutality. When he couldn't escape, he simply went limp, a rag doll for their amusement. He could still smell their breath as they backed him into a corner, hear their moronic jibes as their greasy fingernails dug into his skin.

Solomon stifled a sob, shaking away the memory. Tears were for the weak. His physical and mental scars paled into insignificance when he brought Rebecca to the forefront of his mind. Planning his revenge made him feel empowered, and he'd had ten long years to work out how he was going to repay her misdeeds.

He glanced back at the monitor, and found his mother's sunken face staring back at him, glass of sherry in hand. Her beady eyes seemed to plead with the camera, the corners of her mouth turned downwards in her customary frown. She hadn't known what to do with herself after her domineering husband died. She was lucky Solomon was there to step into the breach. She turned to press the button on the walkie-talkie, which screeched into life on the desk in front of him. 'Your dinner's ready, son.'

'Fine,' Solomon said. 'Put it in the microwave. I'll have it later.'

She turned back to the monitor. The hint of a German accent still floated from her lips, even after all these years. 'I was wondering if it would be all right if I popped out to see Edna, two doors down. She's been poorly and I thought I could bring her a slice of *Apfelstrudel*.'

Ah, apple strudel, his mother's signature dish. Solomon spat the words into the receiver as he pressed it to his mouth. 'What time is it?'

His mother flinched. After taking a deep breath, she turned over her left arm and pulled up the sleeve of her cardigan. 'Oh. It's five o'clock. I just thought . . .'

Solomon screamed, sending the radio skittering across the floor. Throwing open his bedroom door, he roared his instructions. 'What did I tell you? No visiting after four. Get with the fucking programme or I'll put you on lockdown. Understand?'

Tentatively his mother shuffled into the hall, daring a brief glance upwards. 'I'm sorry, *Mäuschen*, I won't ask again.'

Solomon tutted at the smashed radio on his bedroom floor. Silly bitch. This was her fault. The price of a new one would come out of her allowance. The corner of his mouth twitched in a smirk. Now she could feel what it was like to be a rat in a cage. Constantly monitored, not even able to take a shit without someone watching. Not that he wanted to watch her drop her droopy knickers to defecate. She was just a bit player. He ran his fingers through his tousled brown hair, and rolled his chair over to monitor one. *All the world is a stage*, he thought, *and here lie the main players*.

He clicked the mouse, and the image of a child flooded onto the screen, playing on her bedroom floor. It would be worth the sacrifice of leaving home to be near her, and with the sophisticated computer equipment he was bringing on board, he could monitor his mother's movements remotely – when he wasn't busy toying with Rebecca, that was. He had already visited her home unnoticed. He could easily do it again. He stared unblinkingly at the small figure, a tune playing in his head. The same tune he used to mentally hum when he was getting pounded by his fellow inmates: *Hallelujah . . . Hallelujah . . . Hallelujah.*

'Ah, little Lottie.' He tapped the screen, his cracked lips broadening in a smile. 'I'm coming for you.'

CHAPTER TWO
REBECCA

2016

Leaning on my hands and knees, I peered past the pairs of old leather shoes and shone my iPhone torch under the sunken double bed. Curled tightly in a ball on top of a brown leather suitcase was Margaret Bowen's cat, Smudge, her black fur coated in dust bunnies. A low growl emanated from the base of her throat as the blast of light transformed her eyes into demonic yellow orbs.

'Here, puss puss puss,' I said, in my most coaxing voice. Smudge hissed as I extended my arm, taking a swipe at my fingers. I glanced back to see Margaret's wrinkly brown support tights, her two feet plugged into what looked like her dead husband's slippers.

'You'll need this, see,' she said in her thick Welsh brogue, jabbing my boots with the end of a broom. One advantage of being small was that I could easily wriggle into tight spaces, but today I hoped to keep my hand intact. I withdrew from the cat, brushing the dust from my cropped chestnut hair as I stood. I did not miss my dyed blond locks. My reinvention had helped me begin again and, ten years on, I could not have felt any more at home. A sneeze tickled my nose, and I held it in as I turned to Margaret. She stood with one hand on her narrow hip, the other clutching the broom. Her well-lined face was set in determination, her short grey hair wiry and unkempt. Since her husband's passing, Margaret was too busy tending the cats she rescued to fuss about her appearance. I turned my attention back to the broom, the ends thick with cobwebs.

'I'm not sure that's the right tool for the job,' I said, trying to sound professional. 'We've got a humane trap back at the veterinary centre. I'm sure we can coax her into it with a little bit of food.'

'Food? How can she have surgery if she has food?' Margaret said.

Heat rose to my cheeks. Schoolgirl error. I should have known better by now.

'Here,' Margaret said, pulling back the top blanket and launching it in my direction. The smell of cat pee overwhelmed me, and I quickly wrestled it away from my face.

'Throw this on her when she scoots out,' she said. 'I'll rattle the broom under the bed.' As Margaret was the owner of eleven cats, I gave in to her superior knowledge.

Five minutes later, Smudge was safely bundled in the pet carrier on the front seat of the Land Rover, and I was driving back to the surgery. She must have sensed that she was being taken to be spayed, judging by her evil glare from behind the caged door. Catching errant cats was one of the many tasks assigned to me as my husband's part-time receptionist-cum-dogsbody. I glanced up through the muddied windscreen at the dark storm clouds, the sun a dim spark as it set behind the rain-soaked hills. Twilight had descended, bringing with it the threat of the darkness that fell sharply in the winter. I flicked on the headlights, keeping them dipped. Pontyferry was not graced with streetlights like my old suburban home in Essex, and even now, after almost ten years, I approached the country roads with caution as the night drew in. You never knew what you would meet around blind corners: unguarded farm machinery, a herd of sheep, or a quad bike at full speed, its driver racing home to beat the spill of rain. I bumped along the potholed lane, glancing in the rear and side mirrors. It was silly really, after all this time. As if anyone would be watching me here, in the middle of nowhere. But the ghosts of the past were never far away and, in the depths of my mind, a tune whistled. *Hallelujah.* I shuddered, turning the car heating up to full blast. The nightmares had returned, waking me in the night and haunting my days. Signalling at the junction, I swivelled my head left and right before turning off for the road that would take me to the Benedict & Walker veterinary surgery. Old habits died hard, and I was one of the few residents who bothered with indicators down the lonely country lanes.

'Got her,' I said triumphantly as I placed the carrier on the freshly scrubbed counter. 'Hiding under the bed she was.'

'Not the broomstick-and-quilt method?' Sean said. His accent was much less pronounced than Margaret's, softened after a five-year stint travelling.

'Yes, a very pissy quilt, I may add, with extra dust.' I brushed an imaginary cobweb out of my hair. Those things scared me more than any feral cat.

Sean placed his hands on my shoulders. 'I would have brought over the trap, you know. You only had to ask.'

Rugged from years of outdoor work, my husband still sent a tingle down my spine.

'I'm fine, honestly,' I said. 'I'm going to head off now, make a start on the tea. Do you want me to divert the phone so I can pick up any calls?'

'Yes, it shouldn't take too long. We'll keep her overnight and have her back home tomorrow. She'll be terrorising the other cats in no time . . .'

Geoffrey Benedict, Sean's partner in the practice, joined us in the surgery, sipping tea from a chipped enamel mug. He was a similar age to Margaret, but looked a whole lot better for it. His eyes were crinkled in amusement, and his silvery beard embellished the pink bloom rising in his cheeks. I loved his collection of bow ties; today he was wearing tweed. Geoffrey was such a jolly man; it was not difficult to see why he had played the part of the village Santa for seven years in a row (all he was missing was the expansive belly, but a cushion and a length of string soon took care of that). Semi-retired, he seemed to enjoy spending time in the surgery, and we were grateful for his help after Sean bought into the partnership. 'And how is the lovely Becky?' Geoffrey said. 'Did you manage to escape unscathed?'

'I did,' I replied proudly. 'Although I had a feeling Margaret was hoping you would make an appearance.'

Geoffrey smiled. 'The old girl's not made of wood, is she? So how are we being paid today? Timber? Eggs? Sexual favours?'

'Eggs,' I blurted with a laugh, pointing to the basket I had rested near the door.

'Omelette for tea tonight then,' Sean said, with a wry smile. He made enough money from the farmers to accept some bartering. He was too in love with the outdoors to spend all his time on small animals; he carried out twice-weekly surgeries as favours for the village people he had grown up with all his life. Pontyferry was a community. They looked after their own. It was one of the reasons why I chose to live here. At first I had been attracted to Portmeirion in North Wales, with its beautiful quirky buildings and breathtaking views of the coast. But a tourist hotspot would leave me vulnerable to newcomers, I thought. I needed a closed community, and the fact that I was regarded with some suspicion when I arrived in Pontyferry only endeared it to me even more. Not that it took too long to win the villagers over: for some reason they took a liking to me, the mysterious girl renting a room over the shop. And, as much as I tried to keep to myself, I warmed to them too.

So I started my new life as Becky. What had happened in the past belonged to someone else – at least that was what I tried to tell myself.

The wind roared as I made my way home on my scooter, screeching through my visor in ominous howls. Storm winds gathered, testing the naked trees lining my path, swaying them left and right until every leaf had been dislodged. Winters were much harder in Wales than in the flatlands of Essex. But nothing could beat the smell of the heather on the rolling hills in late summer, the bracken-covered slopes, or the soft kiss of the sun in the aftermath of a storm. If only I wasn't living in Solomon's shadow – though it was true that my paranoia had eased somewhat over the years. I truly believed I was past all that. Why, then, had the nightmares returned?

Now, I felt as jumpy as when I first arrived, and not just for me. I didn't want to be dragged into a past I had tried hard to forget. But the past has a way of catching up with you, and I could not ignore the truth. Solomon knew my secret. And he would not rest until I paid for it.

CHAPTER THREE

REBECCA

2016

Bear was doing that thing where he told me off for leaving him. The sound he produced was a mixture between a bark and a growl, a *bowww owww, owww*, and he danced on the slate flagstones as his whole body wriggled instead of his tail. Bear was two years old, and almost up to my waist. He came from a long line of Newfoundland dogs that Sean had owned since he was a toddler, all named Bear because, in the mind of a toddler, that's what big brown dogs were – huge fluffy teddy bears come to life. I ruffled his soft brown fur, squeezing past him as I removed my red polka-dot helmet. I had bought it at the same time as my beloved Vespa, the siren-red scooter I bumbled about on whenever the weather would allow. My helmet safely on its hook, I pulled my key from the thick oak door and locked it from the inside, shoving the bolts and deadlock across. It was hardly any wonder Sean's younger sister, Rhian, looked at me funny, given how safe Pontyferry was.

'Are we expecting guests? Freddy Krueger? Michael Myers? Or is Hannibal Lecter joining us for tea today?' Rhian grinned, leaning on her crutches with a comical look on her face. She was strikingly pretty, with cherry-red hair bundled haphazardly on her head, and bright red lipstick to match.

I hung my jacket on the driftwood coat hook, hastily changing the subject. 'Your MS playing up today? I hope Lottie's not been too much of a handful.'

Rhian had been diagnosed with multiple sclerosis in her early twenties, and five years on was still learning to cope with it. Some days were better than others, but she never allowed it to get her down.

'Lottie's been a star; it's big old Bear here that forgets when I'm wobbly on my legs,' she said, her point proved as he nuzzled her jeans with his head.

'If you're not up for surgery tomorrow, I can step in.'

'And miss Geoffrey force-feeding me cookies and mugs of whisky-laced tea? What's not to like?'

It wasn't that easy and Rhian knew it. Sean treated his sister as if she was still in perfect health, asking for help with the animals, juggling calls, sorting out the accounts, and driving around on errands. But Rhian could hold her own, and outswear the most awkward of clients. We had come to the perfect arrangement, taking turns working in the surgery and sharing the child care. The allowance Rhian received helping out with Lottie meant she could afford to keep her flat in Powys. Sean and I had spent the last five years renovating the farmhouse the siblings had grown up in, but she seldom stayed over, preferring her own independence.

'I've got something for you,' I said, riffling in my bag for a black velvet box. I had brought it to the surgery so she wouldn't find it and spoil the surprise. 'I finished it last night.' I pressed the box into her hand. 'If you don't like it, just say, and I'll make you something else.'

She peeked inside to see a small handmade globe containing a dandelion seed. A tiny silver key hung on the chain.

'It opens the bottom of the globe,' I said, as she lifted the chain from the box and stared, mesmerised, as the glass caught the light. 'Nothing can keep your spirit trapped – you own the key.'

Rhian carefully placed it back in the box before throwing one arm around me for a hug. Tears brimmed in her eyes, and I was relieved that my hard work had touched her in some way.

'Oh, I love it,' she said. 'It means the world to me.' She hugged me again. 'You're so clever. You should really sell these online.'

I smiled at the woman I had come to regard as a sister. 'They're one of a kind, just like you.'

I saw her out, reluctantly leaving the door unbolted after Sean texted me to say he was on his way home.

'Where's my hug bug?' I said, bending down to receive a sticky squeeze from Lottie, who was licking the remnants of a jam sandwich from her lips. Her aunty Rhian was a pushover when it came to her demands, unable to resist her angelic blue eyes.

'Have you been eating in your room again?' I asked, and was answered with a definitive shake of the head.

'No, Mummy, in the kitchen,' she said, sucking her fingers clean. 'It just sticks to me, that's all.'

'Hmm,' I said, doubtfully. My daughter had a queer love of spiders, since watching the movie *Charlotte's Web*. She could often be found 'feeding' them by placing crumbs in their delicate webs. I was constantly checking her room for unwanted inhabitants, having to release them into the wild with the promise that not one of their eight legs would be harmed. 'Best you wash your hands instead of licking them. Do you want me to—'

'I'm all grown up, Mummy. I can do it myself,' she responded, shoving her Anna plush doll under her armpit and marching to the bathroom. Lottie loved *Frozen* as much as *Charlotte's Web*. Like many four-year-olds, her duvet, wallpaper, and even the curtains in her bedroom were a tribute to the Disney movie she had watched hundreds of times over.

I left her singing as she dabbled in the bathroom sink upstairs, and walked across the landing to my bedroom. I flicked on the light switch, the afterglow of Lottie's hug dissipating as I entered the room. My heart fluttered in my chest. Everything looked as I had left it, but there was something I couldn't quite put my finger on. A presence. I sniffed the air. Was that a faint whiff of aftershave? Or the memory of a scent invoked by my paranoia? It was doubtful Rhian had entered the bedroom. I rolled the idea around in my head as I inspected my bedroom. Even if Rhian was well enough to venture upstairs, she would never invade our privacy. I held my breath as I pulled the floral quilt back from my bed, scattering the assortment of pillows and cushions I had assembled that morning. I didn't know what I was looking for, but my personal space felt tainted. I turned my attention to my dressing table, checking its contents. Make-up, the half-empty perfume bottle, a wide-toothed comb, all exactly as they had been that morning. I stared at the Charlie bear Sean had bought me for my birthday two months before. Instead of facing the door in greeting, his head was swivelled around, his gaze resting on the bed. A prickle of fear overcame me. Someone had been in my room. Tentatively I reached out to touch his chocolate-coloured fur, almost jumping out of my skin as a figure crept in behind me.

'Sweetie, you frightened the life out of me,' I gasped, my fingers finding my mother's silver locket as I clutched my hand to my chest.

'Sorry, Mummy,' Lottie said, her eyes wide and remorseful. 'I didn't mean to.'

My attempts at questioning her proved useless. Lottie denied entering my room or playing with the teddy. I told myself I was being silly, that she had most likely touched it when Rhian was downstairs. I peeped through the curtains as the headlights of Sean's Land Rover flashed down the winding lane that led to our home. It was time to make supper, and I put all thoughts of an unwelcome visitor behind me.

CHAPTER FOUR

Diary Entry: 17th April 2005

You've been sitting on my bedside table for some time now, whispering to me to confide my innermost secrets. When Mum presented you to me, I felt a pang of disappointment. I had asked for a piece of art for my birthday, something to remember her by. We both knew it could be her last present. A vintage journal hardly seemed fitting for such a momentous occasion. Only my mother could spend a whopping two hundred pounds on such a thing and present it as art. But then I took a closer look, and fell in love as the meaning behind her gift became clear. I drew you to my nose, breathing in the scent of antique hand-dyed leather, and stroked the heart-shaped silver lock. A vivid magenta, you were different to anything I'd ever owned. Your spine crackled when you opened, revealing warm off-white pages just calling out for my words. Mum smiled, her eyes knowing. She was providing me with a confidante, someone to turn to for the rough times ahead. Yet she made a rule. What Mum and I have will always live in my heart. But my journal is to be filled with new experiences, relationships and fresh starts. And so here we are. I've finally found an entry worthy enough to stain your beautiful pages. The day I plucked up all my courage and ran the London Marathon.

I thought I knew everything about this large-scale event. I'd prepared well in advance, spoken to other runners, and watched past races online. But nothing could have prepared me for the assault on my senses. At the halfway point, I felt utterly exhausted, and wondered what had possessed me to sign up for such a gruelling run. The din of the crowd rang in my ears as I approached Tower Bridge. A skinny Superman powered past, his home-made cloak dappled with the rain. I wished he was real, so he could scoop me up and fly me out of a venture that was surely destined for failure. My trainers, comfortable every day during my training, began to chafe my heels. My Lycra clothing felt like a suit of armour, and, unusually, I had a stitch in my side. Even the cheering crowds flanking my path could not help me, because they were drowned out by the cruel voice of my subconscious. *Look at that woman in the blue shorts, she must be at least sixty-five and she's twice as fast as you. You may as well give up now, before you embarrass yourself any further.* I plodded on, trying to focus on why I had slipped on my shiny Cancer Research vest to pound the streets of London alongside 38,000 other people. We all had our stories of loved ones, still here or gone, and it was their memories that spurred us on. In my case I was running for my mother, Estelle.

It's always been just me and her. I've never known it any other way. But I know that soon she will be gone, and I'll be all alone.

During the marathon, the thought filled me with a terror so deep it weakened my knees. I'm used to its nocturnal visits, but in the sea of faces and clamour of the crowd, I was overwhelmed. The smell of the streets rose up to greet me, and the noises, colours and heat merged into a kaleidoscope. A wave of dread blindsided me, mingling with my exhaustion. I staggered to a halt at the side of the road and leaned with my hands on my knees, taking slow, steady breaths. I hide my panic attacks from Mum, and there was no way I was going to allow them to consume me in public.

I brought my thoughts to a happier place, allowing the memory of the previous night to float into my mind: Mum stroking my hair as I sat by her bed, just as she did when I was six years old, humming her favourite Leonard Cohen song, *Hallelujah*. Except this time her words were wistful and filled with sorrow.

'If I could only see you settled,' she said. 'Just to know you have somebody to look out for you when I'm gone.' And then she leaned back against her pillows and sighed a soft, precious breath. 'That would mean the world to me.'

Unfortunately, all my relationships had been disasters, surely stemming from my skewed sense of what was normal. My mother's on-off relationship with my father had left me confused and bewildered as a child. So many times I had woken up to discover that he had walked out, and I never knew when I would see him again. As much as I wanted to grant my mother her wish, there was something inherently wrong with me, and I didn't know how to fix it. Instead, I had thrown myself into fundraising. When I wasn't busy with my job as a teacher, I spent my time running charity stalls, rattling collection tins and generally being the annoying young woman you crossed the road to avoid.

However, as the bodies milled around me on Marathon day, I felt overwhelmed. Running a charity stall was one thing, but completing the twenty-six-mile route through London was something entirely different.

I reached out to lean against one of the temporary railings lining the pavement, sweat trickling down my forehead, stinging my eyes and blurring my vision, when a cool bottle of water was thrust into my hand. I squinted up to see the face of a man who was tanned, fit and somewhat bemused – what my mother would call 'easy on the eye'.

Barely sweating, he nodded insistently, urging me to take a drink. He was at least a foot taller than me, with soft tousled hair and winter-grey eyes. I, on the other hand, was red-faced and scowling, my thick blond fringe pasted to my forehead. Not exactly alluring. When I spoke, it sounded like I was having an asthma attack, rather than politely thanking him for his help.

'Thanks but . . . I'm going to call it a day,' I panted, looking for a break in the fence, wondering how I was going to get back to the tube station. But my good Samaritan was not having any of it, and gently steered me back into the throng with some encouraging words. A cheer arose from the sidelines, and my face broke out in an involuntary smile. I told myself that I'd get another couple of miles out of the way, then duck out when he got fed up of me and left.

'You're going too fast . . . Rebecca,' he said, eyeing the crumpled name emblazoned on my chest. 'Pace yourself. Come on, I'll help you.'

'There's really no need,' I smiled politely, reading his name in return. Solomon. It struck me as unusual. I wanted to say it aloud, to feel the syllables roll off my tongue. I thought how unfair it was how his sweat gave off a sun-kissed sheen, while mine dripped down my face. But I plodded along beside him, the gentle pace bringing my breath back to what qualified as normal. The stitch in my side disappeared, and I barely noticed the chafe of my trainers anymore. Perhaps he was right, and I had been running too fast. But I had stopped enjoying myself five miles before and wanted to get it over with. I waited for him to leave, but for the next few miles he seemed quite happy by my side. The clouds parted, the light shower of rain evaporated into mist, and suddenly the world seemed a brighter place. But I knew I was being selfish, taking up his time. 'I don't want to keep you,' I said. 'I'll only slow you down.'

'Nah, that's OK,' he said, making my stomach flip as he dazzled me with another smile. 'I'll see you through to the finish line.' Then, glancing down at my unconvinced face, he said, 'You're doing great. Why don't we run another five miles, see how you feel then?'

Five miles. He said it as if we were popping around the corner to buy a paper. I didn't have the energy to argue, and it *was* much nicer in his company, even if I did look a fright. A man dressed as a giant pair of testicles wobbled past, and Solomon and I exchanged a glance and laughed. The next forty-five minutes were spent encouraging other competitors, and watching in awe as a man with a fridge strapped to his back kept one step ahead. Every now and again, Solomon would raise his hands in the air and begin clapping, rousing up a storm of applause from the supporters. Being in his company was magical, and as the minutes ticked by, something told me it was more than a chance encounter, like one of those first dates that you expect to be rubbish but end up turning into something good. I admired his natural ease with strangers. The sense of camaraderie brought a buoyancy to the air, and without my negative thoughts to dampen my spirit, it felt like it was turning out to be a wonderful day.

I relayed stories of my fundraising between puffs for breath, and Solomon seemed to drink in my every word. Nobody had ever looked at me with such intensity before, and I basked in the glow of his smile, trying not to worry about my appearance. But before I knew it, we were on the last stretch, and I knew our time together would soon be over. I ached all over, but it was a bittersweet pain. I wished I could have met him under different circumstances, when I was suitably preened, instead of looking like a sweaty horror-movie extra.

He checked his watch, and I caught a look of fleeting disappointment as it crossed his face.

'I've really messed up your time, haven't I?' I said, taking a swig of water.

'Look,' he said, reaching out to share the bottle. 'I've done this loads, so it doesn't matter. If I help you finish, then it'll be all worthwhile.' He drank from my bottle without wiping the mouthpiece, and I was surprised at how comfortable he was in my presence.

Like everyone else passing the hallowed finishing line, I closed my eyes and raised my tired arms in jubilance. Solomon patted me on the back, not in the least concerned about the fresh sweat drenching my vest. A sudden influx of runners came through, and we parted like waves. After catching my breath long enough to accept my medal, I turned to find him. But he was gone. I cursed my stupidity as I scanned the crowds, swallowing back my disappointment. The whole time we were running, I had spoken about myself. My fundraising, my job. Why hadn't I asked him where he lived? Or at least offered to buy him a drink? Because I was too shy, that's why, and he probably wasn't interested in me anyway. The ugly voice of my subconscious resurfaced. I was given the opportunity to make my mother happy by meeting someone nice, and I had messed it up. But that was me all over, and now here I am, wistfully recalling our time together, wishing I had been brave enough to ask for his phone number.

I've done the whole Internet stalker thing, but I don't know his surname to search his race photo online. I know how pathetic this sounds. Like a lovesick teenager, I'm desperate for a glimpse of his face. It's ridiculous, having a crush on someone I barely know. But the fact that he didn't hit on me makes him all the more attractive. Like a soppy teenager, I find myself playing love songs and dreaming about his smile. I'm wavering between believing we had a connection to the more likely reality that he stayed with me out of pity. But he was so attentive, and unlike most of the fellas I've dated, he seemed genuinely interested in what I had to say. Which is why I'm sitting on my bed, aching and blistered, praying that the fate that has been kind enough to bring us together will do me another good turn.

CHAPTER FIVE
SOLOMON

2016

Solomon chewed the Nicorette gum twice before parking it between his back teeth. The peppery kick brought focus. The trick to complimenting someone was to be polite, courteous, but not smarmy. Eye contact helped, and a generous, sincere smile. Of course, it didn't help if you had cabbage stuck between your teeth or something hanging from your nose. That's why he ensured he was perfectly groomed before he met with his new probation officer. Judging by the smell of the previous visitor, he would be a welcome change. Besides, the officer was female, so he was sure that a little flattery would soon win her over.

But his words fell on deaf ears, as she flicked, stony-faced, through his paperwork. Not that it had been easy to find something to compliment. Her thin, hard face was so pink it looked as if it had been scrubbed with a nail brush and a bar of carbolic soap. Her hair, which was white-blond and scraped into a lengthy ponytail, was her only redeeming feature. Behind her, dust motes sparkled, suspended in slices of sunlight peeking through the office blinds. Solomon counted in his mind, *one, two, three, four* . . . Finding interest in the mundane was a trick he had picked up as a child, as he waited patiently for his punishment to be administered. In his father's presence or his headmaster's study, distraction provided a buffer for what was to come. From counting the leather-bound books pressed into the groaning bookshelf to imagining pictures in the cracks in the wooden floorboards, such acts brought strength. They could imprison his body, but not his mind.

'I'm impressed,' the probation officer said, her gaze meeting his. 'Seems you were a model prisoner. Keep it up and you and me will get on just fine. How are you finding it? Adjusting to the outside?'

'Yeah, good. It's been six months now, so I've gotten my head around everything. Having a job helps, new friends, a fresh start.'

'They're a good bunch at Computech. Very supportive of our back-to-work initiative. They don't often get someone with your education, mind,' she said, her eyebrows raised. 'Still, you were lucky to get in, given the crime.'

Solomon nodded, his eyes on the flecks of dead skin trapped in her brows. The condescending bitch, expecting his gratitude for a minimum-wage job, while his colleagues earned double the amount. Who did she think she was, speaking to him like that? His pulse quickened, and he inhaled a calming breath. This was not the time to lose his temper. As far as probation was concerned, he had moved to Birmingham for work purposes only. His new job as a freelancer allowed him to flit between his office at Computech and his flat, affording him lots of spare time. He had the skills to complete his projects in half the time of his colleagues, leaving him spare time to check on Mother's progress, and most importantly, carry out his plan.

The probation officer droned on, her nasal voice drilling into his brain. Managing to keep his temper in check, he nodded his head in all the right places as she told him to 'keep his nose clean', and he even managed to thank her on the way out.

His shadow fell tall as he walked the concrete streets, his mind entrenched with thoughts of Rebecca. Hacking into her laptop camera remotely had been ridiculously easy, although nothing had prepared him for her metamorphosis. When they first met, she was a young, attractive blonde, with tanned skin and a teaching degree. Now, the fun-loving young woman had been replaced by a homely farmer's wife. Shadows had grown under her eyes over the last ten years, and she seemed to have quietened her disposition.

He gained no enjoyment from watching her undress for her shower. Childbirth had softened her body and rounded her curves. When she held her child she seemed sacred, pure almost. But in the darkness of his room, that concept had lasted just seconds, as reality bit deep. He knew exactly what she was. The hatred he had nurtured for over ten years would stand him in good stead for what lay ahead. He would enjoy stripping away the layers, testing the limits of her morals, until she revealed herself for what she really was: a cold-hearted selfish bitch. He checked his watch. It was time to eat. Not that he felt hungry. That wasn't important. As long as he stuck to the timetable, then everything would be OK. It was lights out at ten, up for a 6 a.m. start. Every movement was mapped with precision, particularly his plans for tomorrow. He smiled. He was looking forward to meeting Rebecca's husband.

CHAPTER SIX

SOLOMON

2016

Solomon pressed down the freshly glued beard as he stood in front of the floor-length mirror. Some baggy overalls, facial hair, and a peaked cap provided a decent disguise. Lifting his jaw, he surveyed the hair on his neck. His own mother wouldn't recognise him now.

He'd had all sorts of ideas about how he was going to install cameras in Rebecca's farmhouse, but in the end he went for the simplest: an email to selected customers only offering a free upgrade to the Walkers' current burglar alarm. That, backed up with the fake website mimicking the original installer's, was enough to encourage her to book an upgrade online. Of course, Solomon had already planned the slot of 'available' times, which coincided with her commitments in the surgery. And now, masquerading as Greg from XLR Security, he found himself driving to Rebecca's home to improve her security. The irony made Solomon laugh until his stomach hurt.

The house was set well back from the twisty road, encompassed by acres of rugged farmland. If isolation was what Rebecca had been searching for, she had landed on her feet with Sean. Solomon had been shocked to discover that not only had she married, but she had sealed the union with a child. How easily she had discarded him and their dreams of a family of their own. Lying in his prison cell, he had pictured Rebecca alone and unhappy or, better still, dead. But reality bit hard when he tracked her down. Such thoughts had been fantasies. She was a woman. And women always abandon you in the end. But the past still returned to torture him. All he had ever done was try to protect her, keep her by his side, and his side alone. His previous visit had been fleeting, granting him enough time to replace her teddy with an upgrade, complete with spy camera installed. But intermittent viewing was not enough to provide him with the control he needed to carry out such an audacious plan. Not if he wanted to keep one step ahead.

The doorbell produced a light chime, alerting the dog he had met before. Slices of fresh ham had won him a new friend during his last visit, but Bear was the last thing on his mind as Sean Walker opened the door. Sean's broad shoulders filled the door frame. He was taller in the flesh, reminding Solomon that he could not afford to be complacent.

'XLR Security,' Solomon mumbled, slipping Sean a flyer. 'I've come to upgrade your alarms.'

'Come in,' Sean said, dragging Bear back by the collar as he tried to burrow in Solomon's overall pockets. 'Sorry, I'll put him in the other room.'

'It'll take about an hour, then I'll be out of your hair,' Solomon said, sneaking a sideways glance at the man he despised by association. The man who possessed the woman *he* had been engaged to marry. He kept his gaze to the floor as he brought in his tools, refusing Sean's offer of refreshments. The job was straightforward enough. All he had to do was take the face off the alarm, drill a tiny hole and fit the camera behind it, then wire it into the system for power. Not that he told farm boy Sean any of that.

The hole, he had instead pointed out, led to an extra sensor which would pick up the slightest movement. The light would remain green as normal, and turn to red when the alarm was activated. Of course, the camera would record regardless of what colour the lights were. It was a shame he couldn't have installed infrared, he mused, as he fitted the first of the eight cameras. But you couldn't have everything.

It pained him to see that Rebecca had set up such a cosy nest. The outside of the house was weathered brick but inside freshly painted walls and newly replaced wooden beams modernised the interior. Spotlights in the ceiling banished the darkness, and soft furnishings, cushions and throws made the living room a welcoming nook. Solomon worked deftly as he finished the downstairs. He was not there to inspect the interior design. Thanks to the stupidity of her country-bumpkin husband, he was able to take an impression of his house keys. Sean was happy enough to leave him to it, and Solomon paused only to stare at the family portrait as he carried his stepladder upstairs. Barefoot and smiling, Rebecca sat against a sterile white background, enveloped by her husband in a loving embrace. At the core of the scene was a cherubic-faced little girl, her blond hair bunched in pink ribbons that matched her dress and jelly shoes. Solomon clenched his jaw. It took all of his self-control not to smash the glass into a thousand pieces. He touched the corner of the frame and shifted it off-centre.

He didn't see a happy family. All he saw was betrayal. Revenge was what he lived for, a healing balm for the pain she had caused. In some ways, it frightened him to think about what he would do when the focus of his hatred had been removed. But at least this way he could savour each moment, each planned attack building like a crescendo, leaving shockwaves in its wake. There would be no happy ever after for the Walker family.

CHAPTER SEVEN

REBECCA

2016

It had been one of those days where I hit the ground running. XLR Security had overrun with their visit, meaning Sean was late for his morning surgeries. Tuesday was small-animal day, and Sean's reasonable fees brought customers from far and wide. Soon the small room was filled with sneezing cats, puppies waiting for their jabs, and a scrawny parrot that turned the air blue. At least everyone took it in good spirits. They had little choice, unless they wanted to go further afield.

With everyone settled, and the dogs a good distance from the cats, I tried to get on with some work. Some of the community still spoke in Welsh, and I allowed the strange language to wash over me. It was quite soothing really, although I'm sure if I knew what they were saying I might not have felt the same way. I had tried picking up the language over the years, but my heart wasn't in it. Sometimes you're better off not knowing what people are saying about you, although every now and again I would give them a knowing glance just to make them wonder.

Sean finally arrived at the surgery, half an hour late and with Lottie in tow. She loved her occasional visits, and could be trusted to behave. The events of the last couple of days had been playing heavily on my mind and I couldn't wait to get some time alone to make some enquiries about Solomon. I needed to know that he was still inside. I didn't do myself any favours when I left, foregoing witness care in exchange for privacy. Never once during the whole process did I allow myself to forget that Solomon's father was a superintendent in the police. Perhaps I had watched too many Hollywood films, but something deep inside told me not to disclose my new address. Unfortunately, the downside of this decision was that I had sacrificed the chance to receive any updates that should have come my way.

Bronwyn, the officer who prosecuted Solomon, could not have been lovelier. She used to talk about Wales as if it were some fairy-tale land, with its own people and traditions. I remember asking her why she moved to Essex; she simply replied that she had done so for love, and that the Essex police force was far busier than the one in her home town anyway. My own experience seemed to have borne this out. Murders and serious crimes were not so commonplace in Pontyferry.

I had been wanting to call her all day, and the card with her telephone number felt as if it were burning a hole in my pocket. It made me sick with worry because it was dragging me back into a past that I'd tried hard to leave behind. But I had to know where Solomon was. It was unlikely she would give me the information if I blocked my number, but I couldn't risk giving it out. She might have some way of tracing me and – although I knew I was getting paranoid again – I simply wasn't willing to take the risk.

Grateful that the wind had died down, I finally made my way outside and took some mouthfuls of bracing air before climbing into the Land Rover for some privacy. A text beeped. It was from Rhian. SORRY, NOT WELL. CAN'T DO THE AFTERNOON SHIFT. I frowned. If Rhian was unwell, then she might need a doctor. Another unpleasant thought crept into my mind. What if *he* was with her? Holding her hostage? *Get a grip*, I whispered to myself, dialling her number.

She sounded breathless, and I pushed my key into the ignition, ready to hare over there in case she was hurt.

'Rhian, are you OK?' I said.

'What? Yeah, I'm fine.' Her sentence cut off with a giggle and my frown burrowed deeper.

'I thought you weren't well. Are you OK?'

'Um . . . yeah.'

I sensed reluctance in her voice. Rhian was proud. Too proud to tell me when there was something wrong. 'I'm coming over,' I said, temporarily forgetting about my urgent phone call. It was then that I heard muffled laughter in the background, followed by a deep voice murmuring in the distance.

'Don't you dare,' Rhian said. 'I'm not alone.' Another giggle.

The penny finally dropped. 'Oh my God, you saucy cow, who have you got in bed with you?'

'Soz,' she said, not sounding the least bit remorseful. 'We had a late night last night. Don't tell Sean, will you?'

There was no point in telling her off. If anything, I was a little bit envious.

'Don't be daft, I'd never hear the end of it. Just as long as you fill me in with all the details later. I'll leave you to it. Bye.'

'Bye,' Rhian said, before hanging up. I smiled. I was glad she had found someone new. It wasn't easy, living in such a rural community, where women outnumbered the men. I ran my finger over my phone, reluctant to dial Bronwyn's number. My pulse quickened at the thought of finding out, and I wrestled with the voice in my head. Why couldn't I leave it be? Why couldn't I forget all about Solomon, put him behind me? He'd never find me now, even if he *was* out of prison. But I needed to know so that I could take steps to protect my family. Although what further measures could I take? Our house was like a fortress. We had a huge watchdog, and I was permanently on alert. Just what good would it do, getting in touch with the police again? What if they somehow traced the call? On and on the argument raged in my head.

Enough, I whispered, sighing deeply. Blocking my number, I called Bronwyn's mobile, muttering to myself under my breath, 'It could all be for nothing anyway. The number probably doesn't work anymore.' But the call was answered after the first ring, and my stomach lurched at the sound of Bronwyn's voice. I held my breath as long-buried memories were released from their box.

'Hello?' The voice responded a second time, carrying a hint of irritation.

Taking another deep breath, I responded. 'Bronwyn? It's me, Becky . . . Rebecca Shepard.' It felt strange using my maiden name, returning to who I was before I married Sean. 'You investigated the Solomon Kemp case,' I said, feeling his name like dirt on my tongue.

'I know who you are. How are you? Why did you disappear like that? We've been trying to get in touch to offer safeguarding.'

I was conscious of my heart, thudding so hard it felt as if it were going to burst through the thin material of my shirt. I rubbed my chest, praying Sean would not come looking for me.

'I felt it best if I disappeared,' I explained. 'Is he still in prison? Lately I've felt like something's wrong. I can't put my finger on it.'

'He's been released on licence,' Bronwyn said. 'I need to put a safety plan in place, just in case. But your neighbours said you've moved away. Are you still teaching?'

'No,' I said. 'I'm sorry, Bronwyn, I don't want to give my location away to anyone. It's nothing personal.' I paused. 'Given his connections in the police, I'm scared he'll find me if my new address is recorded on your systems.'

'His father's dead. You don't need to worry on that score. Not that you ever had to.' She sounded slightly miffed.

My mouth gaped as I forced myself to take in the news of Solomon's release. 'I can't believe he's out there, somewhere.'

'Please, Rebecca, tell me where you are, just so I can flag your address and telephone number, make the local constables aware. Are you still in Essex?'

'No,' I said, biting my lip. 'I've taken precautions. I knew he'd be released one day. I just wasn't expecting it so soon.'

I stared out at the slate-grey clouds rolling over the sun. What had started out as a nice morning had taken on a menacing hue. The colour seemed to drain from the pretty landscape, and for a while I said nothing.

'He's been assigned a probation officer,' Bronwyn said, breaking the silence, 'which means he's got to sign on and stick to the terms of his licence, otherwise he'll end up back inside. So if you hear from him or he harasses you in any way, you've got to report it. They might be able to have him recalled to prison.'

For how long? I thought. If it wasn't now, then it would be later. His thirst for revenge would be just as fresh in five years' time, or ten.

'Where's he signing on?' I said. 'In Essex?' A flicker of hope rose up inside me. It would take him hours to reach us from there.

'Look, you've caught me on the hop here. I'm not in the office, I'm at home. Let me give his probation officer a call. I'll ring you back, tell you exactly where he is. Then we can put some safeguarding in place. You're a high-risk victim, Rebecca. It's important that we . . .'

'Sorry, Bronwyn, I can't do that,' I interrupted. She didn't need to tell me I was high risk. Nobody knew that better than me. 'When can you find out? I hate to trouble you on your day off, but I really need to know. Can I call you tomorrow? Will you be back at work by then?'

'Call me in thirty minutes, in case she's not picking up. I could email you, if you want.'

'Thanks, I'll ring back soon,' I said, dropping the call. There was no way I trusted email. It was the same reason I shunned social media.

Solomon was a genius with computers. He wouldn't have any problem tracking me down online.

It was an hour before I was able to get away to call Bronwyn again, and in that time my anxiety levels had shot through the roof, paling my skin and giving me a haunted expression. Sean cornered me as I stood gazing out of the window, biting the skin around my fingernails when I was meant to be fetching a wormer for Mrs Llewellyn's Jack Russell.

'All right?' he said, squeezing past me to the cupboard. 'You've been standing there for five minutes.'

'What? Oh, sorry, I'm not with it today.'

'Why don't you go home for lunch? Take Lottie with you. I've only got a couple more appointments before we close for the day.'

'If you're sure you can manage,' I said, knowing I wasn't much use to him in this state. Sean's diary had been booked out so that he could spend the remaining daylight hours at his brother Gareth's farm, examining his new breeding stock. He and Gareth spent a lot of time together, and played rugby in the same team. I didn't have a lot in common with Gareth's wife Chloe. Thankfully Sean was happy enough visiting the farm and joining Gareth for a beer after work, sparing me Chloe's company. She seemed to regard me with some suspicion, and spoke Welsh whenever I was around. The fact that she was once engaged to my husband was never far from my mind, especially as her jealousy was quite obvious, despite the fact that she was the one to jilt Sean at the altar. It used to make me smile, knowing I was getting under her skin, because from what Sean had told me about her, she had treated him badly.

It wasn't until I was home with Lottie serving lunch that I summoned up the courage to call the police. I had already convinced myself that Solomon was in Essex, and I should have left it at that. But still the doubt lingered. Reluctantly I tapped in Bronwyn's mobile number.

CHAPTER EIGHT

Diary Entry: 27th May 2005

I'm sorry for not writing sooner. But up until now, I've had nothing good to say. During the last few weeks I've been veering between dreaming about Solomon, back to despairing over my mother, then back to daydreaming about Solomon again. It helps me to sleep at night, having something nice to focus on, rather than the things I am too scared to face. It sounds crazy. How can someone I've only spoken to for a couple of hours make me feel so strongly? Perhaps it's because I met him during the marathon, another soul running for the same cause, as we clocked up the miles in matching Cancer Research vests.

Those were the thoughts that filled my mind as I sat outside the oncology department this morning, waiting for the last cycle of my mother's chemotherapy treatment to end. Unlike patients who attend a day unit, Mum's treatment is so intensive that she has to stay in overnight. Her ever-weakening condition means they have to keep a close eye on her, but at least she's in safe hands. I began suffering from panic attacks shortly after Mum broke the news of her illness. Robbing me of breath, they make me feel as if I'm sinking into thick, black quicksand. Mum is my whole world, and I'm waiting for the sky to fall. It makes me feel horribly guilty to admit that, because she's the one suffering, not me. I've learned to hide my anxiety, diverting my thoughts so I can catch my breath.

So there I was, sitting in the hospital ward, fidgeting in the hard plastic chair. My elbows on my knees, I sat in my customary *shut out the world* position, watching pairs of loafers squeak past on the shiny, tiled floor. That is, until a pair of leather shoes came into view and a takeaway cup was shoved under my nose. The sweet tang of hot chocolate wafted invitingly, and it looked a lot more promising than the brown puddle in the polystyrene cups that the nearby vending machine belched out.

My heart flickered because, even before I looked up, I knew it was Solomon. I smiled, the kind of warm smile you give when you've been reunited with an old friend.

'Solomon,' I said, the word more a statement than a question. He was wearing navy chinos and an open-necked grey shirt which revealed a white T-shirt underneath. I gratefully took the drink, inhaling its aroma before putting the plastic lid to my lips. It tasted every bit as good as it smelt, and was just how I liked it: straight hot chocolate, no cream, no added sugar. I didn't dare close my eyes as I sipped, in case he was gone when I opened them again. I felt like I was dreaming.

'I saw you come in earlier,' Solomon said, taking a seat beside me. 'You look like you could do with some cheering up.'

It's funny how I've memorised his words. But the outside world just disappears when Solomon speaks.

I realised that seeing me in the cancer ward wouldn't have come as much of a shock to him, given how I had basically told him my life story during the race. But I was bewildered. Solomon had never disclosed where he was from, so Colchester hospital was the last place I expected to bump into him. A thought crossed my mind and I dismissed it: as if he would be so desperate to see me that he would hang around the oncology ward.

'Don't worry, I'm not stalking you,' he said, reading my thoughts. 'I'm here for a check-up.'

My mouth pursed into an O and I realised I was staring. 'With the oncology department?'

'Yes,' he replied, with a finality that suggested he didn't like talking about it. He seemed to think for a second, before continuing. 'I'm in remission. I got the all-clear last year; they just called me back in for the latest test results. Still all clear. Something worth celebrating, don't you think?'

'Definitely,' I said, wondering just how long it was since he'd had his news. All clear. The two words my mother had been deprived of. My heart would lurch in my chest as I prayed for a positive outcome to her many tests. But it was not to be. Mum would be her usual stoic self, and I put on a brave front in return. But today, as I sipped my hot chocolate, with Solomon chatting away beside me, I wanted to forget about cancer and all the awful things it had brought to our lives. Instead, I rested my gaze on his face, absorbing his goodness. This was the second time he had come to my aid, and I was beginning to feel like I had met a real-life knight in shining armour. As we spoke, his cool-grey eyes locked on mine, searching my face. Reflected back at me, they contained an intensity I could not escape, even if I wanted to.

'How much longer do you have to wait?' he asked, his elegant fingers playing with the rim of his empty cup.

I had no real plans for the evening and would probably have spent it with Mum, for as long as I could get away with, but I knew it would make her happy if I told her I was going out with a friend. I guessed that's what Solomon was asking, and my heart fluttered at the prospect of sharing some more delicious time with him.

He invited me out for a bite to eat, to a restaurant in Frinton-on-Sea. His face brightened as he told me his dad was friends with the manager, who never refused him a table.

I checked my watch to see it was 7 p.m. My stomach grumbled as it remembered it hadn't been fed, and I thanked him, saying I would let Mum know.

I paused as he rose to follow me down the hall. He caught my hesitation, then gave an awkward smile. 'Sorry, would you prefer me to wait out here?'

'No, come in,' I said, my face breaking out into a grin. I was so used to my friends and family shying away from my mother's illness that I had not expected Solomon to want to come and say hello. I got as far as her door when a thought occurred. 'This is going to sound very weird, but . . .'

'Go on,' Solomon said.

I cringed inwardly. I knew what I was going to say would risk our friendship and probably send him running to the hills. But as much as I liked Solomon, I wanted to please my mother more. I would have done anything to make her happy, and right then I had the power to give her the gift she had always wanted. I cleared my throat. 'Would you pretend to be my boyfriend for a few minutes?' My face lit up in a rosy hue, as a hot flush bloomed on my cheeks.

The corner of Solomon's eyes crinkled as he absorbed my request.

'For my mother's sake,' I hastily added. 'I know we'd be lying, but it would make her so happy.' I stared at the floor as I realised how pathetic I sounded.

Solomon did not keep me waiting very long. 'I'm confused,' he said, and I immediately regretted asking him. I laughed it off, telling him it was a stupid idea. He didn't come to the hospital to be put in such an embarrassing predicament.

Solomon smiled, then reached out and touched my hair. Straightened to within an inch of its life, it was in far better shape than the last time he saw it. 'Silly,' he said, sending a shiver galloping down my spine. 'I mean, I'm confused as to why someone as gorgeous as you is single.'

The blush that had left my cheeks returned in full bloom, and I cursed myself for reacting to such a cheesy line. A nurse walked past, affording us a curious glance before returning her attention to the clipboard in her hand. It was Selina – I had come to know her in the last few months, and sometimes we had a coffee in the hospital canteen. A pretty Asian girl, with no shortage of male admirers, she was fully aware of my dismal social life. I knew she would quiz me later on. I brought my attention back to Solomon, figuring out the most appropriate response.

I told him I didn't have much time for dating, that I worked full time, and that any spare time I had was taken up with caring for Mum and fundraising.

'Besides,' I said, staring at my feet, 'not everybody understands.'

'I found out who my friends were when I became ill. There's not many of them left now,' Solomon said, sadly. 'But it *would* make my day to put a smile on your mum's face.'

I had no idea what I was going to say as I finally opened her door, and figured we would play it by ear. Mum's health insurance provided a basic private room, with a small television and an uninspiring view of the car park below. I took a step towards her bed where she snoozed, wondering what Solomon would make of the age gap. Mum was forty-five when she had me, twenty-four years ago. I was an unexpected gift from my father, who bailed when he discovered she was pregnant. A roadie for a successful band, he had the perfect excuse to duck his obligations. Today Mum was looking a lot older than her sixty-nine years. I knew that the silvery-grey wig she wore was for my benefit, as was the light application of make-up. Mum had long since made her peace with death, and I would not let her down by allowing her to see how much her frailty upset me. This would be her last treatment, given in the hope of extending what time she had left. But I knew I was being selfish, wanting her with me when she was in so much pain. Standing by the side of her bed, I expected a short visit, but Solomon dragged over two chairs and joined me by her side. I took Mum's hand as she opened her eyes, and as her gaze flitted towards Solomon a slow smile rose on her face.

A gentle whirring noise ensued, as she pressed a button to elevate her bed into a sitting position. 'You didn't tell me you were bringing such a handsome visitor,' she said, her eyes twinkling as she spoke. No amount of illness could take that twinkle away.

I introduced Solomon as a friend, as my courage abandoned me.

Solomon gave my mother a warm smile. 'We're more than just friends,' he said, gently shaking her hand. 'It's good to finally meet you, Estelle,' he said, sitting back in his chair. I wondered how he knew her name, then realised he must have read it on the chart at the end of her bed. It was just the sort of kind gesture I had already come to expect from Solomon.

Mum teased me, asking why I hadn't told her about my new boyfriend, although her words were delivered with obvious approval. Solomon brought his hand around to the back of my chair and began slowly stroking my hair, allowing the long blond tresses to glide through his fingers. The summer dress I was wearing dipped at the back, and each contact with my skin sent a shiver down my spine. My mouth became dry. I struggled to concentrate on what I was supposed to say, and swallowed back what felt like a ball in my throat.

'We've been seeing each other for a few weeks now,' Solomon said, lowering his hand from my hair and locking his fingers through mine. 'I've been falling for her since the day we first met.'

I know those were his exact words, because they're ingrained in my brain. Of course, it was part of an act to please Mum, but I allowed myself to fall into the moment, and basked in the glow. I found my voice, under the approving gaze of my mother's eye.

'I didn't want to jinx it by saying anything, but Solomon insisted he come along and say hello. We're going out for a bite to eat, but we can stay if you prefer.'

'I'm all done in, sweetie. You go and enjoy yourself,' Mum said.

But Solomon insisted on staying for another twenty minutes, chatting to my mother about her interest in music, and the bands she used to sing in. I was delighted to discover he was such an aficionado of sixties music, as he invoked a gentle debate on which were the best, the Stones or the Beatles, playing clips of their songs on his phone to prove his point. Mum's eyes lit up at the mention of some of the old musicians she used to tour with in the seventies, and she mentioned her favourite tune, *Hallelujah*. Within seconds, Solomon was playing it on his iPhone, and Mum closed her eyes as the gentle tune invoked old memories, her hand swaying from side to side, conducting the song. I wished that I had taken more of an interest in her old life, before she had me. I was so taken up with her care, and working to earn a crust, that I never really saw her as a separate person, someone who was once my age, her head filled with hopes and dreams. She began to grow tired, and Solomon said he needed to use the loo. He kissed me softly on the cheek, the warmth of his lips making me feel giddy inside.

Mum's eyes opened as the room door clicked shut. 'What a lovely young man,' she said, stifling a yawn before asking if I was happy.

I decided to go along with the dream and nodded in approval. 'I feel like I've known him forever.' That bit was true.

'Yes,' Mum said. 'I can tell he feels the same way. Now I can be at peace, knowing you've someone special in your life.'

I didn't mention Solomon's health, not wanting to burst the bubble. Despite recovering himself, he had plucked me out of my nightmare, and I was happy to let Mum believe he would get me through whatever lay ahead.

And when he came back with the most beautiful bunch of yellow tulips, I melted all over again.

'I thought this place could do with some brightening up,' he said, filling the vase with water.

Mum whispered something about them being her favourites as she squeezed my hand. She must have thought I had told him, but the truth was I hadn't. It was just a coincidence in what was turning out to be a perfect day.

I bent down to kiss my mother's cheek, murmuring that I loved her and would be back in the morning. I trusted the nurse to call me if I was needed before then.

'I love you too,' she said, before telling me to have a lovely evening.

And it was a lovely evening. I had just enough time to go home to shower and get changed before meeting Solomon, who said he was taking me to The Avenues bistro in Frinton. I would have been content with a pub meal, but when Solomon pulled up outside my home in his sleek, expensive-looking sports car, I began to feel like a princess.

We exchanged numbers before the night was out, and as Solomon drove me home I didn't know how I was meant to feel. I was not into one-night stands, but I had the house all to myself and, given our connection, I was ready to welcome him inside. Nervous excitement bubbled within me as I asked him in for a coffee. He brushed his hand against my cheek before reaching in and kissing me tenderly on the mouth. It was warm, soft, and the contact with his tongue made me go weak inside. We broke for breath, and I detected a hint of sadness in his eyes as he turned me down.

'Not tonight, I'm afraid,' he said. But he had my number and promised to call me later. Which is why I'm writing in my diary, as I prepare to sleep alone. Did I imagine the regret on his face? I keep wondering what was so important that he had to turn me down.

CHAPTER NINE
REBECCA

2016

I admonished myself as I grasped for a tissue from under my sleeve. Giving it a shake, I dabbed my lashes dry. In the old days, I was well practised in catching my tears before my make-up ran. And the mascara I used was waterproof in case I failed. Lottie snoozed, her delicate fingers wrapped around her *Frozen* plush doll. I bent to kiss her soft blond hair, the ache in my heart more painful than ever. At four years of age, Lottie's only comprehension of monsters was to do with the ones under her bed. If only a kiss on the forehead and a soft night light were as effective at killing them in real life. I looked to the doorway and could tell by his expression that my husband was reading my thoughts.

'It's going to be OK, you know,' Sean said. 'You can't stand guard over her all night.' His face held nothing but love, but his words carried a harsh reality I didn't want to hear.

Taking a deep breath, I approached him in an effort to quell the anxiety.

'How can I relax knowing he's out there, plotting his revenge? Because that's what he's doing. And don't think for a minute he'll stop at me because . . . because . . .' My words collapsed into soft sobs, and Sean wrapped his arms around me, kissing the top of my head. I buried my head in his strong chest, taking comfort in his muscular frame. Solomon was tall but lean. Muscled from years of rugby and physical activity, Sean could easily take him if it came down to brute strength alone. But Solomon wasn't all about violence. He enjoyed the game, emotionally manipulating people, instilling fear.

'It's been ten years, and he's no idea where you are,' Sean said. 'What was it Bronwyn said?'

I drew in a breath, inhaling the sweet farmyard odour that sprung from Sean's woollen sweater. It came with the territory, and I gladly took it on board. 'She said his probation officer will be keeping a very close eye on him.'

Sean pushed a lock of my hair behind my ear. 'Well, there you go. He's in Essex. He'll never find you here. Now are you going to be all right or do you want me to make a few calls, ask Geoffrey if he'll see to Mrs McAllister's cow?'

I imagined Geoffrey, settled at home with his wife, watching the latest soap on TV.

'No, I'll be fine. You go. Just lock up on the way out.' But I couldn't relax, at least not until Bronwyn was able to confirm Solomon's address with his probation officer, who hadn't answered the phone when she called her.

I envied my husband's naivety, watching him grab his car keys from the hook on the wall. How could I explain that even if Solomon *was* watched 24/7, he would still find a way of getting to me? He was a calculating man who'd had ten long years to figure it out. I tore myself away from Lottie's bedroom and drifted onto the landing, telling myself to calm down. Everything was how it should be. For now.

A howl of wind slammed the bathroom door, causing a streak of terror to run through me. Jittery laughter escaped my lips as I sneered at my own nervousness, remembering that Sean had left the window open. I pulled down the PVC latch, muttering under my breath to the confines of the bathroom. 'How many times, Sean Walker? How many times must I tell you to keep this damn window shut?' Then I heard it. A telephone echoing. The old-fashioned ringtone playing a well-known song. Not one of the pop tunes that emanated from my device, but a haunting memory of the past. *Hallelujah*. It cut deep into my thoughts as my heart began to race. An unwelcome thought struck me. What if Solomon was in my house? My hand reached into the bottom of the linen basket and I gripped the scissors I had hidden. Such hiding places were dotted throughout the house *just in case*. The cool metal felt good in my palm, and I clenched it tightly, following the sound to our bedroom.

I peered through the crack in the door. Perhaps it was Sean playing a trick, or he had bought me a phone as a surprise. But I knew that wasn't true. My dislike of tricks and surprises was one of the first things Sean learned about me. So who owned the phone ringing in our room? *Hallelujah . . . Hallelujah*. It was not going to stop until I answered. As I pushed the crack in the door wider, the noise grew louder.

'Hello?' I called out, holding up the scissors. But there was nobody there. Nobody that I could see. Fear was overtaken by my instinct to protect and, my scissors raised, I stood my ground as my eyes roamed the length of our bedroom. The built-in wardrobes were big enough to house a man, but the sound seemed to be coming from under our bed. No, *in* our bed. Reluctantly, I lowered the scissors and quickly pulled back the thick featherdown duvet. Ripping off the sheets, I found the phone nestled beneath the memory-foam topping that lay on our mattress. I grasped the cold metal, my heart pounding as the display screen lit with the insistent call. It was an iPhone, black and barely used.

With shaking hands, I answered the call, still on alert as I paced the room. The call disconnected immediately, and I jumped as the phone vibrated with a text. My mind raced as I pressed the button to open it. It was one word. Enough to make my legs buckle beneath me.

```
Witness
```

My heart hammering against my ribcage, I checked on Lottie again. Her doll abandoned on the floor, my little girl was sleeping soundly, oblivious to my panic. My eyes were drawn to the window, and I peered past the security lights to the desolate scrubland beyond. The lack of car headlights suggested the winding roads were empty, and the only sound I could hear was the wind howling in the hills. I swallowed, feeling the need to check the doors one more time.

Bear lifted his head from his cushion as I strode into the kitchen, still holding the phone in my hand. It reassured me to see him so relaxed; his tail drummed against the flagstones before he turned his attention back to the important task of sleeping. I bent to pat him, as I thought about calling the police. As if in response, the phone beeped with a text, making me jump for a second time that day. Overcome with dread, I forced my index finger to open the website link attached. A cold white page flashed on screen, with nothing but a few lines on display. Wide and unblinking, my eyes crept over the words:

```
Witness.

Here is your proposition.

Fail to respond and you get hurt.

Talk to police and you die.
```

This cannot be traced, do not waste your
precious time.

Ready to play? You have sixty seconds to
decide.

00.59

Click YES to begin.

'No, no, no,' I gasped, as the clock on the screen counted backwards
from sixty seconds. Fifty-nine, fifty-eight, fifty-seven, it was going too
fast. I barely had time to comprehend the words splashed across the
screen. But one message stood out from all the rest: TALK TO POLICE
AND YOU DIE. Twenty-nine, twenty-eight, twenty-seven, the clock ticked
down with damning finality. I jabbed the YES button three times, my
fingernail pecking against the screen. The page refreshed, producing
another message.

Let the game begin.

Enjoyed playing witness?

You get to do it again. Ten times over.

One crime for every year you kept me
inside.

Who are the victims?

You choose.

I clenched my jaw. This had Solomon written all over it. An act of revenge for my perceived betrayal. I should have been relieved that he was playing his games online rather than in person. But his presence felt as real as if he was standing behind me. I must witness a crime for every year of the sentence he served as a result of my witness testimony. If I refused, I would pay the price for my betrayal. Too scared to blink, my eyes followed the trail of words as they revealed my challenge.

```
Victim number one. Theft.

Margaret Bowen or ?

Enter target here _____

This will default to: Mrs Bowen if
incomplete.

You have thirty seconds to decide.

00:29
```

'What?' I gasped, making Bear amble over, his head cocked to one side. 'What does it mean, *I* decide?' I said, to nobody at all. 'Is this some kind of sick joke?' I blinked, returning my gaze to the website. My time had run out. A new message flashed on the screen.

CHAPTER TEN
REBECCA

2016

Bear's ears pricked up as the rumble of Sean's Land Rover reverberated on the tarmac drive. Wagging his tail, he padded out to the hall to greet his owner. My heart drummed like small beating wings as I stared, open-mouthed, at the phone.

```
Your vote has been counted.

The victim is: Margaret Bowen.

Await further notification.
```

What does that mean? I whispered. Surely not the Mrs Bowen I knew? The woman who took in stray cats and never uttered a cross word. Sean's keys rattled in the front door. I had to keep this to myself, at least until I figured out what was going on. In Sean's eyes, the police could fix everything, but finding the phone in my bed meant Solomon already knew where I was. Thoughts racing, I slid the phone into my jeans pocket, switching on the kettle as I composed myself.

At thirty-eight, Sean had as much of an affinity for Bear as he'd had for his dogs when he was a child. It had been a wrench for him to leave Bear at home rather than have him accompany him on his call-outs, but he was happy to comply if it provided me with some much-needed reassurance. It worked for me, but Bear was not so enamoured of being left behind.

'That was quick,' I said, reaching for two mugs from the hook on the wall.

'False labour,' Sean said. 'She rang me when I was halfway over,' he chuckled softly. 'Can you believe it? Mrs McAllister using a mobile phone. She must be ninety if she's a day.'

I smiled, turning to hand him a steaming mug. I swallowed the tightness in my throat, trying not to think of the ticking time bomb in my back pocket. Margaret Bowen lived alone in a remote area, a harmless old lady who existed for her cats. Surely he wasn't going to harm her, an old dear with a stoop and a dodgy ticker? It was a wind-up, wasn't it? A way of testing the waters.

'Are you all right?' Sean said, his soft blue eyes full of concern. 'You look like you've seen a ghost.'

'I'm fine.' I gave him a watery smile. 'At least I know where I stand with Solomon. I guess tomorrow we can start getting on with things again.' The words sounded hollow, because I knew they were a lie. Solomon was unpredictable.

'Good,' Sean said, giving me a quick peck on the cheek. 'Well, if it's all right with you, I'm going to catch up on that footie match I recorded. I've managed to get by all day without hearing the result, so I'd best watch it while it's still a mystery.'

'Sure.' I pulled the face I used when football was mentioned. 'I was going to take a shower anyway.'

Clouds of steam rose around me as spikes of water cascaded from the shower head. Wrapped in a towel, I used the time to pick through the phone. Apart from the texts and my use of the Internet, it was blank. There were no numbers saved, no history, and nothing stored in the picture gallery. Good. The last thing I wanted to see was Solomon Kemp, although he must have changed in ten years. Perhaps I *should* know what he looked like now, in case he crossed my path. I remembered his swagger. He walked with an air of authority that demanded respect. But I remembered his eyes most of all. Cold and grey, with an intensity that could turn your legs to water. Solomon came from a respectable family, and thought he had everyone fooled.

Using the money from the sale of the house, I had packed up my belongings and left. It was such a heavy price to pay. A new identity meant giving up every facet of my old life. My family, friends, the people I grew up with. All gone. They wouldn't recognise me now: I had merged into this sleepy Welsh village. Meeting Sean had been my turning point, the marking of a new chapter in my life. And now it was about to be all blown apart.

Staring at the screen, I strained to remember the first prompt. My efforts at refreshing the page produced nothing. It was one of those encrypted website addresses, not the usual www sort. I was no techie, but as far as I could see, it was for my eyes only. What had it said? I rubbed the back of my neck, feeling a familiar prickle of anxiety, just as I had a decade ago. Only now I wasn't sitting in a pool of blood. I was holding up the roof for everything I held dear. I tapped my fingers against my chin. There was something about a theft, and having to await further notification. Should I warn Margaret? And say what? She'd think I had lost the plot. My mind racing, I switched off the shower. How did he get into my home without Bear tearing a chunk out of him? I ran through the corridors of my mind, dissecting my day. There was nobody following me. I'd made absolutely sure of that. I frowned. Our narrow bathroom window had been left open, and the house had been empty during the day. Was that when the phone had been planted, stowed in my bed to drive the message home? Our farmhouse was like a fortress, but someone had still managed to find a way in. I pursed my lips, holding back the sob that threatened to escape. Surely Bronwyn would help? She had put him away the first time – there must be something she could do?

I dialled Bronwyn's number, having remembered to block my own.

'Hello,' Bronwyn said. But I couldn't respond. I wanted to tell her about the text, but the words were stuck in my throat.

'Is that you, Rebecca?' she said, her voice growing concerned. 'Are you OK?'

Flashbacks of Solomon invaded my memory. What was I doing? Solomon had made it quite clear. Talk to the police and I die.

'Sorry,' I whispered. 'I'm fine. I shouldn't have called.'

'Listen, don't hang up. It's Solomon. He's moved, for work purposes apparently. I can't share the exact address but he's in Birmingham. Is that anywhere near you?'

Given what had happened in the last twenty-four hours, it shouldn't have come as a surprise. But it did. I sucked in a breath as the walls of the steaming bathroom closed in on me.

'No. I . . . I've got to go. Goodbye.'

'Rebecca, wait, don't go.'

I terminated the call as Bronwyn pleaded with me to stay. But I couldn't take the chance. Not when he was so near. My mind raced with possibilities. He could be at my house in an hour and a half. He could be here right now. What the hell had I just done?

◆ ◆ ◆

I paced the room as all the old memories returned to taunt me. My life was in two halves: before and after Solomon. I knew there was no reasoning with him; he just did not seem to be equipped with the ability to accept responsibility for what he had done. And worse still, he had done it in the guise of caring for me, because his insecurities were satisfied only by power and control. I tortured myself, thinking back over what I had done to make him want to engage with me so completely. I thought about all the times that I allowed him to treat me badly, when I should have walked away. But I could not see it. Because a part of me had wanted the perfect relationship too. Standing up in court and giving evidence was hard, but it was me or Solomon. I had no choice. And now I was being forced to choose again.

CHAPTER ELEVEN
SOLOMON

2016

Apart from the buzzing of the fridge and the traffic fumes that wafted in through his window, Solomon was pleased with his two-bedroom flat. One bedroom for sleeping in, the other for planning the hunt. There was nothing to beat the thrill of the chase, and he had barely slept since his plans gained momentum. As much as he hated his father, being introduced to hunting was one of the few shining moments in his miserable childhood for which he was grateful. Each time he was home from boarding school, a clock ticked backwards in his head, counting down the hours until his return. *Tick, tick, tick* it went, filling him with dread as he realised he had three days left, then two, then one. It was impossible to enjoy his freedom, knowing that in a matter of hours he would be back to the freezing-cold baths, the slice of the cane on his bare behind, and the teachers who enjoyed teaching him a lesson a little too much.

Fox hunting with his father was a ritualistic event in which time stood still. Starting off on a crisp winter's morning, there was no better buzz than following the pack of hounds, their wet noses sniffing the air for a scent. The horses bounced on the road, their nostrils flaring, quivering with the anticipation of what lay ahead. They looked so fine, the riders in their blood-red jackets and leather boots, the wide-hipped women poured into their jodhpurs, eyes sparkling, nerves tingling, as they prepared for the chase. The horn would sound, cutting through the air in a scream that echoed a signal across the flatlands of Essex. His heartbeat thundering in his ears, Solomon would hold on tight to his steed as the hounds yelped and bayed for blood. He was ten years old at their last hunt, and he remembered it like it was yesterday. The horses lathered in foamy sweat as they galloped across the land, jumping streams and ditches, and powering through bracken in a fight to catch their prey. The fox having to use guile to escape being torn apart. Solomon had beaten his horse; it was a slow thing, but thanks to the new whip he'd got for Christmas, he had made him gallop like never before. After an hour he was richly rewarded, watching as the hounds tore their prey to pieces, leaving just enough blood to smear the children's faces and mark their triumph. Some of the children recoiled, but they were soft. Solomon relished the blood as it was crudely daubed on his cheeks, touching it as it hardened into a wrinkled red balm.

Mother fought with him to wash it off. It was his reward for being the best. For seeing it through. That day he hunted with his father had been one of the few times in his memory when he received praise for a job well done. There wouldn't be any more. As a member of the police force, his father's superiors didn't approve. Hunting was frowned upon, thanks to those damned animal rights protesters, his father said, and, without his father's support, Solomon wasn't allowed to go. But it didn't matter now – he had new prey.

Solomon switched on the computer monitors, downing a pint of milk. Who needed *Big Brother* on TV when you had Rebecca cam? He congratulated himself as her image came on the screen. It was time to continue the hunt. Instead of a horn, he signalled with a mobile phone. He flashed a smile in the dim light. The anticipation was almost too much to bear.

Solomon had written lots of letters when he was in prison. But none of them had ever been sent. Privacy was not a luxury afforded to prison inmates. He knew that all letters were read before being posted, and the things he had to say to Rebecca were meant only for her. At first everything he wrote was full of disbelief. Finding out that she had left him to take the blame was a betrayal like no other. All of this had been her fault. It always was. Right from the beginning the only thing he had ever done was try to love her and have the perfect relationship. But perfection comes at a price and humans are fallible.

It took a very special person to live up to his idea of perfection, but he thought he had found it in her. She had seemed intelligent, beautiful, unassuming, thoughtful and kind. All good traits to pass on. It was not that he was the maternal type. Having children was just what people did. But all of that was gone now, because Rebecca had seen to that too. As the years went by Solomon wrote different letters – sometimes, in his darkest days, he almost felt sorry for the way things had turned out. Their relationship had such potential. It was why he got so angry when she did things out of his control, and why he had to keep tightening the reins.

Towards the end she got more and more things wrong, and he found himself enjoying doling out the punishments more than he should. He painstakingly planned their marriage, hoping that if he could just get through to her, they would have the perfect life they both deserved. If only she had not fallen down the stairs, then he could have taught her a lesson, and she would not have invited Jake into their home. They would be married now, living in his Frinton home.

But instead she was with her country-bumpkin husband. A man of average intelligence, average looks, and most likely a very average bank account. Solomon had promised Rebecca everything: the beautiful house and inheritance, once he had his parents out of the way. And they were so close when it all fell apart. It made Solomon all the more determined to make her pay.

He would tear apart her happy home, and show her for what she really was. Forcing her to be a silent witness was nothing short of genius. She had been so keen to step into the courtroom and give evidence against him. Ten long years he had served, after her evidence ensured his incarceration. It was his turn to pay her back, ten times over. The tables were turned, and he would be the one to watch her squirm as everything she loved was taken away.

CHAPTER TWELVE

REBECCA

2016

The phone felt weighty, as if it were going to implode at any moment. I leaned forward as Lottie ran into my room and hugged me, feeling as if contact with the object in my back pocket could contaminate her. In an indirect way, it could. I had so many mixed feelings about Solomon's challenge that I did not know what direction my thoughts were taking me. I hated being a puppet on a string to a man capable of such deviousness. But what choice did I have?

Lottie descended the stairs ahead of me, determinedly gripping the banisters as she took each step in turn. At just four years old, she possessed a streak of independence that belied her age. A wave of protectiveness washed over me and I exhaled the breath I had been holding in. Perhaps it was just a wind-up, a message to say he knew where I was.

'Muummmmy, can I have a glass of milk, please and thank you?' Lottie's voice carried over the cartoons playing on her iPad. At least the noise did not disturb any neighbours. I used to love our rural location but, right now, I would have been grateful for some extra eyes and ears.

'Of course you can. Now turn that down,' I responded, pausing as I descended the stairs, having noticed that something was amiss. A dark sense of foreboding encased me in an icy grip. Our family portrait was slightly off-centre. I reached out to touch it, just as the alien phone vibrated in my pocket. I jerked back, swearing under my breath.

Heart sinking, I allowed the phone to burn a hole in my pocket as I poured Lottie a glass of milk. It was a small act of defiance. He could wait until I saw to my daughter's needs. After checking Sean had locked the doors, I slipped into the bathroom to check the phone. It felt like a block of butter in my grasp as I swiped the screen. Fresh dread enveloped me as the backlight revealed a text. I was desperate to know what was happening, but too scared to take it in. The message was sent in the same cold, abrupt tone as before.

Notification number one. Theft.

Margaret Bowen.

Tonight at 9pm.

Shaftesbury Lane.

You are a Silent Witness.

Talk to police and you die.

Tonight? I whispered. *I've got to go out tonight?* In a way, it made sense. What better time for a crime to be committed than under the cover of darkness? Shaftesbury Lane was the drop-off point for the bingo bus from which Margaret began the short walk to her home. I knew this because she once persuaded me to go along. Feeling sorry for her, I agreed. When I got there, I discovered that Margaret was not a loner after all, and had a whole bunch of friends she called 'the dippy dabbers'. It turned out that *she* was feeling sorry for *me*, bless her. Was Margaret Bowen going to get mugged tonight? If so, how could I just stand back and allow it to happen? I heard Lottie, giggling in the living room, and I knew I couldn't afford not to.

I steered my scooter down the lonely road, away from my family and everything I held dear. Getting away had not been as difficult as I anticipated. With Lottie asleep, I left the house under the pretence of buying milk. I knew there was danger on the horizon and, by not warning Sean, I was putting them at risk. But if I told him, he'd insist on leaving it in the hands of the police. Sean had been brought up in the bubble that is Pontyferry, where people went to bed without locking their doors and everyone knew you by your first name. I sighed. He really didn't have a clue. The torment whizzed around my head as my thoughts voiced their justifications. *Solomon's out there, on the prowl.* The thought prickled the hairs on the back of my neck. I swerved to avoid a hare as it bounded across the road. A flash of white tail told me he was OK, but the same could not be said for my shattered nerves. Taking a few deep breaths, I eased my hand off the throttle, manoeuvring down the narrow winding road, the lights of the town twinkling as they welcomed me in, just as they did years ago. This was how I repaid them, by bringing a threat into the village and standing by.

It took three attempts to park my scooter at the end of Shaftesbury Lane. Each time, the stand sank into the soil, and my bike lurched to one side like an old drunk. I wheeled it a couple of feet, risking the paintwork as I leaned it against a hedge. A sliver of moon made for poor light, but the view of the stars was breathtaking. Without the interference of street lights, the skies above Pontyferry were a joy for my husband, whose interest in astronomy was exceeded only by his love for animals.

The stars were lost on me tonight as I trudged up the lane. My stomach tied itself up in knots as I tried to pre-empt my tormentor's next move. If Solomon didn't see me, then how would he know I had witnessed the crime? Was Solomon even going to be here? He was on licence. Surely he would not risk going back to prison? Hands shaking, I slipped out the black woollen hat from my pocket and pulled it on. Despite the cool night, a nervous sweat slicked my palms. What if I was walking straight into a trap? Margaret could be tucked up in bed, being used as an excuse to lure me down this lonely lane. The rumble of the bingo bus putted in the distance, breaking into my thoughts.

I pulled out the phone and glanced at the time. Five minutes to nine. He was here, watching me right now. He had to be. There was no way he would deprive himself of that pleasure. I wanted to run, to spin on my heel and ride home, to the safety of my husband's arms.

My boots squelched into the muddy path as I trudged on towards the crossroads, eyeing the oak tree as a suitable place to hide. Unless he was already there. The thought of coming face to face with Solomon filled me with dread. In the distance the headlights of the small blue minibus chugged in my direction. Through steamy windows, the bus's overhead lights revealed rows of white-haired bingo-goers, chatting in their seats. Tentatively, I approached the tree, listening for every sound. I breathed in the cool night air, my pulse quickening at the uncertainty. Where was he? I checked the phone: 20:57 glowed bright in the darkness. From the left, the singular pinprick light of a motorbike cut through the night. *No*, I whispered. What if there was *another* witness? Did that mean the crime wouldn't take place? The bus was getting nearer now. I peered out from behind the tree, wanting to shout, *I'm here, you bastard, take me, not her*. But I was struck dumb. My body fought for self-preservation, rooting me to the spot as I carried out my duty. One minute to go. Margaret stepped off the bus as it pulled up on the corner, and waved the driver goodbye. My heart beat faster as the seconds counted down. The bus took a left as Margaret cautiously picked her way down the road, the small beam of a torch in her hand. Then the motorbike came thundering down the lane behind her.

CHAPTER THIRTEEN
REBECCA

2016

The cold trunk of the tree provided little comfort as I watched the drama unfurling before me with horror. Digging my fingers into the moss-covered grooves, I barely noticed a millipede crawl across my hand. My heart was beating so fast I swore Margaret would hear it. Cloaked in a pink woollen hat and scarf, she ambled by, with one hand deep in the pocket of her gabardine coat and the other still holding the flashlight. She was humming something, but the song was drowned out by the approaching motorbike.

It's just a theft, I reminded myself, *nothing more*. Margaret's handbag hung loosely across her shoulder, not clutched in her hands. Grateful for small mercies, I recited a silent prayer of thanks. The motorbike barely slowed as it approached the outline of her lone figure. I wanted to cover my eyes with my hands, but my imagination was working overtime. What if she was knocked down? Could I really abandon her down this lonely country lane? I glanced at the phone. It was dead on nine o'clock. Time had run out for both of us.

As the bike got closer, so did the vision of its leather-clad rider, whose identity was blotted out by the tinted black helmet. It was impossible to tell if the figure was male or female, let alone know who it was. Was it Solomon? Or was he watching my discomfort from afar? Mud was splattered across the licence plate, making it unreadable. It was a well thought-out job. The bike was almost level with Margaret now, and I stood out from behind the tree, the rider noting my presence with a thumbs-up signal. *Oh God, oh God, oh God*, I thought, breathless as I darted behind the rough bark. *Was that Solomon?*

In one swift movement, the bike revved up beside Mrs Bowen, making her wobble. I held my breath as a hand swiped in the moonlight, swooping on her leather bag strap. Stumbling on the dirt track, Margaret shrieked before falling to one knee. A string of obscenities followed as she pushed herself up off the ground. Waving her fist in the air, she bawled, 'Come back, you little bastard! Give me back my bag!' as the driver disappeared into the night. Then her shouting died down, dissolving into a sob as she slowly hobbled up the road.

I leaned against the tree, allowing my legs to give way beneath me. If I ran to comfort Margaret now, questions would be asked, and I risked something else happening if I didn't follow the instructions to the letter. She would soon be home. Her neighbours would take her in and call the police. The thought made me panic as I scrambled for my scooter keys. I had to get out of here.

Ducking down behind the thickets, I ran all the way back to the Vespa and, once I was satisfied Margaret was out of sight, started the engine. A wave of revulsion overcame me as I strapped on my helmet. How could I do that? Sean would have stopped, helped Margaret back to her house. No. Sean would never have allowed it to happen in the first place. But my husband did not know what I knew.

Stopping only to pick up the milk, I sped towards home. I desperately needed to take a bath, to scrub away Solomon and his disgusting act. The memory of the thumbs-up sickened me. It was all a game to him. Tomorrow I would have to face the locals as word of the attack seeped through the community. Sean used to say that you couldn't fart in Pontyferry without someone knowing about it. Could I look people in the eye, knowing I had brought this to their door?

My dark thoughts disappeared like wisps of smoke as I entered Lottie's bedroom. A star projector illuminated her ceiling, transforming the room into a faraway galaxy. I smoothed her hair from her face, and lightly kissed her forehead.

'Sweet dreams,' I whispered, picking up her fallen Anna toy and tucking it under the covers. She snuffled, her dimpled hand bringing the doll close to her chest.

'Can I get you a coffee?' Sean asked, taking the pods from the kitchen drawer. The coffee machine was the one gadget in our home that hadn't ended up dismantled in the cupboard.

I hoisted myself up on the counter, remembering I had Sean's black woolly hat in my coat pocket.

'Decaf, please,' I replied, gripping the lip of the counter to hide the shake in my hands.

'I worry about you, out on that bike at night. There's a nice Fiat 500 for sale on eBay.'

I gratefully took the mug of coffee from his outstretched hand. 'I can't get rid of the Vespa, are you forgetting how we met?'

'I remember you coming off it as you took that corner like a madwoman.'

I pulled him towards me. 'You dressed my wound and said I looked like Audrey Hepburn. Remember?'

'A right knight in shining armour, wasn't I?' Sean put his mug down, his gaze set intently on mine. I could smell his hair, his skin. He belonged to the outdoors, and I wanted to get lost in him. I took another sip of coffee, allowing the froth to ride up my lip before licking it off. I was not well practised in the art of seduction; it usually came off as awkward and tacky.

Sean sighed. 'I'm worried about you. All this business with Solomon. I'd be a lot happier if you were in the safety of a car.'

He moved in close, pushing a lock of my hair behind my ear. It was his ritual, telling me he was looking out for me. I closed my eyes, and when I opened them I could have cried on seeing the level of concern reflected back at me. I hated lying to him, but I had no choice.

'I'm OK, honestly. I just got a bit worked up, that's all.'

'And you've had no communication?'

I dipped my head in my cup to take another mouthful, grateful for the excuse to lose his gaze. 'If I did, I'd tell you.'

'Good. Because I'm not allowing this . . . this thug to come between us.'

What felt like a lifetime of silence passed between us. Solomon was many things, but he was too clean-cut to be a thug. It seemed like a stupid thing to say about someone who had served time for murder, but Solomon was the type of person who could talk his way into an Oscars after-show party. Dangerous, yes. But a thug he was not. My mind began to race ahead to the next victim. The very thought of it made me feel sick to the core. Unless . . . I took a deep breath, trying to appear nonchalant.

'We've never really spoken about what we'd do if' – I checked Sean's expression and carried on – 'if he found us. Would you be willing to relocate with me? I mean, I know it's not easy but—'

Sean broke away from our embrace. I could tell before he spoke that the answer was a definitive no.

'Do you think I'd run away with my tail between my legs?' His face hardened. 'If he tries to hurt my family, I'll finish him for good. And, unlike him, I won't get caught.'

I touched his arm. 'Don't. This isn't you.'

But Sean was still muttering under his breath, his dark thoughts wriggling free into the ether. 'I'd feed the bastard to the pigs. There'd be nothing left but a bellyache to treat.'

The words sounded ugly on his tongue, and I couldn't bear to listen to them. 'Please, Sean, I don't like to hear you talk like this, it upsets me.'

He took a sharp breath, as if just realising he had an audience. 'I'm sorry. Here, let me give you a *cwtch*. Make it all better.'

I closed my eyes as he wrapped his arms around me, but there was little comfort to be found in his embrace. Solomon's poison was already seeping into our family, and he had barely just begun.

'Where's Bear?' I said, sliding off the counter. Craning my neck, I stared through the window and searched the back yard. Our home was built on an acre of land, with an abundance of walkways and friendly farmers who didn't mind when we cut through their fields. Everybody in Pontyferry knew Sean, and I had never met anyone with a greater respect for the land. He was never happier than when he was outside, although there were days when the wind was so cold it felt like it could whip the skin from your face.

I opened the back door, tapping my foot against the flagstones. 'I really wish you wouldn't let him out on his own.'

Sean raised an eyebrow. 'He's just having a gallop around the fields. It's good for him, helps him let off some steam.'

'Anything could happen to him,' I said, feeling a chill descend. 'He's been gone almost an hour.'

Sean soaped his hands at the sink. 'Well, if you'd let him accompany me on my calls, then I wouldn't have to let him out in the evening. He's probably off chasing rabbits. He'll be back soon.'

But it wasn't rabbits I was worried about. It was Solomon, and the lengths he would go to in order to teach me a lesson. A small figure appeared at the door. It was Lottie, her chin wobbling as she dragged her comfort blanket behind her.

'Sweetheart, it's ten o'clock. What are you doing up?'

She shuffled towards me, tears welling in her eyes. 'Has Bear run away?'

I took her in my arms and gave her a reassuring hug. 'No, he's just gone for a run around the fields. Don't worry, sweetie, he'll be back soon.'

'But I want him here, Mummy. What if the bad man takes him?'

I frowned. 'What bad man?' I said, biting my lip for fear of her answer.

'The bad man that hurt Rocky. What if he's got Bear too?' I sighed with relief. She was not talking about Solomon; she was worried about Peter Cantwell. Rocky was his unfortunate dog, seized by the RSPCA as his owner was charged with offences of animal cruelty. There were times when I thought nursing Rocky at home had been a mistake. Introducing my child to the world of animal cruelty had obviously left its mark. Sean told us that Rocky was not expected to survive his injuries. But we could not leave him alone in the surgery at night after a lifetime of abuse. We provided weeks of intensive treatment in an effort to extend his life, and during that time Lottie was his constant companion. It was nothing short of a miracle that he survived. His new family still kept in touch, sending us regular updates on his progress. But his previous owner received nothing but a fine and a lifetime ban against owning animals, and now Lottie was scared he was on the prowl.

It was not Peter Cantwell I was worried about, though. It was Solomon Kemp. But my daughter did not need to know that more than one 'bad man' prowled the land. I spun around as a loud *woof* echoed in the back yard. Sean flung the kitchen door wide open, grabbing Bear's collar as he ran towards Lottie. 'Steady, boy! Pwoar, what have you been rolling in?'

I bent down to greet him, allowing him to plant stinky kisses on my face. I didn't care if he smelt of poo. He was home safe, and that was all that mattered.

CHAPTER FOURTEEN

Diary Entry: 24th June 2005

I've picked you up so many times, with the intention of putting my feelings down on paper. But the truth is I can't. It's too soon to talk about Mum dying because once I start crying I can't stop. If it weren't for Solomon that night, I don't know how I would have coped. He must have thought I was crazy, texting him just hours after leaving me. Two words, MUM'S GONE, were all it took to bring him immediately to my side, and he's barely left it since. He knows that I can't stand to be alone.

Getting his own key cut was a good idea, and I could see why he didn't want to bother me by asking for permission. It's been lovely to find my dinner on the table every evening and the house all warm and clean. These days Solomon listens to classical music. It's a vast contrast from the Beatles tunes he talked about with Mum on the day she died. I know he's being considerate, not wishing to invoke painful memories on my part. It's almost a month since the funeral, and our relationship is taking its own course, without any direction from me. Solomon's been so kind. Nothing is too much trouble. He even contacted my family and friends, telling them I was too upset to socialise. I would have liked to have said goodbye to my aunt before she went back to York, but Solomon was so thoughtful, visiting her on my behalf and telling her that I was not up to it. The house seems so bare now he's bagged up Mum's things, but he was kind enough to let me pick out some of her jewellery, before taking everything to the charity shop. To me, jewellery is a personal thing. I made my mother lots of special pieces, starting from when I was just four years old, right up until she got sick. I know he meant well, but it hurts to see the house stripped of Mum's personality. She left our three-bedroom semi to me, and it's mortgage-free. But it's in desperate need of some TLC, and I don't have the finances or the energy to carry it out.

Solomon is a stickler for timekeeping and, having been brought up in such a regimented lifestyle, it's hardly surprising. I'm afforded little insight into his schoolboy years, but my gentle probing revealed that disobedience of his father's rules would result in Solomon feeling the sting of his cane. 'Spare the rod and spoil the child' was a much used phrase in Solomon's household, and his adherence to timekeeping has carried over to every aspect of his life. Dinner is served at 6 p.m. on the dot, and today was no different. The dark, restless sounds of Beethoven's Symphony No. 5 provided the backdrop for our meal as he laid the table. My offers of help were silenced as he told me to relax and enjoy the music. He placed a small pot of garlic butter down, and I inhaled the smell of freshly baked dough balls as he took them from our little gas oven in the kitchen.

'This looks delicious,' I said, trying to muster up an appetite. It made me feel guilty – the fact I'm moping around while Solomon's sorting out the house on his days off.

Pulling a rickety wooden chair in to join me, he relayed his morning's work of mowing the lawn and clearing the rubbish in the garden while I was still in bed.

'You shouldn't have,' I said, apologising for sleeping in. 'It's those sleeping tablets, they knock me out.'

Solomon laid his hand over mine and told me not to be sorry. He talked about my old workshop, which he had discovered under the tree at the bottom of the garden. I hadn't mentioned it to him before, because I stopped making jewellery after Mum fell ill. I stopped because I was scared of what I might produce. It's my craft, and I pour my soul into the intricate little pieces, each one so very personal that I'm unable to sell them to strangers. I told him about the little miniature globes I used to make, how I filled them with sand from the beach and crafted tiny silver starfish, which I dangled on a chain. Then there were the moon and star necklaces, and the tiny silver mouse and cheese necklace, with matching earrings. I lifted my right hand to show off my dainty white daisy ring and matching bracelet. 'This is from one of my collections,' I said, admiring the way it caught the light.

Solomon returned his attention to his food, telling me that a hobby would help ease my troubled mind.

I nodded as our conversation turned back to the house. That was when I realised he was cleaning the place because he expected me to sell.

'Given its location near the seafront,' Solomon said, pausing to chew his food, 'this house could be worth in the region of £190,000. I know it's a bit shabby, and the furniture is worthless, but the structure seems sound.'

I did not share his excitement. It was too soon to think about money, and a feeling of unease crept up my spine. I don't know about the afterlife, but I'm sure I felt Mum's disapproving glare as Solomon picked over the bones of my inheritance.

He sensed my discomfort and jokingly rolled his eyes as I squirmed in my seat. I failed to see the funny side, then reminded myself how lucky I was to have a boyfriend who was so interested in my welfare. I twirled the pasta around my fork as I tried to pluck up the courage to discuss the thing that had been niggling me all day. Nora, the headmistress from school, had texted me. She said that Solomon had rung her, telling her I wasn't going back to work. I appreciated his concern, but it wasn't his decision to make.

Solomon raised an eyebrow as I blurted out my concerns. My heart fluttered in my chest. His displeasure at being questioned was obvious, but I had to know why he said it, when I had been keen to go back to work.

In a curt voice, he informed me that Nora rang the house phone while I was visiting Mum's grave. 'She's a bit pushy,' he said. 'Asking how soon you're coming back. You've just lost your mother. How heartless can you be?'

'Oh,' I paused, wondering if I had got it wrong. 'She said you rang her?'

Swirling the wine in his glass, he took a gulp. When he spoke, his voice was terse.

'You've not been very well lately, and I was just trying to help by answering the phone. If you prefer me to keep my distance, all you have to do is ask.'

The thought of being on my own scared me. While I was with Solomon I did not have to think too hard about facing a future without Mum. A wave of sadness overcame me and I instantly regretted my words. I apologised profusely: I must have taken what she said the wrong way – I wasn't thinking straight, that's what it was. Embarrassed by my ingratitude, I mumbled my thanks. Taking on all my troubles was such a big ask, especially so early on in our relationship.

But the truth was, I didn't know what sort of a relationship we had. Solomon had pretty much moved in, although he was sleeping in the spare room. I knew from the minute I met him that we shared a special connection, but we hadn't yet slept together. He was such a gentleman; he probably did not want to take advantage of me in my grief. But intimacy was something I craved. We were yet to go beyond kissing, though he was very affectionate in public. However, alone in the privacy of my home, I did not know where I stood. I swallowed back a mouthful of wine, needing some Dutch courage to bolster my next move.

'Solomon,' I began, figuring now was as good a time as any to ask, 'are we actually *in* a relationship?'

He rested his fork and pushed away his plate. I found it hard to read his expression as the candle flickered between us, and was relieved when he reached across and took my hand. It was soft and warm to the touch, and he rubbed his thumb against my palm. 'Do you have to ask?'

I thought of all the flowers he had bought me since the day he came into my life. And then there was the jewellery, like the necklace he bought, which he told me to wear at all times. It had broken my heart to remove my mother's silver locket from around my neck. It was a sterling-silver pair of guardian angel wings, which opened to reveal a heart. One of my finest pieces, it had taken me months to make. Mum had never taken it off, and now here I was, swapping it for a mass-manufactured piece that carried no history. But I could not be so ungrateful as to refuse his gift. It proved this was more than friendship, but I still felt confused. I supposed the death of a parent was not the best starting point for any relationship.

'Sorry,' I said, realising it was the second time I had apologised to him that day. I blamed my head, which felt stuffed with cotton wool due to the cocktail of antidepressants and sleeping tablets I was taking. Solomon had driven me to the doctor the day after the funeral, his face full of concern. It was unusual for GPs to prescribe drugs so quickly, without suggesting counselling first. But Solomon had told me what to say in order to get the medication I needed to get me through the days ahead, and I was too upset to talk to anyone about the pain I felt inside. Now I was beginning to wonder if the drugs were doing me any good. I felt groggy and stupid all the time. Solomon said it was natural to feel that way, when I had been through months of caring for somebody and all the stresses it involved. It was the same reason he wanted me to take a long break from work, and I felt guilty for questioning his conversation with Nora.

'It's just that we haven't, you know, been intimate yet,' I said, for want of a better word.

'Darling, I'll do whatever it takes to make you happy. That's all I want for you. It was all your mother ever wanted too, someone to look after you. I'm happy that I'm here to carry out her last wish.'

His comment of 'doing whatever it took' sounded odd, and it left me more confused than ever. Was this really how he felt about taking me to bed? But I saw genuine concern in his eyes. I must have read his words wrongly. But still, I wonder. My ratty little kitchen isn't the most romantic of settings, but I hadn't expected him to schedule our bedroom activities with the same precision with which he runs his life. I guess that's why I'm writing this diary entry. Solomon's popped home now for some more spare clothes, then he's coming to bed at 10 p.m. So here I am, sitting on my bed, nervous as hell and wondering what to wear. Hopefully the next time I write in, I'll have something positive to say.

CHAPTER FIFTEEN
SOLOMON

2016

Solomon could not remember the last time he had felt so excited. As he sat before his screens in his boxer shorts, he could not tear himself away from the action, not even for one second. He grabbed the empty milk bottle on the counter and, with the other hand, pulled out his flaccid penis and dangled it inside. A wave of relief fell over him as he filled it with hot yellow liquid. The smell of piss didn't bother him anymore. Not after ten years on the inside. You lost your dignity when you went to prison. You lost everything.

He placed the bottle on the side, missing his mother for the first time. The place was getting to be a tip. She was always useful when it came to clearing up. And who would wash his clothes? Tomorrow he would grab a bin bag and give the place a clean. But not tonight. He was having far too much fun watching Rebecca. Up and down she paced, checking doors, windows, locks, then back to Lottie, downstairs, upstairs

– she was leading a merry old dance, and here he was, like God, watching down and deciding her fate.

If she was this rattled after a simple theft, what would she be like by the time they got to the juicier crimes? A slow smile spread across his lips. Margaret Bowen had merely been a taste of what was to come. He would make Rebecca's heart beat like the fox on the hunt. He imagined dipping his thumb in her blood and smearing it on his face. But physical revenge was too easy. First he must torture her soul. And if she got the better of him? He chuckled to himself. That wasn't likely.

There were nine steps to go, each one more succulent and rewarding than the last. It wasn't difficult to find details of her friends and associates. The veterinary clinic's operating system was positively antique. At first he had been tempted to mess up the appointments but, fun as that would have been, it might have encouraged them to upgrade the computer software. Besides, why throw a snowball when you can unleash an avalanche?

Rebecca had finished pacing now, and stood by the window, her face devoid of emotion. Did she know he was watching? She must have felt his presence, judging by the number of times she rubbed the back of her neck.

The corner of the screen was plunged into darkness as she switched off the light. He stared at her silhouette as the light of the full moon embraced her form.

'It'll take more than the darkness to save you from me,' Solomon whispered, leaning back in his swivel chair.

He turned to screen two, pulling up the spreadsheet he had devised. Names, addresses, phone numbers and IP addresses of people she knew. Lists of proposed victims, back-up plans if something went wrong. The crimes were planned with military precision, taking forensic evidence into careful consideration. There was nothing to pin him to what lay ahead and, thanks to his old man popping his clogs, he had enough money to fund his enterprise.

Technology had developed at such an exciting rate, and there was no shortage of people to carry out his bidding, due to the contacts he had made on the inside. The first crime was a taster, and Rebecca had not let him down by calling the police. But there were other, meatier endeavours he had planned to carry out himself. Still, with the GoPro camera attached to the motorcyclist's helmet, it was almost as good as being there himself. The expression of fear on Rebecca's face when the driver turned to give her the thumbs-up. Solomon smiled. Saved to his memory bank, it was one he would treasure for some time. At least, until they met in the flesh. The alarm on his phone beeped a reminder. 11 p.m., time for lights out. His late night had been scheduled into his timetable, so it was nothing to fret about. He opened the window before slipping into bed. Below, a symphony of car engines and pedestrians lulled him to sleep. And then he was back there, to the day his mother abandoned him.

The engine of the Mercedes-Benz purred as they entered the driveway to the imposing building. Father sat poker stiff as he drove, his hat covering the bald patch that was beginning to form. Solomon clutched his brown leather suitcase on his knees. Teddy was in there, and he didn't want him to fall off the back seat. Mother glanced back with a reassuring smile. 'This is going to be a real treat, *Mäuschen*,' she said, then turned to face forward and sniffed into her hanky.

'For God's sake, Anna, how many times? I didn't bring you over here to speak German,' his father said, pulling up the handbrake as the car came to a halt. 'Pull yourself together, before you show me up.'

Solomon knew what his mother meant. 'Little mouse' was a nickname she had given him since birth. He knew other German words, but he wasn't allowed to speak them in front of Daddy. Such insolence would earn him a stinging slap on the backside. Mother continued sniffing as they climbed the concrete steps, stopping only when they reached the long, columned corridor that seemed to stretch for miles. The bad feeling that had begun in the pit of Solomon's stomach increased with every step. He gripped his mother's hand, drawing on the warmth through her lace glove. He didn't like this place. It smelt of disinfectant and seemed very old. He wanted to go home, to his tree house, and the smell of freshly cut grass. To the warmth of his bed, and the books on his shelves. A bell shrilled, making him jump, while his father and a thin-lipped man discussed the importance of timetables and discipline. Mother bent down to speak, her voice soft and comforting.

'*Mein Schatz*' – she glanced up at Father's disapproving look – 'my precious child,' she continued. 'Don't look so scared. Why don't you go with that nice young man and let him show you around? We'll see you soon.' She released her hand from Solomon's, which was immediately encased in the tight cold grip of an unhappy-looking boy in a striped blazer.

'But, Mummy,' Solomon protested as he was marched up the foot-worn steps towards the cramped dormitory. His mother gave him a tinkly wave, smiling broadly as he left, but there was something behind her eyes. Something that made his heart all jittery and scared.

'This is where you'll be sleeping from now on,' the boy said flatly, picking at a spot on his chin.

Solomon stared in disbelief. Rows of identical metal single beds lined the dank room, with candlewick bedspreads encasing the thin mattresses. 'I want Mummy,' Solomon said, dropping his suitcase. Tears filled his eyes as his sense of panic grew. He was four years old. Too young to be away from his mummy for very long.

'Well, she doesn't want you,' the boy retorted, folding his arms as he blocked Solomon's path. A cold chuckle escaped through his parted lips. 'They haven't told you, have they? This is where you'll be staying from now on.'

Solomon ran to the window, blinking back the tears as he stood on his toes for a view of the grounds below. Outside, a car door opened, and he pressed his face against the cold glass. 'Mummy!' he screamed, his voice echoing in the confines of the dormitory. 'Don't leave me, Mummy! I'm up here!' Clenching his fists, he beat the pane, making it rattle in its frame. But Mummy and Daddy got in the car and began to drive away. Solomon waited for the brake lights to illuminate as they remembered their son. But the car got smaller and smaller, and a scream rose in Solomon's throat. He hadn't heard the *clack clack* of hard leather heels enter the room behind him. Bony fingers grasped his neck, peeling Solomon from the window and throwing him on the floor.

Solomon lashed out, grappling with his bedside lamp. He was no longer in a boarding school, but alone in his two-bedroom flat. It had all been a nightmare: part of a past that would haunt him forever, unless he fought back. His bare chest rose and fell as he drew in breath. The outside breeze filtered through the curtains, bringing comfort as it chilled his back. There were no open windows in prison or school. But part of him was still trapped, imprisoned by the women who betrayed him. He turned over his pillow and basked in the midnight breeze. The truth was as strong now as when he left prison. The only way to stop the nightmares was to seek a satisfying revenge.

CHAPTER SIXTEEN
REBECCA

2016

Rubbing the sleep from my eyes, I turned to find Sean's side of the bed empty. Rhian had volunteered to work the early-morning surgery, to make up for slacking off with her latest squeeze. I was looking forward to spending the time with Lottie. This was her last year before she attended school. Having turned four in October, she would be one of the oldest girls in her class in Pontyferry primary next year. I treasured our time together, and couldn't bear to think of her being out in the big wide world, where I would entrust the school to keep her safe.

I pushed the thought away. I was not going to allow anything to spoil today. Not even Solomon. But it was like trying to hold back the tide, and his memory resurfaced as I took a shower. As I drew the razor over my legs, I remembered how Solomon had always insisted I wax. At first I used to think I was so lucky, having a boyfriend who paid for my beautician. But it wasn't as if I had a choice. As Solomon used to say, what was the point in having a trophy if you didn't polish it? And he was quick to point out if I was letting myself go. I gasped as I dropped the razor. Red ribbons of blood poured from the nick in my leg onto the white tiles below. It wasn't a big cut, but enough to bring me into the present moment. What was I doing, allowing him to invade my thoughts like this? But I was trying to put off the inevitable. I had to face the fact that he would be occupying my mind space for some time to come. The idea of revisiting our past sickened me to the core. If Sean knew about what I'd done, what *we* had done when we were together . . . The pancakes I'd had for breakfast made themselves known. I rinsed the conditioner from my hair, allowing the water to cascade down my back. I needed to draw on my strength if I was to get through this. *One down, nine to go*, I thought, full of foreboding. Solomon was dangerous, angry and fresh out of prison. The best hope I had of keeping alive was to carry out his wishes.

The rest of the morning passed in a flurry of baking, reading, and watching *Paddington Bear* on the television. I had just finished cleaning the kitchen when Rhian rang the doorbell. Bear bounced in the hall, recognising the clack of Rhian's crutches on the tarmac outside. I checked the peephole just for good measure, before opening the door and allowing her inside.

'Morning,' I said cheerfully, glancing behind her as I checked the yard was clear. 'I really must get you a spare key.'

Rhian arched an eyebrow as she entered the hall. 'Oh God, no, don't do that. Sean would want one back, and there's no way I'm letting him into my flat.'

'And what have you been getting up to, Miss Walker?' I said, with a knowing smile. 'I hope that fella you skived off with was worth the effort.'

'Young men always are,' Rhian replied, taking a seat at the breakfast bar.

'Please tell me it wasn't another teenager,' I said, cringing as I poured her a coffee.

Rhian huffed a sigh. 'Well, how was I supposed to know? He looked a lot older in the nightclub,' she said, her heavy kohl eyes blinking with mock regret.

I stifled a laugh. 'Student, was he? I bet you met him in Viva, didn't you?' Known for its cheap booze and student clientele, Viva was a nightclub situated around the corner from Rhian's flat.

Rhian groaned. 'Oh, don't laugh, I can't bear it. He was nineteen, quite cute, but he saw my crutches the next day and got all funny when I told him about my MS. I don't think I'll be seeing him again.'

'Oh, I don't know,' I joked, enjoying making her squirm. 'A few of them have applied for work experience at the surgery. I think it would be quite sweet.'

Rhian glanced around to check Lottie was out of earshot. 'If you dare tell Sean, I'll, I'll . . .' she said, but her tone was soft, and backed by a giggle.

I noticed she was wearing the necklace I made, and I reminded myself to start another piece. I had plans for a silver ring for my husband, indented with tiny planets orbiting the stars.

I checked my watch, sorry to leave my sister-in-law's company. Rhian was the closest I'd ever come to having a sister. I adored her from the moment I'd met her. Having come from a family of brothers, she seemed to feel the same.

'Seriously, though, why don't you try to find someone a bit older? Someone with a bit of life experience who'll think nothing of that flipping disability. It's not as if you let it hold you back,' I said.

'I'm trying,' Rhian said, the corners of her mouth turning up in a smile. 'I registered online a few weeks ago. I've been chatting to one guy, a bit shy, but he seems lovely.'

My thoughts returned to Solomon and alarm bells began ringing in my head. 'That's a bit dodgy,' I said, sucking in air.

'Why?' Rhian said. 'I can't afford to keep going out, and I'm not gonna meet a dreamboat in the surgery, am I?'

She was right. Most of the men that attended the surgery were weathered farmers with questionable growths sprouting from their ears and noses.

Rhian leaned on the counter, her chin resting in the palm of her hand. 'Besides, it's not one of those shag sites. It's a proper one with a good reputation. I'm being upfront about my MS so there's no horrible experiences later.'

'OK,' I said. 'Just be careful. Those places are full of scammers and psychos. Don't give out your home address and make sure you meet them in public.'

'But we can't have any fun in public,' Rhian purred. My face fell, and she raised the palm of her hand in a gesture of reassurance. 'Just kidding,' she said, but as I noticed the twinkle in her eyes, I struggled to believe her.

I shook my head, then glanced at the clock on the wall. 'I'd best be off. Lottie's in the living room watching—'

'*Frozen*. Yeah, I heard,' Rhian said, sniffing the air. 'Have you two been baking again?'

'Yup, there's some cookies in the fridge, help yourself. Any problems—'

'Give you a ring,' Rhian replied. 'We'll be fine. Enjoy surgery, we've got quite a few booked in.'

I smiled at her habit of finishing my sentences. We had known each other long enough that she didn't have to try hard to guess what I was going to say. The same could not be said for my thoughts. I had to keep those all to myself.

CHAPTER SEVENTEEN
REBECCA

2016

The veterinary-practice kitchen was big enough to squeeze in three chairs, a table, sink, microwave, and a fridge. There were no fancy sofas or televisions here, and sitting in one of the tatty wingback chairs released an aroma of cigar smoke and a scattering of biscuit crumbs. I reluctantly lifted myself up and went back into reception, where Margaret Bowen was holding court. The place was buzzing with news of her mugging, as she attended a check-up for one of her cats. Eyes wide, she relayed the events with theatrical embellishment.

'It was them Hells Angels,' she said, crossing her legs under her chair. 'All on drugs, they were, yelling and whooping down the road.'

Geoffrey leaned against the counter, biting back a smile. He had said it a hundred times. *If a story in Pontyferry begins as a mouse crossing the road, it'll be an elephant by the time it gets to the other side.* Margaret's audience gasped in horror, fearing they were about to be invaded by drug-taking, handbag-snatching, sex-maniac bikers.

'But I was on the bus,' a thin woman with a wire-haired terrier piped up beside her, 'and I only saw one motorbike.'

'They came after that,' Margaret sniffed. 'Out of their heads, they were. One of them tried to make a grab for me, but I sent him off with a flea in his ear. Look!' she said, rolling her thick support stocking down over her knee. 'Tried to take me down, they did. But I wasn't having it.'

'You shouldn't be stripping off in front of me,' Geoffrey winked. 'You'll get me going, and we can't have that, now can we, Margaret?'

'Get away with ya.' Margaret beamed, coyly rolling up her stocking.

I allowed myself a smile. She would dine on this for some time. She seemed none the worse for wear, apart from the bruised knee. Her bag had been found just a few feet up the road, its contents strewn in the mud: house keys, purse, everything was there.

The guilt of walking away would never leave me, but it did make me feel a bit better to know that Margaret was all right. I would need my resolve for what lay ahead. Especially when I had to focus on the next victim. The whole criminal element hadn't escaped me either. The rules were clear. I was meant to be a silent witness. I couldn't get involved with the police. But wouldn't they start to get suspicious if I turned up at every crime? Perhaps it was what he wanted all along.

To win this game I would have to be like him and detach myself from the people I chose. I ran through my acquaintances, realising just how insular my life had become. The surgery had become my life, and I divided my time between there and home. We didn't go to church, I wasn't a member of any clubs, and Lottie wasn't starting school until next year. On the rare occasions we went out, it was with Sean's friends, who became mine by proxy. Gareth and Chloe, Sean's brother and his wife, featured more in our lives than anyone else. But did Solomon know all this? Any second now the phone could ring, bringing with it my chance to nominate. But who? I felt like I was on an episode of *Big Brother*, with one manic viewer.

I cast my mind back, to people I came in touch with as I carried out my day. The drug reps that came to the practice visited regularly, but they weren't local. I bit my lip. If I was falling at the first hurdle, what was I going to be like later on?

The text didn't come until later, when I was locking up the surgery. Sean was washing down the operating table, while I chatted with Geoffrey in reception. I felt the buzz in my pocket, and I stood with my arm extended, clinging to the CLOSED sign like a mannequin in a shop window.

Geoffrey prattled on for a while, before he realised he had lost his audience. 'Are you all right, love?' he said, rubbing his beard. Geoffrey had been like a dad to Sean and me, which was a comfort to us both, given we had both lost our own fathers – Sean's through a tragic accident, while mine just left one day and never returned. He could be dead for all I know, and it's been easier for me to tell people that he is.

I should have carried on speaking as normal, but my words would not come. I was too busy staring through the surgery door, my eyes flitting to the car park and beyond. Was he watching me? Getting off on my reaction? I reminded myself not to give him the satisfaction.

'Sorry,' I said, rubbing the chill from my arms. 'I just remembered something I need to do.'

A call from his wife distracted Geoffrey long enough for me to get away. Bathrooms were my new sanctuary, and the toilet in the practice was marginally private. Set at the end of a chilly tiled corridor, the questionable smell emerging from the pipes ensured visits were kept short. I had barely locked the bathroom door before I slammed down the toilet lid and flicked on the phone. *Please be OK, please be OK,* I whispered under my breath. The screen lit up as it revealed a text sending me to the same encrypted site as before. I quickly took a picture with my other phone. I had just seconds to respond, but the contents of the previous message were a blur in my mind. I had to remember the messages, if I had any hope of keeping ahead. Biting my lip, I read the text.

CHAPTER EIGHTEEN

Diary Entry: 25th July 2005

I can't believe it's been four weeks since I've written. I feel bad for not using you, when Mum intended you to be such a precious gift. My old hatbox has proved to be the perfect hiding place, especially after Solomon asked me to remove my 'women's things' from the bathroom. Nestled underneath my packets of tampons and sanitary towels, I have no concerns about him reading my thoughts. Perhaps I should feel bad, hiding you away, but sometimes when he looks at me, it's like it's not enough for me to tell him how I feel. He wants to be inside my head too.

So much has happened since last month, and I don't know where to start. Looking back at my previous entry, I was hopeful this update would be romantic prose about our first precious night together. I couldn't have been more wrong.

Perhaps it's because I've been through the wringer over the last few weeks, but sex with Solomon was not what I expected. To me, it felt cold and almost mechanical, as though he was going through the motions. Given our connection, I had expected fireworks. But our first night together felt flat. He seemed to sense my disappointment, because he said it was only natural that I hadn't put my heart into it when I was feeling so unwell.

The next day I decided to cut back on my medication and try to get my life back to some semblance of normality. Solomon had got into the habit of answering all my phone calls, keeping the cordless phone by his side. I was surprised to hear him speaking to Selina from the hospital. I was used to the term 'Rebecca's anxiety' coming up during his phone calls, like I had invented a new disease. He spoke in low tones, as if I was asleep, instead of curled up on the sofa beside him. But I was too fuzzy-headed to see anyone, and I knew he was deflecting the calls for my own good. I missed work, but I had a couple of weeks left on my doctor's fit certificate before I had to go back. Solomon's birthday came, with little fanfare from his family. I was yet to meet any of his friends, which often struck me as odd. I planned a very special evening for us both, surprising him by booking us into a swish London hotel, opposite St Paul's Cathedral. It felt good to get away from the house that had held so much sadness over recent weeks and, as I slipped on my black chiffon dress, Solomon thought it would be a lovely idea if we ordered room service, instead of eating in the restaurant downstairs. I was surprised, because I had spent a lot of time getting ready, and when I came out of the bathroom, the food was already there. But by the time I was halfway through my main course, I could barely stay awake. I checked the blister pack of pills, and saw that two more were missing. But I didn't remember taking them. Then darkness closed in.

I woke at ten the next morning, blinking from the sudden flash of sunlight, as Solomon parted the curtains. He was showered and dressed, and our bags were packed ready to go home. I lifted the duvet. Instead of the silky lingerie I bought, I was wearing his T-shirt. The night had been and gone, and I had missed it all. I blinked, vaguely remembering Solomon undressing me, and the gentle stroke of cleanser as the cotton pad brushed against my skin. I touched my face. Had he really removed my make-up? What else had he done? I looked at my nails. They were painted red. I didn't own a red nail varnish. I cleared my throat, which felt like I had swallowed a cup of sand.

'What happened?'

He handed me a glass of water, then sat on the end of the bed and sighed. 'You don't remember? You fell asleep during dinner. To think, I was so looking forward to spending my birthday with you, and you end up face down in your food. Not exactly an ego boost.' He said it like he was joking, but I knew he was serious, and I felt a pang of guilt for letting him down.

I sat up, rubbing my eyes to try and gain some clarity. All I could do was apologise profusely, despite not being able to remember a thing. I asked why he hadn't tried to wake me, given it was such a special night.

Solomon patted my hand as I reached out to him, but would not look my way as he told me that he'd tried. Apparently I swore at him before cleaning myself up in the bathroom and going to bed.

'Worst. Birthday. Ever,' he said.

Shame washed over me. It had to be the drugs making me act strangely, because that didn't sound like me at all. What must he have thought of me?

I searched my brain as I tried to claw back the memory. But it simply wouldn't come. All I could do was to salvage our day and make it up to Solomon. I leaned over him and kissed his cheek.

'We have a couple of hours before checkout,' I said, trying to sound alluring as I rubbed his back.

'Your breath smells,' he replied flatly, rising from the bed.

My tears mingled with the soap as I stood under the jet of warm water. I ached all over, but I did not know why. Just what had happened that night? Had I really overdosed on tablets and passed out in my dinner? And the swearing? That did not sound like me. But what was the alternative? That Solomon somehow drugged me? I immediately dismissed the thought: why would he do such a horrific thing? He wasn't that sort of man, and had been looking forward to our night as much as me. I clenched my fists and pressed them against my forehead, cursing my stupid brain. No more tablets. I would find another way of coping. But when I came out, Solomon was holding a glass of water and a small white pill dotted the palm of his hand.

'I think I should take control of your medication from now on. We can't have you overdosing again, now can we?'

Still stinging from his earlier rejection, I told him I wanted to stop taking them for good.

But Solomon wasn't having any of it, saying it was best we do it gradually.

'You can't stop taking strong medication just like that, Rebecca. I'll help you cut down. Now swallow,' he said, shoving it under my nose.

I nodded, offering a thin smile as I took the glass. 'This is going to sound silly but . . .' I said, staring at my bright-red nails as they wrapped around the glass. 'Did I put nail varnish on last night? It's just that I don't wear this colour.'

Solomon frowned, 'Jesus, Rebecca, you really are losing it. You didn't paint your nails last night.'

I sighed, more in relief than anything, because I knew I hadn't put the varnish on. But then another thought struck me, one that made my heart skip a beat. If I didn't paint my nails, then who did?

Solomon handed me my clutch bag, and opened it in front of me. 'See? You did your nails yesterday, before you changed into your dress. Are you telling me you really don't remember?'

I looked into the bag to see a bottle of 'Big Apple Red' varnish. But as I looked back up at Solomon I shook my head, feeling even more stupid than normal. I didn't remember buying it, never mind putting it on.

Things thawed between us on the way home, and he surprised me by taking me to meet his parents that evening. I was thrilled. Meeting Solomon's family was something I had asked about several times, but he had not told me where we were going until we were virtually at the door. I fiddled in my make-up bag and applied some fresh lipstick as his sports car drove down the pretty tree-lined Central Avenue. The smell of the sea air lifted me, and I put my earlier concerns to bed.

I stared, open-mouthed, as he pulled up outside the impressive two-storey Edwardian home. I had been to Frinton many times but, on a teacher's wage, properties such as these were out of my reach. Before he met me, this had been Solomon's home, and I could not understand how he could go from living there to my humble house in Clacton-on-Sea.

'Turrets,' I gasped, pointing to the house. 'You have turrets.'

Solomon smiled. 'They're one of the original features of the house. Beautiful, isn't it?'

I nodded, admiring the mature gardens and the pretty honeysuckles lining the path. He seemed to delight in my reaction, and we both stepped up to the front door. Nerves rose inside me like freshly hatched butterflies, and Solomon squeezed my hand, before putting his key in the latch. I hoped a visit to his family home would fill in the gaps and provide me with details of a past that I knew so little about. A diminutive woman met us in the hall, and her face brightened in a smile. She was smaller than me, with little button eyes and greying auburn hair, rolled into a bun.

'*Mäuschen*, why didn't you tell me you were coming, and with a guest too,' she said, her German accent endearing her to me even more. I watched Solomon roll his eyes, as he told her to call him by his name. I wanted to tell him off for dismissing the mother he was lucky to have. But instead I shook her hand as introductions were made.

'I knew he must have a girlfriend,' she said, her eyes sparkling with delight. 'It's so good to meet you.' I followed her down the long corridor, the scent of lily of the valley trailing in her wake. I took in the impressive wide stairs, which were fit for a ballroom. Rich tapestries lined the wall, and my heels echoed as they clicked on the parquet flooring, making me feel as if I was in a stately home.

'I didn't know you were half German,' I whispered to Solomon, as we were shown into the living room.

'There's a lot you don't know about me,' he said, squeezing my hand for the second time that day. I picked up a hint of nervousness in his voice, and I squeezed back. This was his family home; why did he look so worried?

I instinctively knew the tall elegant man at the bay window was his father. They looked strikingly alike, and he strode over with a cold aloofness, looking me up and down before shaking my hand with regimented vigour. He regarded Solomon with a nod of the head, and instructed us both to sit down on the leather Chesterfield sofa. I thought of my mother, and how she had welcomed my past boyfriends with a generous hug, mugs of tea, and chocolate digestives. This meeting was so formal I felt like I was at a job interview. The living room was grand, although it smelt like a library, and the leather furnishings and oil paintings seemed expensive, but out of date. Solomon's mother remained silent until his father spoke, and I wondered if that was a family rule. Watching Mr Kemp make conversation with his son was almost painful, their words stiff and awkward as they spoke. It was as if they were strangers, thrust together to act out a family scene. I delighted in speaking to Mrs Kemp, who insisted I call her Anna.

'James and I met in the seventies,' she said, when I asked about her background. 'He was serving in the BAOR, the British Army of the Rhine. We got married, and came to Britain ten years later. It was very strange at first, but I soon found my way around.'

'And then you had Solomon?' I asked, keen to dig up whatever history I could.

'Yes, in 1982, shortly after his father joined the police. It's been just the three of us ever since,' she said, and I bit back the urge to ask why he didn't have any brothers or sisters. It seemed such a waste, the three of them rattling around in a house as large as this.

'I had hoped Solomon would have followed in my footsteps, instead of that computer nonsense he wastes his time on,' Mr Kemp grunted from his chair, voicing his disapproval.

'Computers are the future, Mr Kemp. Like them or loathe them, we can't live without them,' I said. Answering back was a daring move, given that I found the man intimidating. But it hadn't looked like anyone else was going to correct him. Silence descended as Mr Kemp stared down his nose at me with disdain.

'As you know, it was my birthday yesterday,' Solomon said, arching his eyebrow towards his father, who had given him nothing. 'I had something special planned for our night away last night, but unfortunately Rebecca was taken ill,' he continued, reaching into his trouser pocket.

I looked at him, quizzically, wondering where he was going with this.

'So I thought that now would be a better time to do this, here in the house where we will one day live.' His hand came out of his pocket and I could see he was holding a small black velvet box. A rush of panic shot up inside me, and I told myself I was getting it wrong. Any minute now, he would produce a pair of earrings, or a delicate brooch.

Solomon pushed back the chair and dropped on bended knee. His mother gasped, his father coughed, and a gasp locked in my throat as he spoke the words.

'Rebecca, I want to spend the rest of my life with you. Will you marry me?'

CHAPTER NINETEEN
REBECCA

2016

Another text, another challenge. I gripped the phone as I scanned the words on the screen.

> Victim number two. Common Assault.
>
> Geoffrey Benedict or ?
>
> Enter target here _____
>
> This will default to: Geoffrey if incomplete.
>
> You have thirty seconds to decide.
>
> 00:29

The mention of Geoffrey's name took the air out of my lungs. So Solomon knew about the practice too. Geoffrey rarely visited our home, joking that he spent enough time with Sean at work. There was no way I would allow him to be the victim of an assault. But the clock counted down mercilessly as I struggled to find a replacement. Nineteen, eighteen, seventeen . . . There was one name in reserve, and I pulled it from the back of my mind. Biting my lip, I tapped it into the box. Peter Cantwell: the unsavoury character whose Staffordshire bull terrier, Rocky, we had treated. Despite prolonged neglect, Rocky had still had it in him to lick the tears that fell on my hand as I comforted him during Sean's examination. Every cigarette-butt crater, every scar, each broken bone. All documented for court. If anyone deserved a slap, it was Peter Cantwell. My hands were shaking as I tried to hold the phone steady, but it was not registering my input as I typed.

'Fuck's sake,' I swore, frantically pecking at the phone with my finger. Eleven, ten, nine. Taking a breath, I started again. Five, four, three. A low whine emitted from my throat as I typed the final letter, just as the clock flashed zero. *Please please please*, I mouthed, hearing a pair of heels clacking against the tiles in the hall. The screen flashed and, with shaking hands, I prepared myself for the message of response.

Your vote has been counted.

The victim is: Peter Cantwell.

Await further notification.

'Yes,' I said with a groan, pushing the phone back into my pocket. A clanking noise echoed as a metal object tapped against the bathroom door. I winced, recognising the sound. I had barely noticed her come in. I opened the door to face Rhian. She was leaning on her crutches, with a quizzical look on her face. She was wearing her usual biker jacket and black jeans, with her lustrous red hair tied up with a red scarf. I felt positively dowdy in my tunic and trousers, with a smidgen of foundation to brighten my skin.

'Are you all right?' she said, her manicured eyebrow raised. 'I thought you were having a *Harry Met Sally* moment in there.'

'Oh, the gossips *would* be talking if that was the case.' I blushed, realising what it must have sounded like. Not that Rhian hadn't made enough of her own gossip in recent months.

I grasped for the first excuse I could think of. 'I erm . . . thought I was pregnant. I did a test . . . it's negative.' I could have kicked myself for coming up with such a daft excuse, but I knew Rhian would not question my obvious relief. It was not the right time for another child, now Sean was getting the practice off the ground.

Rhian gave a slow nod of understanding. 'Sounds like a drink is in order. Fancy hitting the pub?'

'Where's Lottie?' I said, knowing Rhian would have brought her to reception. The routine had been the same for years. But knowing Solomon was watching the surgery made me uneasy.

'In reception. So what say we take a trip to the Horse and Jockey to check out the new barman?' Rhian asked with a twinkle in her eye.

At that moment I would have loved nothing better. The realisation that I would not be able to drink until all this was over hit me like a slap in the face. I paled, wondering if my life would ever go back to normal again. 'Sorry, I can't.'

'More like you want to go home with Sean. Just make sure he puts a raincoat on it the next time, eh?'

'Ewww,' I said, snapping out of my daze. 'That's your brother you're talking about.'

Rhian snorted with laughter. 'Too far?'

'Too far,' I grimaced. 'Has he finished with the last of the clients? I'm sure they only come for the gossip.'

'Oh, that bunch of reprobates. They're gone. I gave them the death stare and told them to make a quiet exit.'

'Thanks,' I said, noticing Rhian wince as she leaned on the aluminium crutches. 'Still playing up?'

'It's being a real bitch. Still, nothing a few shots won't cure. But if you won't accompany me down the pub, I'm sure I can find a willing young man,' she said, winking a kohl-lined eye.

I shook my head. 'Are you sure that's wise? Drinking with your medication?'

'Of course not, since when have I been wise? Now, if you'll excuse me, I have to go pee.'

As I took a notebook from the stationery cupboard, I realised that my entire network of friends and family were all at risk. I had to compile a list of potential victims, and figure out where Solomon was going with all this. I was no Miss Marple, but even a small understanding would help. As long as I could keep it hidden. The last thing I needed was Sean finding out.

'Hey, hun,' he said, coming up from behind me and nuzzling the back of my neck. 'I'm all done here. Why don't we leave Rhian to lock up and get home? Lottie's pretty tired. We could pick up a takeaway on the way home and have an early night.'

'Oh, you should have said. I've told Rhian I'll go out for a couple of drinks with her, keep her company.' I swivelled around and wrapped my hands around his waist. 'I'll only be an hour. Why don't you go home with Lottie, get her to bed, and I'll pick up some food on the way back?'

'OK. Just don't let her lead you astray. I know what she's like once she starts drinking.'

I lowered my voice as the echo of her crutches filled the corridor. 'I'll just go for a couple and get her packed into a taxi for home. We can have a nice long soak in the bath after our food,' I said, just before he took my words with a kiss. I closed my eyes, savouring the moment.

I explained to Rhian that I was accompanying her after all. A quick couple of drinks would be enough to pacify her, and I could ensure she got home in one piece. But it was just a cover to get away. I wouldn't be going straight home. I had someone important to visit first.

CHAPTER TWENTY

REBECCA

2016

Darkened clouds rumbled overhead, threatening another spillage of rain. That was the downside of living in Wales. The variations in green were breathtaking, but if you didn't accept the rain as a friend, then you were in for a miserable time. I held on tight as a blast of wind made my scooter wobble. Shaftesbury Lane did not seem as intimidating in the day as it did at night, although evening was closing in already. November nights were a dark and gloomy affair in Pontyferry, and my heart gave a little start as I thought of the festive season. How many people's Christmases would be ruined this year because of me? I could blame Solomon Kemp all I wanted, but deep down I knew it was my fault. When I first moved into Pontyferry, the close-knit community appealed to me instantly. And the landscape – I had never known such freedom. The air was so fresh and crisp I could taste it. Not that I went too far – bumping into Sean had been a blessing. Both battle-scarred from previous relationships, we fell into an easy friendship, without any pressure to take it further. He introduced me to shortcuts that only the locals knew about: where to buy the best sandwiches, and the best coffee shop in Pontyferry. It was our little joke, because there was only one. I settled in, too enthralled with my new-found freedom to be anything but happy. In contrast, the guilt I felt now at bringing harm to Pontyferry's residents felt heavy on my shoulders. Starting with Margaret Bowen.

Easing up on the throttle, I crawled past the tree I had hidden behind the day before. Margaret had seemed so full of life when she had visited the surgery, yet I had caught something in her eyes that made me go cold. Counting out her change and straightening her scrunched-up notes, she'd paid her bill when it was time to leave. Her watery eyes had filled with sadness as she mentioned going home to an empty house. 'It's times like this I miss my Archie,' she'd sighed, referring to her long-deceased husband.

My stomach rumbled and I realised I hadn't eaten since breakfast. It was tying itself up in knots, just like it did when I moved here. I revved the throttle, and didn't slow until I reached Margaret's home.

I drove down the dirt track by a copse of trees, passing the first two stone houses, which looked as if they had been there since Pontyferry came into existence. Margaret lived in the third, a little further down the road. I killed the ignition as I parked on the grass verge. It was prettier in the summer, when the bloom of rose bushes added some much-needed cheer. It was so remote, as if three Lego houses had been pushed into the earth, out here in the middle of nowhere. Pontyferry covered such a vast open space; there were lots of little clusters like these. The roads had been built for horses and traps, not the heavy farm machinery that was commonplace today.

Margaret did not need a doorbell, as the cluster of cats caterwauled as if the Grim Reaper was knocking on their door.

'Who is it?' Margaret called out, her voice strained.

'It's me, Rebecca Walker,' I said, wiping my feet on the mat. 'From the veterinary surgery.'

A shuffling noise ensued, along with more meowing and the sound of something being knocked over. 'Benny, Betty, shush!' she commanded, as a bolt was pulled across on the other side.

I entered the gloom of the hall, following Margaret into the living room. The smell of cat rose up to greet me; half-a-dozen litter boxes lined the floor. I eyed the orange curtains, tightly shut against the outside world. Margaret gestured to the sofa, and I perched on the edge.

'I won't stay long. I just dropped by to see if you're OK.' I caught her puzzled expression and continued. 'I know you've been in the surgery, but . . . sometimes it's easy to put on a brave face. How are you, really?'

'I'm all right dear. I've had quite a few visitors, people have been very kind,' Margaret said, absentmindedly stroking a kitten that had jumped up on her lap.

'We're worried about you. I heard you got quite a fright.'

Margaret rubbed her knee as the memory came back to haunt her. 'In all my years of living in Pontyferry, I've never been a victim of crime. Can you believe that? I don't understand what they were doing out here.'

I wished I could offer her comfort, tell her it was a random attack. But I found myself struck dumb when it came to the incident itself. 'Probably just kids, mucking about.'

'That's what the police said,' Margaret replied, appearing to have forgotten her tale of Hells Angels and drug-fuelled sprees. 'But I can't help thinking they'll be back. They didn't get anything of value this time. Perhaps they'll come to my home instead, go rooting for my jewellery.' Her hand touched the pearl necklace nestled on her collarbone.

'Is that why you've got the curtains drawn? The door locked? You're worried they'll return?'

Margaret nodded sadly. 'My son's asked me to go and live with him in Edinburgh. I don't get on very well with his wife. She's very sharp.

But maybe it would do me good to be near them. It's very isolated around here.'

'But you've got your neighbours.'

'They're older than I am, and I'm no spring chicken.' She pointed at her chest. 'What good are they going to be if those hooligans come back?'

I chewed my bottom lip, wishing I could give her some much-needed reassurance. 'They won't. I'd hate to see you give up your independence. And what about the cats?' I said, as one wound around my legs, its long black tail tickling the backs of my knees.

Margaret sighed, her shoulders dropping an inch as her eyes roamed over her beloved companions. 'My son said he'll help me rehouse them. His wife's allergic to the fur. It's why they never visit.'

They'd be quick enough to come when you pass on, I thought. I had met Margaret's son and wife once before, when Sean conducted a call-out. She seemed more interested in the value of the property than Margaret's welfare.

'I'd hate to see you leave. Won't you reconsider? I'm sure you've seen the last of them,' I said, as guilt seeped in.

'That's very kind of you to say, but unless you can guarantee they won't return, then I have no choice.'

I dropped my gaze to the floor. I could have given Margaret those guarantees, but I chose not to. 'I brought you this,' I said, pulling out a small bottle of gin from the inside of my jacket. 'To help you sleep.'

Margaret's face lit up in a smile, and she thanked me profusely as I handed it over. But it was bought out of guilt. I swallowed, feeling lower than the dirt I had dragged in on my shoes.

CHAPTER
TWENTY-ONE
REBECCA

2016

'What are you looking for up there?' my husband called up, no doubt perturbed by my pyjama-clad legs sticking out from the hatch. The sight of me poking around in our spider-infested loft was unusual enough, but at three o'clock in the morning, it was downright odd.

'I lost my marbles,' I said, trying to keep my voice light-hearted. 'I thought I'd find them up here.'

Our takeaway meal and the shared bath that followed had made for a cosy night. But restless thoughts drove me out of bed in search of my old journal, the one Mum had presented me with before she died. I bent down to face my husband, who was standing at the foot of the ladder, wearing nothing but his Calvin Kleins and a quizzical expression as he waited for a rational explanation.

'It was meant to be a surprise,' I whispered, so as not to disturb Lottie. 'I'm making you a special piece, and there's a three-inch burnisher up here that I need.' It seemed like a poor excuse, but Sean knew how funny I could be about my jewellery-making when inspiration hit.

'At *3 a.m.*?' Sean asked, his words breaking into a yawn. 'Come back to bed, love. You can look for it in the morning.'

'And have Lottie lecture me for disturbing the spiders? I'll be with you in a minute. You go ahead,' I said, throwing him a reassuring smile before disappearing into the gloom. I listened to him pad back into the bedroom, and I exhaled a sigh as my body slowly relaxed.

When I first poked my head up into the darkness, I half expected to see the whites of Solomon's eyes as he reached out to ensnare me. Like a giant shoebox, the long shaft of space was easily big enough to act as a hiding place for unwanted visitors. But the undisturbed cobwebs reassured me that the only predators present were the spiders that had created them. I glanced at the abandoned crates, filled with things deemed too good to throw out but not good enough to occupy our living space below. Sitting next to the shaft of light from the open hatch, I drove my elbow deep into the box nearest the door. I knew exactly where I had left it, because it was never far from my mind.

Just as I had on the day I was given it, I brought the vintage-leather cover of my journal close to my nose. It smelt just as good now as it did all those years ago, when my mother had urged me to fill it with the breathings of my heart. Little did I know then what lay ahead of me. I had no intention of bringing it down. There were secrets in here that would never be shared with my husband. *Dywed yn dda am dy gyfaill, am dy elyn dywed ddin.* It was one of Sean's phrases that I had learned off by heart. It translated as 'Speak well of your friend; of your enemy say nothing.' It was Sean all over, and the reason why he could never read my damning entries. His need to know more about me had once been the root of many an argument between us. It came to a head on the eve of our wedding, when I had given him an ultimatum: accept me as I was or not at all. Thankfully he chose the former, although it didn't stop him asking from time to time, desperate to glean a little more knowledge of my old life. He could not comprehend that there were parts of me he knew nothing about. Like him, the occupants of Pontyferry were completely transparent. What you saw was what you got. But their lives had not been like mine. And, unlike me, they had nothing to be ashamed of.

I still treasured the locket belonging to my mother, but could not bear to put her picture up on the walls of our home. Another foible Sean could not understand. Pictures of his parents smiled at us from almost every room in the house. It left Sean with the opinion that I'd had a nasty fall-out with Mum before she died. But he was wrong. All wrong. I could not bear to see her face, asking me why I had brought a murderer to her door. I traced my fingers over the cover of the journal, trying to invoke brighter memories of the past as she handed over the gift she had so painstakingly chosen. But I could not think of my mother without Solomon clouding my mind.

I sighed, inhaling the stale loft air. Did I have a right to feel so sorry for myself, when my mother and Jake were dead? At least I was alive and had the chance to start again. Unlike Jake, with his rumpled shirts and lopsided tie, who was told off for his lackadaisical attitude more than once. If he had not called round that day, he would still be alive, probably still teaching. He had asked me out once, for a drink. But I was too busy looking after Mum, and turned him down. Sometimes we chatted in the teachers' staff room, where he would tell me all about his band, and how he was waiting for his big break. An image of his open coffin flashed in my mind, causing goosebumps to rise up on my bare arms. I had hoped that going to his funeral would exorcise the demons running around in my head. But seeing him like that, his black hair parted to one side, clean-shaven, and his pale, bloodless skin . . . it didn't look like Jake at all.

I realised I was crying, as the patter of a tear hit the leather journal, enriching the deep magenta colour as I swiped it with my thumb. Why had I come up here? Had I really hoped to draw comfort from a present that contained so many horrific secrets? Turning, I shoved my diary deep into the crate. If only it were as easy to bury the memories in my head.

CHAPTER
TWENTY-TWO

Diary Entry: 11th August 2005

I have so many mixed emotions. It's a blessed relief to be able to turn to you and allow my thoughts to bleed all over the page. I always come away feeling lighter, as if I've sat down with a friend. And, in a way, I have. Recounting my experiences with speech, sights and smells helps me untangle my thought processes and ease my troubled mind.

My last entry came to an abrupt end as Solomon came home. When he proposed, I was rendered speechless. I had fallen hard for him, but it was so soon, and I needed time to think. A solitaire diamond set in white gold, the antique Berganza ring was the most exquisite thing I had ever seen. I tore my eyes away, preparing the words that would break his heart. *It's not a no, it's just a not right now*, I thought. My feelings must have been written all over my face, and I opened my mouth to speak. Solomon's eyes pleaded with mine. I glanced over at his parents to see Anna nodding encouragingly, while a sly grin crossed Solomon's father's face. He thought I was going to say no. I gazed back at the ring as it sparkled under the light of the chandelier. I loved Solomon, and he had done so much for me. This was the first time he had asked something of me in return. I told myself that we could opt for a long engagement, and it was not as if I ever wanted us to be apart.

'Yes,' I said, my words a hoarse whisper. 'Yes, I will marry you.'

I had hoped that the excitement of the engagement would inject some passion into our sex life. I felt gutted that my grief had deprived us of the early, heady days, when you can't keep your hands off each other. Things were perfect between us in every other respect, and I knew how lucky I was to have someone like Solomon in my life. Public displays of affection came naturally to him, but in the confines of our home he was distant. I wondered if his boarding-school upbringing had anything to do with him being unable to give himself completely to me. In public, he threaded his fingers through mine, kissing me on the cheek and touching my hair. So why did he only go to bed after I was asleep, and shrugged me off if I so much as touched him in the night? We were engaged now – was this the best I could hope for? And then I wondered. Was it because in public he was safe, and it could only go so far? I tried to tell him that not every cuddle had to end in sex. But it always came back to me. He told me that I was needy because I was grieving, and things would sort themselves out in the end. But sometimes he said it with a hint of irritation in his voice, and I knew that he felt I should be getting on with things. So I hid my tears for the loss of my mum, and spoke again about coming off my medication. Solomon said I was not well enough for that yet, but he would alter my dosage. He was so caring and attentive, I had no reason not to trust him. But the niggle persisted, and I set out to get answers, because I still believed he was deflecting a problem that lay firmly at his door.

Solomon was not a big drinker. But when he came home from work saying he'd had a crappy day, I purposely set out to get him drunk so we could discuss our sex life. I know it was wrong, pouring vodka doubles into his glass. But I needed to know what the problem was, or if he just didn't find me attractive in that way. We were both slightly drunk when I brought it up over dinner, and my heart flickered in my chest as I tried to broach the subject of sexual fantasies. 'Is there anything you'd like to try in the bedroom department?' I said, trying to be seductive as I nibbled an asparagus spear.

'You've got butter on your chin,' he said, passing me a napkin.

'There must be something you'd like to try,' I replied, not ready to give up on the conversation just yet.

Solomon knocked back the dregs of his vodka.

'I don't think you'd like my tastes,' he said. 'Bondage isn't for everyone.'

'As in sex games?' I said, feeling a tingle of excitement. 'Why don't we give it a try?'

He snorted, but did not dismiss it out of hand. He seemed to regard me for a moment, steepling his fingers against his lips as he mulled it over. 'All right then, but not here. I know of a nice hotel in Hertfordshire. I'll book us a room. Make an appointment at the beautician's and get your legs waxed. I know you're in mourning, but you've really let yourself go.'

I dismissed his hurtful comments, because it was how he dealt with my insistent probing. I hope that in time we'll be more like a normal couple, with a consistent mutual respect. So we've planned another weekend away, without the sleeping tablets this time.

CHAPTER TWENTY-THREE
REBECCA

2016

'Sean,' I whispered in the darkness, 'can you hear that?' A faint whistle echoed up the stairwell, chilling the flesh on my bones. 'Sean,' I rasped, shaking his shoulder. 'Wake up. There's someone in the house.' But my husband snored softly, the excess hours working in the surgery taking their toll.

Sitting up on my elbows, I strained to listen. Nothing. I exhaled. It was just my imagination. I lay back down, taking slow breaths to calm my drumming heart. But my respite was short-lived as the whistling resumed, louder this time. My eyes snapped open. It was his signature tune. *Hallelujah.* Solomon was in my home. Leaden footsteps dragged up the stairs, the tune growing louder until it halted outside my door. Darkness enveloped me, stealing the breath from my body as I opened my mouth to scream. I was rooted to the spot, unable to move. The footsteps shuffled across the landing towards Lottie's room. I willed my husband to wake up. Why couldn't he hear it? And where was our dog? Solomon's intentions flashed in my mind like a distorted horror movie. Bear wasn't here because Solomon had killed him. He would slaughter my child, and then come for me. I clawed at the sheets, forcing air into my lungs, finally emitting a desperate scream. A pair of hands clasped my shoulders, their eyes flashing in the darkness. He was here, in my room, and I was blinded by the night. Fists clenched, I pummelled his chest, stopping only when his strong arms enveloped me, whispering in my ear that everything was all right. The reassuring smell of freshly soaped skin instantly relaxed my muscles. It was Sean, telling me *shh shhh, hush now, my love, it's just a bad dream*. I drew in a shuddering breath, my wet lashes blinking against his bare chest. Only when my trembling stopped did he release his grip. Illuminating the room with the soft glow of the lamp, Sean took a breath, resting his palm against my cheek. *You're safe now*, he whispered. I lay back down. He knew better than to ask me about it. I had this irrational fear when it came to nightmares, that somehow talking about them would make them come true. Sean switched off the lamp. His hand slipped around my waist as we settled back down, and soon his breathing lulled into a slow, steady rhythm. But there was no way I could get back to sleep. I peered over my quilt at the teddy, wishing I had turned its head back towards the door. Its cold glass eyes glinted with knowing, enveloping me in a fresh layer of dread. I rested my head on my pillow. My eyelids grew heavy and I succumbed to tiredness as my thoughts grew weak.

I went through the motions of making breakfast, rewinding my nightmare from the night before. It had been chillingly lucid, and I prayed it was not a premonition of things to come. The smoke alarms shrilled, snapping me out of my daze, and I grabbed a tea towel, wafting it against the oven before pulling out the offending tray of burnt toast.

'Shit,' I swore under my breath, barely noticing that little ears were present, taking it all in.

'Mummy said a bad word!' Lottie exclaimed, before coughing as the blue-black plume of smoke wafted up her nose.

'Naughty Mummy,' Sean said, opening the back door wide and allowing the fresh valley air in to scoop out the smell of burnt bread. 'I don't know why you don't use the toaster.'

'It's nicer under the grill,' I replied. 'I packed you a lunch. Don't forget to bring it.'

Mornings were always a rush, and I looked forward to my day off, leaving me some much-needed time to think things over. I had barely slept last night and, when I did, I inhabited the same awful nightmare. Solomon climbing the stairs, whistling *Hallelujah*, stopping outside my bedroom door, then turning for Lottie. I had been trapped, helpless to respond as my breath refused to come. At least I could blame my behaviour on the news that Solomon had been released from prison.

Sean buttered up a plate of toast that he'd shoved in the toaster, offering one to Lottie.

'I don't feel very well,' she said, declining Sean's offer of toast.

I felt my pocket, wondering if the phone had just vibrated, or if I had imagined it. A soothing breath cleared my mind. No, it was just my imagination. I would pack Sean off and then have time to . . .

'Rebecca, did you hear what I said? You *are* in a daze today, aren't you?' Sean's softly spoken voice cut into my thoughts.

'Mmm? Sorry, what was that?'

'I said, Lottie's got a temperature.'

Lottie coughed in response. She *was* flushed. How had I not noticed?

'I feel sick,' she said, as I put a hand to her forehead.

'Why didn't you tell me?' I said. 'Does it hurt anywhere else?'

'It's scratchy,' she said, touching her throat. Sean placed a depressor on her tongue and shone a light down her throat. He might have been a vet but he had a good handle on childhood illnesses.

'It's inflamed. Best she stays inside today.' His warm hands fell on the shoulders of my dressing gown as he kissed me on the cheek. 'Time I was off. I don't think it's anything to worry about, as long as she gets lots of fluids.'

'I'll give her some Calpol,' I said, reaching into the kitchen cupboard. Panic loomed as I remembered what lay ahead. Solomon's texts. What if another challenge came through? God, it was bad enough I had to witness a crime; I couldn't bring Lottie too. My hand wound around the silver locket on my neck. Apart from the journal, it was one of the few things of my mother's that I possessed. Solomon had thrown out most of her stuff, when I was in bed in a drug-fuelled haze. I missed her so much it was painful. If she were here, she'd know what to do.

'Why don't you go into the sitting room?' I said to Lottie, as I waved Sean off. 'I'll bring you some ice-cream and jelly.'

'Yeah!' Lottie squeaked, kicking off her slippers and trotting off. I was about to tell her to change out of her onesie, when I realised we might have to go out. But how? I bit my lip as frustration built, the phone held tightly in my hand. The familiar theme tune of *Frozen* wafted from the living room, and I wished life was as simple and uncomplicated as a Disney movie. I tried to pre-empt Solomon's plans as I pulled out the tub of ice-cream. Our giant American fridge was jam-packed with food, thanks to the two-hour weekly shop. When I was twenty, I was as far removed from a maternal housewife as could be. Things were different now. I loved my life, and prided myself on a clean home and a well-stocked fridge. I was nothing without my family.

The phone buzzed, making me jump as a sense of dread filled my every cell.

Notification number two. Common Assault.

Peter Cantwell.

Today at 9am.

Ash Grove.

You are a Silent Witness.

Talk to police and you die.

Ash Grove was a small council estate on the border of Pontyferry, one of the few built-up areas in the village. I thanked heavens for small mercies; at least the victim was Peter Cantwell and not Geoffrey. Common assault was low level, wasn't it? I settled Lottie before searching Google. It listed the various types of violence against people. Common assault was a simple push, or even spitting at someone. But my heart sank as I realised the offence was at the bottom of a sliding scale, which meant the only way was up. Actual Bodily Harm, Grievous Bodily Harm, Murder. Was Solomon going to work his way to the top? And, if so, could I really do as he said? With the names of my friends being put forward as potential victims, I had no choice. I checked my watch. It was time to go.

CHAPTER
TWENTY-FOUR
REBECCA

2016

Anger bloomed as I imagined Solomon laughing at my dilemma. It would give him a little thrill to know that he had upset me in another way. 'How about we go out and get you some ice-cream, would you like that?' I said, pulling on my coat.

'But I *have* ice-cream, Mummy,' Lottie said, curling up on the sofa.

I rested my hand on her forehead, which, thanks to the Calpol, had cooled. 'I need to go for a little drive, sweetheart, and I can't leave you alone. You can leave your onesie on. Just pop yourself into the car, we won't be long, I promise.'

'I need a wee,' she said, pushing off her blanket and slowly walking to the downstairs toilet.

I checked my watch again. Lottie took ages in the toilet at the best of times, but as she dragged her toy behind her, I knew this visit would take twice as long. Not that any of this was her fault. It was mine. I was drowning in guilt and it had only just begun. I gazed through the window at the overcast skies, still belching rain from the night before. The toilet flushed and I was gripped with indecision. What would happen if I didn't go? Rain hit the windowpane like spiked nails, with no sign of letting up. But I couldn't afford to anger Solomon. He knew where I lived. I clapped my hands, plastering on a fake smile.

'C'mon, sweetheart, we've got to hurry, before the rain gets worse. Here, we'll wrap you up in the duvet like a big sausage roll. You can sit in the back and stretch out.'

By the time I strapped Lottie into the car, another five minutes had passed. I had just ten minutes to get into the outskirts of town before my time ran out. An internal clock ticked backwards in my head, keeping time with the wipers as they fought to keep up with the rain. What was Solomon going to do? Knock on Peter Cantwell's door and slap him in the face? The car jolted as I bounced into a pothole. I hated driving Sean's old Volkswagen estate, but I had little choice, if I needed to reach my destination. Worn from animals and farm machinery, the road was a series of dips and hollows, testing the rusting suspension as we bumped along. I looked at the clock on the dashboard and put my foot down. Lottie was very quiet in the back. Too quiet. She was bound to tell Sean of our excursion. But what was the alternative? Could I ask my daughter to lie?

Focus, I thought, thinking ahead. It's just a common assault, nothing major, and in ten minutes it'll all be over. *Yes,* my conflicting voice replied, *but who's next?* I ran through some names in my head. The shabby homeless man who shouted abuse at passers-by outside the bus station – rumour had it that he acted a bit strange around children. He was never sober, so he probably wouldn't feel a beating the same as a normal person, would he? My thoughts halted as the flash of a blue light caught my eye.

My pulse quickened as I slowed the car at the junction into town. A sign was embedded in the mud, reading, DIVERSION – GWYRIAD. I usually found the Welsh signs and road names charming, but today my heart sank. A diversion could run for miles, adding precious time to my journey.

A thickset police officer leaned into my car window, sprinkling me with droplets of rain. 'You'll have to take the diversion, there's been an accident.'

'What sort of an accident?' I said, over the rattle of my motor. 'My husband's a vet, he drives a Land Rover. It's not him, is it?'

'No, a smash between a motorbike and a sheep. Driving too fast in the rain, no doubt. Just continue up that road and take the next left towards Welshpool, then you can cut back to the town, if that's where you're trying to go.'

Welshpool? I would never make it at that rate.

'Oh, and Miss?' The officer gave me a disapproving glare. 'You're lucky I don't give you a ticket for speeding, the way you've raced up that road – with a child in the back as well.'

'I'm sorry,' I said, heat rising in my cheeks. 'My daughter's not well. I was going into town to get her some Calpol.'

'Well, best you slow down or you'll have far worse things to be worrying about.'

'Of course, thank you,' I murmured, before jamming the stiffened gearstick into reverse. If only he knew.

'Are you OK, sweetie?' I said to Lottie, who mumbled a soft 'Yes.'

I turned the heating up high, blinking back the dust that blasted out of the old-fashioned vents. My heart sank as I took the turn for the diversion. I wasn't going to make the deadline. Perhaps that was what Solomon wanted all along. Tears pricked the corners of my eyes. I was allowing myself to be controlled by him all over again. The police officer's words replayed in my mind. A motorbike accident, he said. A small flicker of hope lit inside me. Could Solomon have been involved on his way to the scene?

By the time I got to Ash Grove, I was fifteen minutes late. I slowed to a crawl, passing Cantwell's dingy bungalow. It wasn't surprising the rain-drenched streets were empty. He was probably still in bed. I peered at the stuffed bin bags outside his gate. The courts had imposed a lifetime ban against him owning dogs, but without anyone to police it, there was nothing to stop him getting another one. Empty beer bottles and takeaway cartons overflowed through the split bin liner, but there was no sign of the cheap tins of dog food he occasionally fed the last poor creature under his ownership. I sighed, hoping Cantwell was alone in his misery. I couldn't bear to think of another animal going through that pain. The rain began to ease and was now being driven down the gullies into the street grates. A couple of pedestrians passed, shaking their rain-battered umbrellas. There was no sign of any motorbike. I glanced back at Lottie, who was now fast asleep. Perhaps it's over, I thought, wondering if the motorbike collision had been fatal. As I clicked up the car indicator to turn around, the phone buzzed in my pocket, and all hope inside me died.

CHAPTER
TWENTY-FIVE

Diary Entry: 28th August 2005

My dearest journal, I can't tell you what a relief it is to be able to turn to you for support. I know it seems daft, speaking to you as if you're real, but sometimes these random entries are the only things keeping me sane. I'm blushing at the prospect of recounting our night away. But I'll burst if I don't get my head clear of the thoughts spinning around in my head. God knows I can't speak about my sex life with anyone else.

We were sitting at the bar of the Manor House Hotel, me in my little black dress with the lace on the collarbone, and Solomon in his suit. I remember him telling me not to look so scared as I downed my third glass of wine. I had barely been able to eat my meal, because he had given me no indication of what lay ahead. The hotel he booked was so grand, but old-fashioned, with oak-panelled walls and stairs instead of a lift. The tinkle of piano keys echoed in the distance. There was no tinny muzak playing through the foyer speakers here. Solomon rose from his seat and coolly took my hand before leading me out of the bar. I tried to control my nerves as we ascended the stairs to our room. Caressing the dark wooden banister, he seemed somewhere far away. I fiddled with the strap of my shoe in the hall, and he barked at me to hurry. It was as if he did not want whatever spell had overcome him to break, and I trotted to catch up as he shoved the key card into the door. But there were no passionate kisses waiting for me when we stepped into our room. Instead, he bawled a series of instructions in a regimented manner. I glanced at the bed, to see a pair of black lace-top stockings resting on the duvet. A pair of red stilettos were neatly placed on the floor.

'Take off your clothes, and put those on. Leave your hair down. Then get on your hands and knees on the bed.'

I nodded sharply in response, my heart beating wildly in exhilaration. The shoes matched the red nail varnish he had asked me to wear – the same varnish that appeared in my bag the last time we went away. Any reservations I had were masked by the alcohol, and I took off my clothes and did as he said. He disappeared into the bathroom, and I could hear him undressing. I had no idea what to expect, and I prickled with anticipation, the cool night air from the open window chilling my bare skin. Solomon opened the bathroom door, naked and fully aroused.

That night, he slept soundly beside me, as if what we had just done was the most normal thing in the world. But an uncomfortable choice arose as I stared at the ceiling. I had to decide if I was willing to sacrifice the intimacy I craved for Solomon's cold and demanding sexual desires. Sex did not include beatings or whips, and for that I was grateful. But I had been completely at his mercy, and did not trust him as much as I should. My scalp hurt from when he wrapped my hair around his fist, and my wrists were sore from being bound together. But part of me was turned on by seeing Solomon so passionate, totally lost in the moment. For the first time in our relationship, we had climaxed together, before collapsing in a heap on the bed.

◆　◆　◆

Solomon was animated as he spoke about our wedding on the way home the next day. He seemed excited about our nuptials, and I wondered if he was relaxed because of our activities the night before. It had opened my eyes in a different way, and I replayed each moment in my head with growing unease. There was a point when he pulled hard on my hair, and shifted my gaze to the mirror on the dressing table. The intensity of his expression frightened me. His face was hard and cold, but as I whimpered in pain, a salacious smile spread across his lips. He was enjoying my discomfort, and it did not sit within the realms of what I thought a normal relationship should be. I tried to tell myself that lots of people enjoyed rough play, but there was more to it than that. I could have gone along with his sexual tastes, perhaps even got used to them. It was the fact I did not *trust* him that frightened me. The red shoes he had given me smelt like they had been worn before, and I could not shake off the feeling that something had happened when I passed out during our last hotel stay. And there was something about his behaviour, as he touched the panelled walls of the hotel. I wondered if his fascination with the place was connected with his past.

But there was no getting through to him. Whatever haunted Solomon was strictly out of bounds, and further probing produced nasty, scathing remarks as he lashed out at me, the source of his annoyance. I still loved him, but I knew in my heart that our relationship was not a foundation to build a happy marriage on. I waited for a week before telling him that I wanted a long engagement, and he asked me if it was because of our sex in the hotel. 'No,' I replied, not wanting to hurt his feelings. 'I just think we should have some more money saved so we can have a proper do.'

'Don't worry about money, I'll get my parents to pay for it. They're loaded,' Solomon said, with a smile. He hadn't even taken my opinion into account, and he was not finished yet. 'Last weekend was so good, I thought we could try it again, with a little variation this time.'

I arched my eyebrow. 'Oh yeah? Like what?'

'Would you be willing to wear a blindfold? And maybe talk dirty?' He stood behind me as I stared out of the kitchen window, pressing soft kisses against my neck, and blowing in my ear.

I smiled coyly, arching my neck as he sent shivers down my spine. It was good to feel attractive. And maybe I had been hasty. I was an old-fashioned girl who had led a sheltered life. To me, sex was hearts and flowers, and mutual appreciation. But perhaps I was wrong. I decided to give it another chance, before voicing my reservations. That week, Solomon couldn't do enough for me, and even talked about me going back to work. My job was hanging by a thread, due to the amount of sick leave I had taken, and I knew I would have to make a decision one way or the other. I missed my colleagues, and was too embarrassed to speak to Selina about what was troubling me. All my friends seemed to have dropped away, which was all the more reason to make my relationship with Solomon work.

But sex the following weekend made me feel dirty and used. We did it at home, in our bedroom, and Solomon told me beforehand what he wanted me to say. It turned my stomach to voice the words, and he was rougher than before, unspeaking as he satisfied his needs. Blindfolded and bound, I was completely at his mercy, and it seemed to go on forever until he was finally satiated, and set me free. As he fell asleep beside me, silent tears fell down my face.

And now, as I read back my freshly written words, I know I have come to a decision. Solomon tells me I am his only love, yet his actions do not demonstrate his words. There are too many things wrong with our relationship to carry on. I'm growing stronger, and I need some time on my own. As much as I love Solomon, I have to let him go.

CHAPTER
TWENTY-SIX
SOLOMON

2016

Solomon watched with disdain as his colleague Felicity Armitage shuffled past. The pencil skirt that was at least two sizes too small put her arse on full display. The popularity of big backsides was one of the things that baffled Solomon since his release from prison. To him, a woman should be petite, and well proportioned.

She turned on her heel at the water cooler, sashaying past his cubicle. He reminded himself to smile as she leered, her red lipstick coating her teeth. For one horrifying moment he thought she was going to stop. He shook his mouse as he waited for his computer to power up. The last thing he wanted was to be overpowered by her stale breath. Not when he had better things to do. His cubicle was nicely placed. Backed against a wall, his viewing material was not visible unless someone, like Felicity, went the long way around on a visit to the water cooler.

Today was about showing willing, and just as he had been the model prisoner for the last few years, he would be the model employee. They didn't need to know what he was planning on the side, and he had easily overcome their pathetic computer safeguarding systems so his Internet activities weren't tracked when they checked out his history. He smiled to himself. This morning's events had been a joy to behold. Rebecca had already botched up the second mission, by failing to arrive at the rendezvous on time. Which left Geoffrey as the default victim. Solomon smiled. He might not be earning very much in his new job, but his flexible hours made it very easy indeed.

He swivelled his head left and right as he brought up Facebook on his computer. It used to be so difficult, keeping track of Rebecca before they met. But now you could find out everything you needed to know with just the click of a mouse. It really couldn't be more perfect, Solomon thought, as he clicked on Rhian's profile.

Rhian's silly duck-faced pout featured heavily in photos taken with various men. Like Felicity, he had her down as a slut, denying her impending disability with mindless sex. To him, intercourse was something to be traded. It brought pleasure to others, but it was rarely an experience he enjoyed. Not that he wasn't good at it, of course. In his relationships before Rebecca, he had taken great pains to film his experiences. There had been no need to gain his partners' permission, because he was doing it to help. On his days off, he would review the tapes, checking the positions, timing and appropriate contact. He could not understand what his girlfriends were so upset about when they found out. It was not as if he was going to show them to anyone else – at least that was not what he had intended at the time. Their sex was normal. Boring. Not like the tape he made with Rebecca. He sighed. That had been his ultimate fantasy. Sadly never to be repeated. He caught Felicity's eye as she stared from her workstation. The way she was sucking on that pen, she was going to end up with a mouthful of ink. It would be easy to get someone like her to comply with his demands. But where was the fun in that? It was Rebecca's reluctance, her fear, that turned him on.

He was first introduced to sex at boarding school. Being a good-looking boy, he often drew people's attention. He was not strong enough to fight off their demands, so he figured he was better off getting good at it and making something in return. The quicker it was over, the quicker he could be left alone. But he was not a victim, because his favours did not come for free. It left it as less of a shock when he entered the prison system and it began all over again. This time he knew what to expect. His thinly padded single bed was not much different to the one he slept in at boarding school all those years ago. For there was one thing he could not stand, and that was to share the place he slept. To find another person touching you in the night, when you were at your most vulnerable. It made him shudder. He had put up with it in the early days of his relationship with Rebecca – at least until he got what he wanted. Now, as he glanced over Rhian's pictures, he was prepared to do it again.

He brought up the dating site on another tab. It was helpful of Rhian's friends to have commented about it on Facebook, and it did not take him long to find her profile. The description of a quirky, fun-loving young woman was the image she portrayed online. With daring red hair and sparkly eyes, she arched a perfectly curved eyebrow at the camera as she toasted whomever was taking her picture. He would take great pains, matching up their interests as he created his profile. A love of Morrissey, all-night parties and cocktails was a good start, and with a hint of wealth and a good sense of humour, it should be enough to pique her interest. Tired of one-night stands . . . wants to meet someone special . . . *blah blah blah*. Everything she wanted to hear, judging by her Facebook conversations with friends. He had even taken his profile picture, ready to upload for her viewing. An overnight growth of stubble stopped him looking too clean-cut, and a visit to the hairdresser's provided him with a trendy cut, long on top, short on the sides. He still looked young enough to use gel, and his hair had grown enough to shape it into a fashionable tousled style. Choosing clothes had been a little trickier. In the end, he went for a shirt and scarf, and took a blurry photo in the park.

Rhian would have had her share of arrogant young men trying to lure her into bed, so he decided to take a different tack. The handsome but shy, misunderstood young man would be the perfect persona to introduce to the young woman who had to battle with her own demons by coming to terms with her disability. Because, despite the bravado she put up in front of her family, he recognised a little piece of himself in her. Not that this was going to be any great love affair – he no longer believed in such things – she was just a vessel to get him what he wanted.

A friend of Rebecca's was an enemy of his, and he would show no mercy when the time came; stamping out his betrayers was the only way of easing the pain. There was no need to rush. He would savour extinguishing the life from those bright eyes.

CHAPTER TWENTY-SEVEN
REBECCA

2016

The vibration of a phone notification was quickly establishing itself as a symbol of something ugly, and my body reacted in an instant. It was as if all the air had been sucked out of the car. I opened my window just enough to enable me to catch my breath. The gritty smell of the streets whooshed in, and I welcomed it – anything to distract me from my distress. Sliding my thumb across the screen, I awakened the phone, and reluctantly gazed at the text.

```
Notification number two. Common Assault.

Defaulted to

Geoffrey Benedict.
```

Await further notification.

Tack tack taka tack, another shower of rain hit the car bonnet, sounding more like hailstones than the fat wet droplets bearing down. I closed the window, shutting Lottie and me in with my panicked thoughts. The crime in this sick game had defaulted back to Geoffrey, with the promise of further notification. *Not Geoffrey*, I whispered, clasping my hand to my mouth, as if saying his name out loud made it real. I leaned my head against the steering wheel as a sense of injustice rose. All of this – taking Lottie out, driving too fast – it had all been for nothing.

'Mummy?' Lottie said, stirring from her slumber. 'Where are we?'

I tucked the phone back into my pocket, swallowing back my emotion.

'In town. We'll be home soon,' I said, reaching back and lightly touching her forehead. It was still cool. Good. I would say nothing about our little excursion. I began to think ahead to the next victim as I carefully negotiated the journey home, past the outskirts of Welshpool and through Pontyferry town. I could receive another notification any time now, and I could not allow another friend or family member to get hurt. It was bad enough that Geoffrey was getting caught up in my mess. Common assault could be classified as a push or a shove, but actual bodily harm was much worse. I had to choose my next victim, and I had to do it now. Peering through the wipers as they swished across the windscreen, I stared out into the streets. As if someone would just come into view, and go *woo hoo, I'm your next victim, come get me right here.*

But in a way they did, in the form of the homeless man sleeping outside Starbucks. He constantly pestered shoppers, swearing and shouting abuse. I tapped the steering wheel as I wondered about his name. But, then again, did it matter, because Solomon was unlikely to know it either. I sighed. This was too serious to mess up. But what if I gave some random name? Someone Solomon wouldn't know. Would it default then? No. I had to make it easy for him, because even a hint of me getting smart would make him come down hard. I parked next to the kerb, pushing my hand into the side-door pocket. Scooping up the change, I counted it before winding down my window and shouting over, 'Here, do you want some change?'

The toothless old man blinked a couple of times before realising I was talking to him. 'Fuck off,' he said, waving a dirty hand in the air. His other hand was nursing an empty bottle of whisky. His skinny frame was bulked out by numerous layers of clothing, reminding me of one of those Russian matryoshka dolls.

I sighed. He was pissed. I didn't want to get out and leave Lottie in the car. I rooted in my jeans pocket, and found a five-pound note. Straightening it between my fingers, I waved it like a metronome. 'Here, five pounds. Do you want it or not?'

His eyes lit up at the prospect of paper money, and he shoved himself off the cold pavement, staggering in my direction as the empty bottle rolled towards the gutter. Muttering something that sounded like it belonged to a different language, he leaned against the window of my car.

I pulled back the note, hoping he would not wake Lottie with his rant. 'You got money?' he said, stinking of whisky and unwashed skin.

'I do. You just have to answer one question for me and this five-pound note is yours.'

'Whaddaya want?' he said, reaching in with crusty fingerless gloves.

'Your name,' I said, closing my palm over the cash. 'I'd like to know your name.'

He frowned. 'Nobody's ever asked me name before.' A shadow passed over his face, and then, in the depths of his eyes, I saw a spark of humanity. 'George. My name is—' he said, taking a deep breath. 'George Fairshaw. Thank you for asking.'

'Well, George, it's your lucky day,' I said, handing him the five pounds and the change I had accumulated in the car. But, as I drove away, I knew it was anything but. I had just sealed his fate. George Fairshaw would be victim number three. And I would be there to watch.

CHAPTER TWENTY-EIGHT

REBECCA

2016

'I don't know what Pontyferry is coming to,' Sean said, throwing his rugby kit next to the washing machine. His bad mood was painfully evident.

The aroma of garlic and tomatoes hung tantalisingly in the air, and I stirred the bubbling pot of Bolognese, throwing in a sprig of rosemary for good measure. 'I thought you were training tonight,' I frowned, presuming he'd lost a game. 'Did you lose?'

Sean cracked open a cool can of beer from the fridge and took a swig. 'What? No, I'm talking about Geoffrey,' he said, swilling back a mouthful of beer. 'Some cyclist spat at him in the street today.'

Of course. I should have known. The threatened common assault had already taken place. But instead of feeling disgust, I was overcome with relief. Being spat at was unpleasant, but would cause no lasting harm. Geoffrey seemed to have aged in the last few months, and I was grateful that this attack was something from which he'd recover.

Sean caught my expression. 'You don't seem very surprised.'

'Oh no, it's horrible,' I said. 'I was just thinking, poor Geoffrey.'

'Well, I think it's disgusting. First Margaret and now this. I don't like it. I don't like it at all.'

'Probably just kids,' I said, which seemed to be my standard reply. It was better than the truth. If Sean got this worked up over a couple of low-level offences, what was he going to be like when the serious stuff started happening? I had to brush up my acting skills, or my husband would see right through me.

'He was wearing a cap,' Sean said. 'Geoffrey reckons he had one of those video cameras attached to it. What do you make of that?'

So Solomon had got someone to do his dirty work for him, then watched the footage from afar.

'Did he call the police?' I said, knowing full well he wouldn't.

'There was no point,' Sean said, taking a swig of beer. 'He was getting out of his car when this fella cycled past on his bike, spat at him, then disappeared around the corner. By the time he gave chase, he was gone.'

At least I had been spared having to watch. 'Should I give him a ring? Debbie must be upset.'

'No, don't do that. He doesn't want to worry her.'

It was just like Geoffrey to keep it from his wife. I turned to Sean, taking the empty can from his hand. 'Well, if anything ever happened to you, I'd rather know about it.' It was only when the words left my lips that I realised what a hypocrite I was.

'The same goes for you,' Sean said, pulling me in for a hug. 'Although you've never really told me what went on between you and your ex to make you so scared of him.'

I rolled my eyes as I broke contact. 'For God's sake, Sean, he served time for murder. I think it's pretty self-explanatory, don't you?'

Sean spoke softly, tiptoeing around my emotions. 'But that was years ago. You don't really think he's going to look for you after all this time?'

My sudden spike of anger faded. 'You don't know him like I do.'

'Tell me then. At least give me an idea of what we're up against.'

'I can't,' I said, turning away from him. 'Some of the things he did . . . I can't talk about it.'

'But, babe, maybe now's a good time to start. Perhaps if you talk about it you'll be able to move on. Let's face it, you've been looking over your shoulder since you met me. Why don't you let me in? We can go through it together. Did he beat you? Is that it?'

'I can't say,' I said, my words a whisper.

'Why not?'

'I'm sorry, I can't,' I said, choosing to hide behind an invisible wall. Sean did not push me any further, but I caught the look of disappointment on his face.

The curtains softly billowed through the open window as we lay in bed, bathed by the moonlight. Sean liked the smell of the hills. He knew I'd get up and close the windows when he fell asleep. It was one of the habits we never spoke about. He opened the window, I closed it. He undid the bolts on the door, I put them back on. He answered the phone, I let it go to answer machine. He would never comprehend what I was going through unless I told him, but he'd never look at me the same way again if I did. I wasn't an easy person to be married to, I knew that. Yet up until now, he accepted my foibles without question.

I eased my hand across the void between us, onto the curve of his chest. I knew from his breathing he was still awake, trying to make sense of my behaviour. Unlike Solomon, he welcomed my touch, and I often awoke feeling protected as I found he had wrapped himself around me. But there were no shades of grey in my husband's reasoning, and I fell between the cracks of his black-and-white world. He hesitated only for a second before turning to face me. But I didn't want to talk, I just wanted to forget the horrible day. I leaned forward, pressing my lips on his, before he could speak. I tasted the toothpaste lingering on his teeth as he opened his mouth to accept me. Slowly I pushed him back, straddling his body. He moaned as I bent over to taste his skin, gifting soft kisses on his neck. My slow rhythmic movements removed all thoughts of Solomon from my mind. By the time we finished, our bodies glistened with sweat.

But my relief was short-lived, as I rose to close the window and heard the vibration of my secret phone. My eyes darted to the clock beside my bed. It was 1 a.m. A chill rose across my naked body and I shut the curtains tight. Was he out there? Watching through our bedroom window? Had he been watching all along? Or was he closer to home? He had installed hidden cameras before. I shook the thought away. I could not bear to contemplate Solomon invading my home, watching my child.

With shaking hands, I pulled my dressing gown from the bedpost and wrapped it around me. Sean was snoring softly now, oblivious to my fear. And I had to keep it that way. It was no coincidence that the message had come just as we finished making love. Solomon was a genius in the art of manipulation. My breath was coming hard now, in through my nose and out through my mouth, as I forced back the panic welling in my chest. My fingers moved quickly as I picked up the phone and tiptoed into the en suite.

I expected a text from Solomon to say that he had been watching, or a threat to say he was coming to get me. But instead, it was another text. Cold and impersonal, in the same style as before.

I braced myself to read the next message.

CHAPTER
TWENTY-NINE

Diary Entry: 31st August 2005

It was nice speaking to Nora yesterday, although I sensed a hesitancy in her voice. I told her Solomon was mistaken when he said I was quitting my job. But it's sorted now and, as Nora said, it'll do me good to get back into a routine. Besides, I'll need my full wages if I'm going to live on my own. Living on my own. God, I can't believe I'm even thinking it. But after what I've learned today, I know it's the right thing to do. All this time I've been blaming myself for the problems in my relationship. It turns out I was wrong.

Yesterday morning Solomon talked about selling Mum's house, and moving in with his parents once we're married. Like all the big decisions, it was not up for discussion, and it didn't seem to occur to him to ask me how I felt. He could not wait to move me into Frinton, and spoke about redecorating the house after his parents died. It's so unfair. I would give anything for another day with my mum, and there he was, counting the days until his parents passed away. As much as I like his mother, there's no way I'm moving anywhere, and his suggestion just strengthened my resolve.

There was no easy way to break the news, and I was so sick with nerves by the time he got home from work that I hadn't been able to cook. I waited in my bedroom, in the hope that, when I told him, he would pack his things and go. The first thing I noticed when he joined me was the estate-agent paperwork in his hand. He dropped it onto the bed, frowning at the sight of me standing by the window.

'Where's dinner?' he said. There was a sliver of irritation in his voice. I allowed him to moan until he ran out of steam, but he irked me as he suggested I was using Mum's death as an excuse to mope around.

'It's not about Mum,' I said, taking a deep breath.

'Your engagement ring. Where is it?' he asked, shrugging off his suit jacket and sliding back the wardrobe door. A memory returned to mind, of Mum being so excited that she finally got rid of my shabby wardrobes and replaced them with 'slide robes' to cram in all my adolescent clothes. I watched Solomon hang up his jacket. It was her last wish that we be together, but if she were here, I would tell her that she was wrong. There are worse things in life than being alone.

'That's what I want to talk to you about,' I said, wringing my hands as I told him I wanted us to have a break.

Solomon slipped off his tie and placed it on the hanger. 'We've just had a weekend away.'

'No, you're not listening,' I said, wishing he would turn around and face me. 'I want a break from our relationship. I need some time to be alone.'

I watched as his shoulders tensed, and he took a step backwards as he turned to face me. The expression on his face was one of disbelief, but an intense fire burned behind his eyes. 'After all I've done for you—'

I was ready for this reprisal, and interrupted his flow. My words were well prepared; I had practised them all day.

'I'm grateful for everything you've done, Solomon, you know that. All I'm asking for is some time alone. Things have been moving so fast. I feel like I can't breathe.'

Solomon's words fell to a whisper. 'You know, don't you? That's why you're doing this.'

'Know what?' I said, a sickly feeling churning my gut.

'About my test results,' he said, dropping onto the bed as his knees seemed to give way.

'What test results?' My hand flew to my mouth as his meaning became clear.

Solomon looked at me with haunted eyes. 'The hospital's been in touch. My cancer's come back.' His head fell into his hands, and I sat on the bed beside him, easing my hand over his shoulder. My mind raced as I tried to take it in, and all thoughts of us separating evaporated into thin air. I didn't know anything about Solomon's cancer, as he had flatly refused to talk about it, wanting us to move on from the past.

'It's OK, I'm not going anywhere.'

'Do you promise?' Solomon said, staring at the pink carpet that had been there since my teens.

'I swear,' I said softly, pleading with him to talk about it so we could face it together.

'Tomorrow,' he said, rising from the bed and kicking off his shoes. 'I'm getting a shower. Can you order in a Chinese? I'm starving.'

I nodded dumbly, watching him close the en-suite door behind him. How could he eat after the bombshell he had just dropped? I stood at the bedroom doorway, wondering what the hell had happened.

By the time I woke, Solomon had already left for work, and I wished I had not taken the sleeping tablet he insisted on giving me. I might as well have been awake all night, but at least I could have spoken to him this morning. *No more tablets*, I thought. I needed a clear head from now on. Throwing on my coat, I made my way to the hospital and headed for the oncology ward. I was stronger now, and could cope with the old familiar smells and sounds as they rose up to greet me. I pumped the antiseptic dispenser on the wall, rubbing the foamy substance between my fingers as I recalled the last time I was there. I recognised the bucket chairs Solomon and I had sat in, and the old coffee machine I had drunk from, before he brought me my hot chocolate. It all seemed like a lifetime away, and for a fleeting moment I allowed myself to believe that Mum was still in her old room. Sometimes when I was in town, I would see someone who looked like her from behind, and follow them for a short distance, pretending she was still alive. But now Solomon infiltrated my thoughts, and the uncertain future that lay ahead. I had thought that perhaps he might be here, then realised I was being silly, blaming my fuzzy head. I turned to leave, and a friendly face came into view. It was Selina, and she trotted down the corridor to meet me, pulling her cardigan across her nurse's uniform.

'Hey you, how's it going? Long time no see,' she said, walking towards me.

I finger-combed my hair from my face, realising I must have looked a sight. 'I'm getting there,' I said. 'Good to see you. Are you starting or finishing?'

'Finishing,' she said, masking a yawn with the back of her hand. 'I've just overrun on the night shift. Fancy a coffee? I need something strong to stop me falling asleep on the drive home.'

I insisted on treating her to a Starbucks. 'So how's things?' I asked, taking a seat in the booth beside her, with two cappuccinos in hand. 'Still taking photos?'

Selina rolled her eyes. 'Chance would be a fine thing. There's not much time at the moment, with work and everything. What brought you to the hospital? Nothing to worry about, I hope?'

I shook my head, but felt a sadness descend. It had been so long since I had spoken to anyone apart from Solomon, I didn't know where to begin.

'How long have you got?' I replied, my burdens weighing heavy on my shoulders.

'Aww, mate, is it your mum?' Selina said, gently putting her arm around me.

I shook my head, biting back the tears as a lump rose to my throat. All the worries of the last few months built like a crescendo inside me. Perhaps it was being in the company of another woman, or just seeing a friendly face, but I found myself blurting out everything that had happened since we last spoke.

Selina seemed amazed to hear I was engaged, relaying her disbelief by shaking her head. She seemed to think I was with Solomon out of pity, but I tried to explain how there was so much more to our relationship than that.

I reached for the tissue in my pocket. 'I can't leave him, not now he has cancer.'

Selina took a mouthful of her coffee and licked the froth from her lips. 'Really? That's weird, though, isn't it? Getting the news the same day you tried to leave him.'

I nodded slowly, feeling disloyal for talking about the man who had got me through so much. 'I feel like such a bitch, talking about him like this, but . . . the thought had occurred to me too. But surely he wouldn't stoop so low?'

But Selina didn't answer the way I expected. She hesitated, before turning her gaze on me. She looked thoughtful as she asked me if I was OK, checking that the stress of losing Mum wasn't affecting my thinking. It seemed an odd thing to say, after what I had just told her, but I let it go. I scribbled down my mobile number on a napkin and passed it over. My old phone got broken after Solomon dropped it into the sink, and I hadn't got around to passing on my new number.

Selina's words played on my mind when I got home, and I was surprised to get a text from Solomon saying he was finishing work early. Guilt consumed me as I realised he was coming to talk about his illness, and I lifted my phone to text Selina, to tell her to disregard everything that I'd said. I jumped as it vibrated in my hand and, like magic, her number appeared on the screen.

Her voice was breathy as she whispered down the phone, and my heart lurched as I wondered if she was in some kind of trouble. 'Are you alone?' she asked, sounding like she was outside.

'Yes, what's wrong?' I said, pressing the phone against my ear.

'You need to finish with him, Rebecca. Just pack his bags and leave them at the door.'

'What are you talking about?' I said, a nervous titter rising up inside me.

'After you left, I went back to work. I hacked Solomon's medical records to see if he was telling the truth.'

'Hellfire, Selina, you'll get the sack for that.'

That's when she told me that Solomon was lying. He didn't have cancer. I barely heard the rest of her words as she reassured me that she had covered her tracks. She ended with an apology, relaying how terrible she felt for doubting my story.

I gasped down the phone, searching my mind for a rational explanation. And then it clicked. Selina had got it wrong. I remembered Solomon saying his test had come up a false negative. It's why they had to call him back, to break the news that he wasn't in remission after all.

But Selina was adamant. Solomon *never* had cancer. The most serious illness he'd ever had was a burst appendix. There was nothing wrong with him. He'd been lying to me all this time.

'No. You're wrong,' I gasped. But I remembered Solomon showing me the scar from his appendix operation.

'I've checked it through,' Selina said, as a gust of wind distorted her words. 'Just what sort of person pretends to have cancer?'

But now Solomon's car is rumbling on my front drive, and I'm about to find out.

CHAPTER THIRTY
REBECCA

2016

I squinted at the message as it lit up the screen.

Victim number three. Burglary.

Margaret Bowen or ?

Enter target here _____

This will default to: Margaret if incomplete.

You have thirty seconds to decide.

00:29

Each communication brought a rising sense of dread. Burglary? I blinked to make sure I'd read it properly. Everything about this knocked me off kilter. I'd presumed an act of violence, but this seemed more against a property than a person. And Margaret Bowen, again? That threw me. I'd presumed it would be a different person each time. If that was the case, could I use the same victim? I bit my bottom lip. How could I play the game if I didn't know the rules? And what about poor Margaret? I'd already failed her once; could I gamble with her safety again? Burglary. That took the homeless man out of the equation for starters. Had Solomon been watching as I lined up my next victim? The clock ticked down, the numbers counting backwards. But I had somebody in reserve. I typed the name in the box, hardening my resolve. I had to be tough to get through this. And I would be.

Eleven, ten, nine. I typed in the name. Nigel Evans. A farmer that owed Sean thousands of pounds and had no intention of paying. Sean had given up sending payment reminders, and couldn't bring himself to sue. He would get over being burgled, and a dose of karma would do him no harm. I knew it was wrong, but I had to justify it in my own mind. Because I had to stand by and watch. Out of all the people I knew in Pontyferry, Nigel Evans was one of the ones I would lose the least sleep over. I awaited the notification, which seemed to be taking longer than before. Shivering in the darkness, I heard Sean murmur my name. I peeked through the crack in the door. 'I'm in the loo, I'll be out in a minute,' I said, willing the phone to beep a response.

Notification number three. Burglary.

Nigel Evans.

Tomorrow at 2am.

Ardwyn Farm.

You are a Silent Witness.

Talk to police and you die.

I heaved a sigh of relief. Had he been delayed because he was looking up the address? How did he even know where the man lived? Whatever it was, I had won this round. Just. Margaret was already living on her nerves. Being burgled would finish her. Her son would put her in a home and her cats would have to be put down if they couldn't be rehomed. Nigel Evans . . . he would get over it. It was the least he deserved. Surprisingly, I fell asleep. It would occur to me much later that my thoughts were unsavoury and unkind. I had vowed not to allow Solomon to change me, and yet I was undoubtedly changing, drawing on my darker nature to get me through what lay ahead.

Sleep came at a price, filling me with nightmares of seeing Solomon's face. He was Solomon the charmer, egging on runners on London Marathon day, sharing my water and getting me over the finish line. Solomon the perfect boyfriend, bringing my mother her favourite flowers. But it melted away, the colours and sounds morphing to a lifeless grey. He was in the confines of a prison cell, staring at me. Solomon the tortured, dark soul. I was on the other side of the heavy metal door, pleading with him for mercy. *We were different people now. It wasn't like how it used to be*, I begged, knowing my words were falling on deaf ears. He lifted a mirror, and I gasped at my reflection. My long blond hair had returned, and with it the red painted nails he liked so much. Then I was back in my bedroom, kicking off the red stilettos and frantically trying to cut my long hair short. But the more I cut it, the longer it grew, until it twisted around my neck. I awoke, finding the cord of my nightgown wrapped around my throat. Anxious hands unwound it, and I gulped back the sobs that had started in my sleep. There were no words to comfort me, only the strength of my husband's arms. I gave in to his embrace, finally falling back to sleep.

The first thing I did when I awoke was to touch my hair. Its shortness brought me comfort. I would never grow it long again. I came downstairs to the smell of coffee and pancakes, served with fresh blueberries and maple syrup. I joined Lottie at the table. She was wearing her *Frozen* pyjamas, her long blond hair like a nest on her head.

I muttered a *thank you* to my husband and filled my mouth with pancakes, a ready excuse not to talk. I wondered how long he would let me continue with these nightmares before he insisted I attend counselling. He plated up the last of the pancakes, and his hands found my shoulders.

'You're so tense,' he said, gently pinching my muscles.

I recognised the cue to speak, but this was not something to be discussed in front of our daughter. 'Ouch,' I said, shrugging off his hands. 'Sorry, but I'm a bit stiff. I think I slept funny.'

Sean murmured something about not sleeping at all, but I let it go. We were both due at the surgery, and Rhian had promised to take Lottie to the park. I looked out through the kitchen window, hoping for rain, which would make her cancel. Disappointingly, the skies were clear. I thought about my 2 a.m. start. A burglary of all things. Surely that was taking a chance, even for Solomon? I could have called the police and caught him in the act. He would be recalled to prison to serve the rest of his sentence. Wasn't that what I wanted? But at least one of the acts had been carried out by a masked man. There were no guarantees that it was Solomon. It wasn't just as simple as calling up and sending him back to prison. The police would need solid proof.

And even if I did call the police, what then? First, they would ask how the hell I knew a burglary was going to occur, and then I'd have to confess about nominating the victim – all because he hadn't paid his bill. Solomon had money, and money could buy you all sorts of things. Perhaps the burglary was a test, the cheese on the mousetrap. If I gave in and called the police, he would snap my neck, as quick as any metal spring. I touched my throat and glanced at my daughter. If I had to risk the welfare of others against my family's lives, then so be it. But the burglary was happening tonight, and soon there would be a request for another victim . . . and another . . . and another. Could I really go through with it?

Sean rattled his keys, seeing me standing at the door with one of Lottie's shoes in my hand. It was happening more often, him finding me half absent when I should have been tending to my family. If only he knew. But I would have to carry the burden of the truth alone. There was far too much at stake.

CHAPTER
THIRTY-ONE
SOLOMON

2016

'I can't believe you're actually sitting opposite me,' Rhian said, seductively crossing her legs. She looked amazing in her fitted red dress, and wore it with confidence.

Solomon had taken great care choosing the restaurant. Somewhere classy, without the intrusion of CCTV. Their table was situated in the far corner, away from prying eyes. He knew from the emails he had hacked that it was one of her favourites.

'I've never done this before,' Solomon said, filling her glass with Pinot Grigio. 'Internet dating, I mean. But once I found your profile, I didn't look anywhere else. I guess I struck lucky first time.'

Rhian flushed. 'Thanks, although I don't know why you're Internet dating to begin with, being from Birmingham. There must be lots of great clubs and bars around there.'

'I'm new to the area. I don't really know my way around yet.' Solomon gave a shy smile. That was something else Rhian had mentioned, in an email to a friend. She wanted to meet someone understated, who wasn't 'up their own arse', as she had so eloquently put it.

'Where do you come from originally?' Rhian said, picking at her dessert.

Solomon looked her over. The whole red hair, red lipstick and red dress would have been overkill on anyone else, but with her pale skin and high cheekbones, she carried it off with ease. 'Here and there. I've been travelling for the last few years, but I think it's time I settled down now.' *Mysterious and wanting to settle down – more boxes ticked,* Solomon thought, slowly bringing the forkful of cheesecake to his mouth.

'So what's brought you here?'

'Work. But let's not talk about that, it's boring. I want to hear all about you.'

Rhian waved him away. 'I'm bloody boring too! Grew up in the village all my life, managed to get away for a few years before I was struck down with MS, came home, got a dull job. The end.'

'The vet practice,' Solomon said, having learned all about it from their online chats. That, and the fact he was stalking the owners. 'Any children?'

'No, although I look after my niece a few times a week. I job share with my sister-in-law. It's really nice being an auntie. You get the best of both worlds.'

'And your sister-in-law? Do you get on?'

'Really well,' Rhian said. 'Why do you ask?'

Solomon patted his mouth with the napkin. 'Just making conversation.'

'Do you?' Rhian said.

'Do I what?'

'Have children?'

Solomon frowned, but it was so fleeting he hoped she had not noticed it. Thoughts of his baby were never far from his mind. The baby that Rebecca killed. 'No. Not yet. I'm an only child, so I don't have the benefit of nieces or nephews either.'

'That's a shame. Do you get to see your parents at all?'

'They're both dead. What about you?'

'Same. Sucks, doesn't it?'

'Yep.' He swirled his wine before taking a large sip.

'God, this conversation's taken a bit of a nosedive. How about we have some cocktails and talk about something else?'

'Like what?'

'Dunno. Sex? That always keeps me interested,' she said with a wink.

CHAPTER THIRTY-TWO

REBECCA

2016

It was good to get lost in work for a few hours. At least knowing the time of the next incident left me the day free from worrying about another notification. I was too wrapped up in VAT returns and spreadsheets to afford it too much time, but I knew that I would have to plan my nightly excursion. The next victim lived just a mile from our house, and I could drive a good distance on low beams without fear of coming across anyone. Certainly not at two in the morning. I would tell Sean I had a migraine, and ask to sleep in the spare room. He would most likely welcome a decent night's sleep, and I could sneak out in plenty of time to get to the house. But where would I watch from? Surely he didn't want me inside the house? No. I was not going to incriminate myself that way. I would watch from a distance, near enough to be seen, but far enough to escape should the police turn up. I had been so busy worrying about Solomon, it hadn't occurred to me until much later on that I could be arrested myself. I couldn't afford for the police to be poking around in my past. Things didn't stay a secret in Pontyferry for very long.

It was a relief that there was no small-animal surgery today. My duties consisted of trying to make sense of our awful accounts system and feeding and caring for the caged animals recovering from surgery. At least I was spared the gossip about Geoffrey's run-in with a mystery jogger. Sean seemed to be the only person he had told, and he seemed slightly embarrassed when I asked him how he was. He popped into reception every day, even on days there was no surgery. He waved my concerns away, although I wondered whether, if I showed him a photo of Solomon, he would recognise him as the person who spat in his face. Probably not. Why else would the person have been wearing a camera, if not to feed back to Solomon, allowing him to indulge in his sick power games? But Solomon would not always be so distant. I could feel it on the horizon, a darkness drawing near. And I was powerless to stop him. Geoffrey would never talk to the police, and Solomon was surely clever enough to create an alibi for each involvement. I froze as the phone buzzed in my back pocket. Another text message left me in no doubt about the lengths Solomon would go to. It was not like the others, and consisted of just six words.

Text received. Let's play some more.

What text? I thought, frowning as I tried to take in the words. Just what was he up to now? I jabbed at the slim black phone, checking the sent box, which was empty. I would never communicate directly with Solomon, and even if I did, this phone was not set up to send him a text. Unless . . . the surgery phone rang on the desk, scaring me half to death and making me jump from my chair. It was someone moving their appointment, and I dealt with it swiftly, trying not to sound too jittery on the phone. My subconscious was already working out the reason for the latest text and, by the time I hung up, I knew to check my personal mobile phone. My fingers pressed and prodded as I called up the texts I had sent in the last few days. There it was. A text sent to a mobile number, which was saved in my address book as 'Sol'. My eyes widened as I opened the text and read the screen.

> Miss you baby. Wanna play? Teach some people a lesson, so we can be together. Margaret Bowen. Geoffrey Benedict. Nigel Evans. I love a bad boy. Show me how bad you can be. XXX

The words filled me with horror. Somehow, Solomon had accessed my phone and sent a text. The words sounded nothing like me. 'Teaching someone a lesson' was Solomon's turn of phrase. I had heard the words enough times from his lips. It incriminated him, but it also incriminated me. And I knew why he had gone from being totally anonymous to risking his apparent involvement. I made him uneasy. He could see I was happy, free of medication and anxiety attacks, and not the subservient little Rebecca he used to know. The text was his way of saying, 'If I go down, you go down too.' I racked my brains, trying to think when he could have sent it. I brought my phone everywhere I went . . . but yesterday I had taken Bear for a walk and mistaken Sean's phone for mine. I had been gone less than an hour. Had he really accessed our home in that short time? Solomon was beginning to feel more like a phantom than a real person. How was he able to slip in and out unseen?

The message was received loud and clear. There was no way I was risking being reported to the police. I would have to find another way of stopping Solomon but, in the meantime, I would force myself to go along with his plans.

That night I was grateful when Sean went to bed early and believed my excuse of a migraine attack. I had suffered with them before, so it was not far from the truth, and the only cure was lying down in a darkened room. I did not need to set an alarm to wake myself at 1.30. Lately sleep had been evasive, and the fact Solomon had been in my home was enough to keep me awake. Some black lingerie was missing from my drawer. Had Solomon taken it when he broke in to use the phone? Or was I getting paranoid? It made my flesh creep to think of Solomon touching my private things. I roamed around the house like a ghost, setting crooked pictures straight, trying to quell the panic rising in my throat.

CHAPTER
THIRTY-THREE
SOLOMON

2016

In a room lit only by the backlight of a computer monitor, Solomon jabbed the left click button on his mouse. The movement brought forth a fuzzy black-and-white image of his home on the screen. He tutted under his breath. Mother had spent most of the day under the covers, and was yet to complete her housekeeping duties. Twice, she had managed to haul her lazy carcass out of bed, and judging by her stooped shuffle towards the kitchen, she seemed to have come down with some sort of bug. A caring son would arrange a visit to the doctor. But he was not a caring son. He enlarged the image of her bedroom, focusing on the small mound under the covers. Peering closer, he felt a tiny flicker of excitement. Was she breathing? A frail hand reached out from the duvet, turning over her sweat-stained pillow before moving to face the wall. *Still alive.* Solomon sighed, flicking over the channel to something more interesting.

But Rebecca was absent from her bed, and it took several panicked clicks of the mouse to locate her on the landing. Motionless, she watched over her child, before straightening the pictures he had skewed during his visit. He had been taken aback by her suggestion of Nigel Evans as a victim. For one thing, he hadn't been on his list of potential nominations. It delayed his response, as he trawled the database of villagers he had compiled to date. He was about to default to the original candidate when he found him, in the surgery software as a client with a bad debt. Solomon slid a black silky negligee from his open desk drawer. It felt soft and comforting against his cheek, and he inhaled deeply, catching the scent of Rebecca's flesh.

He had watched Rebecca's earlier love-making with a mixture of anger and disbelief. He should have known farm boy would have been subservient in bed, but it was not the Rebecca he knew. She liked it rough, and as for the other stuff they got up to . . . it was doubtful there was much of that going on in Pontyferry. She could pretend all she wanted – he knew what she was, and it was only a matter of time before she reverted to her true self.

Yet he couldn't ignore the small pang of jealousy that watching them had evoked. He thought he would find her anxious, just like she was after the funeral. It had taken a lot of guts for her to stand up in court, then leave everything she knew and start again. And there was something about her defiance that continued to turn him on. He still wanted her, despite everything she had done. Or perhaps because of it. He looked down at his hands, realising he had wound the negligee tightly around his fist. It was too late for a reconciliation now, because his anger and revenge took priority over anything else. He had learned a lot of things on the inside: how to pick a lock, when to delegate a crime, and the importance of an alibi. He had also learned the virtue of patience, and planning his revenge on Rebecca was one of the things that kept him sane. His contacts from the inside had proved very useful indeed. Some freshly released inmates would do anything for a wad of cash.

Of course, they could be walking into a trap, and there was nothing to physically stop Rebecca calling the police and pointing the finger at him. She would turn her big doe eyes on them, and fill them up with tears, just as she did the day she testified against him. Lying bitch. She was as much to blame for this situation as he was. But if he was going down, then so was she. If the police got involved, they would see the text sent from her phone, goading him to hurt Geoffrey, Margaret and Mr Evans. He even typed some kisses at the end, just to rile farm boy, if it ever came to light. From now on, they were both up to their necks in it. He couldn't pass up the opportunity when he saw her phone on the bed during her walk with Bear. He had not been far away, so it took him just thirty minutes to reach her house and let himself in with his key, then quickly send the message. He even helped himself to her underwear, before slipping out the back and through the field to his motorbike. He was back in his flat before he knew it, congratulating himself on his ingenuity.

He slept soundly until his alarm sounded at one, and he shivered as he realised the blankets had fallen to the floor. Delicious anticipation seared through him as he pulled on his dressing gown. He had never felt so alive. The adrenalin rush was a strong addiction and, with the beauty of technology, the venture was almost risk free. Switching on his computer, Solomon smiled as a feed was streamed live to his screen.

Like most people in Pontyferry, Nigel Evans had too much faith in the small community where he lived to avail himself of a burglar alarm. Brambles and thistles lined the entrance to the rear garden, and Solomon watched from the safety of his terminal as a crumbling two-storey house loomed into view. Steve had been released from prison just weeks before him, and was keen to earn extra money in any way he could. It had not taken him long to master using the GoPro camera, and he was well paid for the risks he took. Solomon peered at the screen, searching for Rebecca's presence through the gloom. Steve stifled a cough as he entered the smoky living room. The balaclava-wearing ex-convict was no stranger to allowing himself into people's homes, but Farmer Evans most likely had a gun. Breaking into this shitty house seemed like a good enough way of getting himself shot. Solomon had not been willing to risk his own neck, when someone else was prepared to do it for a fee. He barely blinked as he stared at the screen. The best thing Steve could do would be to take something quickly and leave. But there was nothing much of interest in Ardwyn Farm. Solomon watched as Steve's broad gloved hands poked through the cabinets, finding nothing but cheap ornaments and a yellowed dinner set. But his actions were halted as a trigger clicked from behind. The camera panned the room as Steve turned to face a man holding a double-barrelled gun.

'Put your hands up where I can see them, or I'll blow yer brains out.' The farmer spoke in a low growl, through a gap-toothed mouth. Wearing nothing but a pair of stained baggy Y-fronts, he squinted over the barrel of his gun.

Solomon held his breath, watching the scene unfold. He almost forgot about Rebecca as the stand-off continued. Steve's lack of response must have unsettled Nigel as he tightened his grasp on his shotgun.

Steve took a step towards him. 'I've been sent here to deal with you. Shoot me and there'll be consequences.'

Nigel's features twisted in torment as he lowered his gun. 'Take off your balaclava. I want to see your face.'

'That ain't going to happen,' Steve said, shifting his weight.

'Who sent ya? Was it the bookies?' Nigel said, but no response was returned. He stepped back to reach the dust-encrusted phone. 'Keep yer hands in the air, I'm calling the police.'

A sudden scuffling noise from the back drew Nigel's attention away. The camera image shook as Steve lurched forward, grabbing the barrel of the gun. But Nigel was not willing to relinquish his weapon, and a shot rang out, making Solomon flinch as he watched. Debris rained down on them both as part of the ceiling caved in. The force of the shot sent Steve flying backwards, and Nigel, who had hit his head against the table on the way down, was out cold.

Steve clambered to his feet, running straight into Rebecca as he ran to the back door. Her eyes flashed wide. But there was no time to delay. Grabbing her wax jacket with both hands, he dragged her off her feet and pushed her outside. No words were exchanged; there was just the sound of his heavy breathing as he ejected her from the property, and he left her there, standing open-mouthed in the moonlight.

'Go!' he shouted, twisting the key of his motorbike into the ignition. The engine roared into life, spurring her into action.

'Hey! Come back here,' Nigel shouted from inside the house. He was up, and he was still armed.

CHAPTER
THIRTY-FOUR

Diary Entry: 1st September 2005

I wish I could dive into your buttermilk pages and disappear where no one would ever find me. Such an escape would be preferable to recounting the horrors of yesterday. I can't stop my fingers shaking as I set down my thoughts with my pen. As painful as it is, I've got to record them while Solomon's words and gestures are still fresh in my mind. I prepared for confrontation in my last entry, but I could never have imagined the depth of Solomon's deceit. And I can't believe what I'm about to say.

Finding out that Solomon had faked his illness felt like a punch to the stomach. How could he lie to me like that? And he did it so effortlessly. If I even attempted to fib, he knew. But Solomon lied as easily as breathing, making me doubt myself time after time, passing off my grief as an illness so I would leave my care totally in his hands. He decimated my friendships, and tried to force me into giving up my job. I know how unbelievable this sounds. How could this be the same kind, loving boyfriend who stood by me through the toughest of times? I wish it wasn't true. But by the time I've finished this entry all will be clear.

As I heard his key in the front door, I stood firm. For once, I was furious, filled with red-hot emotion, instead of the drug-induced numbness that smothered my feelings. This time he was leaving, and I would not take no for an answer.

'I can't be with you anymore,' I said, standing in the hall with my arms folded over my chest. 'I want you to leave.'

Solomon frowned, dropping his car keys on the small oval table next to the door. He tutted as he approached, laying his hands on my shoulders. Sighing, he threw me a pitiful look as he asked if I had stopped taking my medication. It was messing with my head, he said, making me paranoid and thinking all sorts. Then he offered to get me a sleeping tablet, so I could have a 'little lie-down'.

Dumbfounded, I followed him into the kitchen, where he was filling a glass of water at the tap. Frustration rose as he refused to listen to what I had to say. I stood in silence as he talked over me, telling me not to worry, that everything would be all right.

'Remember at the hospital, when we visited your mother? I committed myself to you that day; I knew that, no matter what, we would always be together. Do you think that was an easy time for me? You were so lost in your grief, totally wrapped up in yourself. But I stayed because I loved you. Because that's what couples do.' He reached into the cupboard and pulled out my sleeping tablets. Pushing two through the foil pack, he gave me a gentle smile, telling me I needed to rest.

I stood there agog as he handed me the water. It was as if a veil had dropped from my eyes. How dare he mention my mother, and act as if I was losing my mind? Finally, I could see Solomon for what he really was: a manipulative and controlling man. A dormant anger rose inside me. I would not be a victim anymore.

'You can stick your tablets,' I said, throwing back my hand and smashing the glass against the wall behind him. 'Now will you listen?' I stepped back from the shattered glass. 'There's nothing wrong with me. It's you. It's always been you.'

Solomon's smile evaporated in an instant. 'So you're finishing with me because I have cancer? How admirable, after everything I've . . .'

'Done for me, yeah, I get it,' I said, feeling alive for the first time in months. I jabbed my finger in the air. 'I know all about your fake cancer, Solomon. How could you do it? Pretending to be sick, when so many people are fighting for their lives. You disgust me. And I want you out.'

But, instead of leaving, he simply rolled his eyes. 'You've got it all wrong. But if you want to believe the source of your information over me, then go ahead.'

It was a waste of time arguing with him. I told him what I knew, without mentioning any names. Then I pointed to the door, my arm rigid as I ordered him to leave. But he just stood there, staring at me as if I had lost my mind.

I strode into the living room, hoping Solomon would go upstairs and pack his bag. But instead he followed me in, and I jerked forward as I felt a sharp, hard poke to my back. I swivelled around, gasping as I realised he was almost on me. Gone was the expression of compassion and sympathy. In its place was a face twisted with rage.

His words were laced with venom as he raved about women looking for the perfect man, yet when they found them, dumping them for being boring.

'I'm "too nice", isn't that it?' Solomon said, making quotation marks with his fingers in mid-air. He snarled the words, sounding anything but nice. 'You never saw me until the marathon; you were too busy with your fundraising, and playing nursemaid to your mother. I did you a favour, because I wanted it to be special. That's how much I loved you.'

'That's why you never showed up on any of the previous marathon records,' I said, flatly, the fizz of my anger evaporating under his shadow. 'You trained for the race just for me.'

'Yes, I did,' he said, abandoning his lies as he confessed the plans he had put in place to ensure our perfect meeting. During all his training sessions, he told me it was my face that had spurred him on.

I should have been shocked, but I'd questioned everything since receiving Selina's call. Now I wanted to know the truth, all of it.

'So you orchestrated meeting me at the hospital, when I was at my lowest ebb?'

Solomon laughed, making me flinch as he threw his hands into the air. 'There you go twisting it all again. Don't you see? It was *you* who dragged *me* in to see your mother, and begged me to tell her we were in love. I was happy to go along with the dream, because I had every intention of making it a reality. Her favourite music, the flowers she liked, I researched it all for you, just to bring you comfort. She was such a big part of your life. And I wanted to be that big part. But now,' he said, grabbing my hair in his fist and making me squeal, 'now you've gone and ruined it all, because you're just so . . . fucking . . . stupid.'

He shook my head with each syllable, making me yelp in pain. I dug my nails into his hands, trying to prise his fingers from my hair. 'Get off me, you nutcase,' I said, the words tumbling from my mouth.

A chill ran through my body as he locked his eyes on mine. 'What did you just call me?'

He shook my head again, almost lifting me from the floor. My scalp stung like it was on fire as my hair was plucked by the roots. Tears rose in my eyes as I stood on my toes, and I tried to appeal to his better nature, the part of him that was buried deep inside.

'Please, Solomon, let me go. I'm sorry, I didn't mean it.'

'That's right, you didn't,' he said, releasing his grip. I staggered backwards, watching him shake the loose strands of blond hair from his fingers.

I knew I should leave it at that, just accept what he was saying, given he was in such a vile mood. But I'd had enough of living my life in quiet acceptance, and could not let things go. Like a fish hook, his words had yanked me back to the past, to the day my mother died.

So I asked him the question playing on my lips. He said he wanted to take Mum's place, to be that big part of my life. Was he pleased when she died? Was that what he wanted all along?

Solomon laughed, a thin, cold cackle. 'You really don't have a clue, do you?' He took another step towards me, until the backs of my knees hit the leather sofa. 'I told you I'd go to any length to make you happy. Instead of watching your mother die a slow, painful death, I gave you both the perfect moment.' He smiled, brushing the palm of his hand against my cheek. 'I did that for you.'

My chest began to rise and fall as the meaning of his words finally became clear. I dug my nails into the palms of my hands, remembering what the nurses said about Mother's demise. How they had not expected her to go so quickly. She was as weak as a lamb, but full of fighting spirit, and the treatment was expected to earn her a few more months of life. That night when we had kissed, Solomon said he had something to do. I took a deep breath, feeling as if I had been punched in the gut.

'Are you saying . . .' – I cleared my throat to allow the words through – 'you killed my mother?'

I stiffened as he began to smooth my tousled hair. '"Killed" is such a harsh word. Think of it as euthanasia.'

I could barely comprehend the confession that followed. He seemed to enjoy telling me how he returned to her room that night. He spoke about doing her a kindness, describing her peaceful features as she slept. He watched me closely as he spoke, and as tears welled in my eyes, a satisfied smile crept on to his face.

'. . . So I pinched her nose and covered her mouth. I even hummed her favourite song, *Hallelujah*. She didn't put up much of a fight.'

'No,' I gasped. I wanted to block the words, but the scene was already playing out before me. My mother being deprived of air, the last face she sees that of a killer. A killer I had brought to her door.

'I don't believe you,' I said, rejecting the thought as too horrific to contemplate. But the words rebounded in my thoughts, over and over again. What had I done?

Solomon shrugged. 'I don't care if you believe me or not. But I'm telling you the truth. I did it for you and I'd do it again.'

My hand rushed to my mouth, and I retched as my last meal threatened to make an appearance. I tried to take slow steady breaths, but dizziness overcame me, and I felt like I couldn't breathe.

'Here,' Solomon said, his composure fully regained. 'Let me get you another drink of water.'

He was gone just seconds before he returned with a plastic tumbler. 'Drink it.' His free hand rested on my collarbone, his thumb rubbing the base of my throat. I took the tumbler from his hand. Overcome by shock and fear, I drank, noticing the bitter aftertaste as I smacked my lips.

'Have you put something in this?' I said, wiping my tears with the back of my hand as the world spun around me.

'I told you, Rebecca, I'd do anything for you. Do you really think I'm going to let you go?'

He dragged me by the hand as he strode up the stairs, but my legs were weak and I tripped on the step, trying to organise my thoughts as I plotted my escape. But all I could see was my mother's face, and Solomon's hand clamping down hard on her mouth. Had he been telling the truth, or was he just trying to frighten me? Either way, I needed to get out. But my legs wouldn't carry me. Solomon wrapped his hand around my waist and dragged me into the bedroom. He unceremoniously threw me on the bed, then locked the door. I watched as he rooted under the bed and pulled out a laptop I didn't know he had. My eyelids drooped like leaden shutters, and I was suddenly awoken by a sharp sting as his palm made contact with my cheek.

'Wakey wakey,' he said, activating a CD in the laptop as he spoke about his insurance policy.

Insurance policy? I thought, trying to stay awake. What was he talking about? His fingers moved nimbly over the keys as he instructed the CD to play. I pushed myself up on the bed and peered over his shoulder. A video flashed up on the screen.

Solomon smiled, seemingly enjoying himself as he told me how he had prepared for this day. I caught the triumphant glint in his eye as he swivelled the laptop to show me a better view. 'I'd like to show you a movie. Another reason why we should stay together.'

I could not breathe. I could not function. For there, on the bed, was me, naked except for stockings and a pair of red heels. I clamped my hands in front of my face as nausea washed over me all over again. 'Oh no you don't,' Solomon said, pulling my hands down. 'You don't want to miss your starring role. And you had lines too. Listen.' He jabbed the sound button, loud enough to hear the filthy words spewing from my mouth. 'No,' I retched, and Solomon slapped me hard across the face.

'Stay with it,' he said. 'I've got one more thing to show you and then you can sleep.'

Shame washed over me as I listened to the language so alien on my tongue, and I realised how it looked. In the heat of the moment I had put my reservations aside to please my boyfriend. Despite the blindfold, you could clearly make out it was me. I prayed for the video to end.

'Watch,' Solomon hissed, as he grabbed my jaw and forced me to look at the screen. What happened next made me want to curl up and die.

CHAPTER
THIRTY-FIVE
REBECCA

2016

I fought to maintain an appetite as I chose from the pub menu. It was Sunday, and we had agreed to meet with Sean's brother Gareth and the 'delightful' Chloe in the Hare and Hounds for some food. But Gareth had rung to say he was running late, and for us to start without him.

'I don't know why you're looking,' Sean smiled. 'You always order the Sunday roast.'

I lowered the menu and returned his grin. 'You're right. Sunday roasts all around. Would you order me a Diet Coke with that, please?'

Sean took the menu and walked to the bar. I liked the Hare and Hounds. It had a relaxed ambience and warm, comforting furnishings. Plus, it was disabled-friendly, something Rhian appreciated on the rare occasions she joined us for dinner. Today she was recovering from a late night with her new boyfriend, and I was glad to hear it was going so well.

Lottie sat beside me, her tongue sticking out of the corner of her mouth as she concentrated on colouring in Donald Duck. I was really not in the mood for Chloe and her little cutting remarks. I had far more important things on my mind. But I was not going to allow Solomon to spoil the family time that was so precious to my husband. The smile I had been wearing for Sean's benefit slowly slid from my face as I contemplated the previous night. It had left me feeling lost, as the lines between Solomon and Sean blurred. Solomon used to be a separate entity, and I had fooled myself that I could cope with the threat that he posed. But since last night, I could not get the burglary out of my mind. As he stood there, in dark clothes and a balaclava, I told myself that I knew this man. It was me he wanted. There was no need for anyone else to get hurt. But then he yanked me from the house, and his grip was so strong that he lifted me from my feet. A thick black beard peeped from under his balaclava, and I realised that the gruff voice did not belong to Solomon, but to someone he must have hired to commit the deed. If that wasn't proof enough, then the small camera attached to his chest harness was. In the shadows of darkness, I worked it out. Solomon had just been released from prison, and he had not served his time alone. I was bringing a whole host of unsavoury characters into this gentle little town. I looked into the man's eyes and saw nothing but emptiness. It was as if he was a robot. A cold, mechanical chunk of steel, capable of crushing bone and draining blood. I hated that the next set of eyes I looked into were my husband's. That some jailbird had been the last person to touch me before Sean. I showered before bed, and again in the morning, trying to wash the feeling away. But it stayed on my skin, bringing back memories of when his fingers bit into my flesh.

I should have hoped for the best, when I walked in to discover a gun pointed at the intruder's face. But all I felt was horror at the prospect of another life lost. Deep down, I still hoped for a positive resolution, for Solomon to see sense and walk away. It was why I made the noise that distracted Nigel. But why did the bearded man pick me up and tell me to run? Was it out of concern, or was he just obeying orders? God knew that Solomon prepared for every eventuality. As the bike drove away, I had jumped on my scooter, cutting through a hiking trail to avoid crossing his path. At least I had managed to tick another crime off the list.

I focused hard on watching Lottie finish her colouring. The most frightening thing about having children was the all-encompassing love you felt for them. With love comes fear. Fear that someday you will suffer their loss. I could cope with whatever Solomon threw at me, but the thought of him touching my daughter frightened me to the core. That was why the bearded man's reaction scared me so much. Rather than hit me, shout, or spit in my face, the stranger had lifted me up and taken me out of danger's way. I lowered my head as I tried to figure it out. Solomon wasn't interested in inflicting violence directly on me, not when he could cause more pain by forcing me to watch him hurt the ones I love. He fed from my horror, like some evil vampire who leeched on fear instead of blood.

Sean mumbled something into his phone, which was cradled between his chin and shoulder as he placed our Cokes on the table. My ears pricked at the mention of the name Nigel, and I took a sip of my drink, catching the tail end of his conversation. It was Geoffrey, and he had news.

'Well, I never expected that. Thanks, Geoff, I'll speak to you later.'

'Everything all right?' I said, allowing the cool drink to slip down my throat. My stomach tightened as I forced it down.

'You'll never guess what,' he said, lowering his voice so Lottie wouldn't hear.

'What?' I looked at him dumbly, keeping my guesses to myself.

'You know Nigel, that farmer that owed us all the money? He's only gone and paid his bill.'

'Really?' I said, trying to sound surprised at the mention of his name. 'And the bookies too?' I asked, pursing my lips as the words escaped. How stupid was I, offering up the information on the tip of my tongue? 'I remember hearing Maura gossiping about it in the practice. Apparently he has debts all over Pontyferry.'

'Well, not anymore. He visited Geoffrey with a wad of notes that smelt like they'd been stuffed under his mattress over the last few years. Minted, he is. Who would have thought it?'

'I wonder what made him pay up,' I said, knowing full well it was the night-time visit that must have played on the farmer's mind. Nibbling my bottom lip, I thought about the phone nestled in my back pocket. I jumped as Sean touched my arm.

'Sorry. Are you all right?' he said. 'I was just saying, he must have had an attack of conscience.'

'I was listening,' I said, even though I wasn't. 'That should take some pressure off the business. You can buy that new equipment you've been talking about.'

Sean smiled in agreement, and I comforted myself with the fact that some good had come from the incident at the farm.

I had sworn I wouldn't drink, not with everything going on, but I had to down two glasses of wine just to get through the ritual of our Sunday dinner. It wasn't that I didn't get on with Gareth, but Chloe seemed to think that her history with Sean gave her some God-given right to tell him what to do, even though she was the one who jilted him all those years ago. Marrying his brother must have been like another slap in the face to Sean, but her loss was my gain, and I continuously bit my lip in her company, only because I wouldn't give her the satisfaction of knowing her catty remarks had hit home.

I knew lots of farmers' wives in Pontyferry, and Chloe was the only one I knew who hated animals. Most grew up with a healthy respect for the land, their stock, and the power of nature. They knew the crops that took so long to nurture could be taken away in a storm. Chloe treated the farm as if it were something she had to put up with. Granted, she was a pretty woman, in a long horse-faced sort of way. At five foot eight she was my polar opposite. Her long shiny ash-blond hair was the result of hours in the hairdresser's, and her face never went without make-up. As for me, I was always clean, but most days my beauty regime didn't go much past a dash of tinted moisturiser, heavy-duty lip balm, and a little mascara to highlight my best features, according to Sean.

I was too distracted by the phone in my pocket to notice Chloe's barbed comments. That's when she wasn't speaking Welsh. I was going through a list of potential victims in my head when Chloe broke through my thoughts. She was sitting across from me, having somehow managed to squeeze herself in beside my husband, leaving me sitting beside Gareth, with Lottie in between us.

Sean had the decency to look embarrassed as she squeezed his knee, telling him how great he looked at rugby training. A plate of salad lay before her, and she looked at me smugly as I polished off my roast dinner.

'I didn't know you went to rugby training,' I said, breaking off a piece of Yorkshire pudding and popping it in my mouth.

'Oh, I always support our boys,' she said, giving Sean's knee another squeeze. She had called Sean and Gareth 'our boys' for as long as I had known her.

'What were *you* doing that day?' she sneered. 'Making some more of your fantastic jewellery?'

Chloe's tone made it clear that this wasn't meant as a compliment. Her eyes rested on the quirky owl pendant pinned to my lapel. It wasn't one of my best pieces, but Lottie loved it, so I always wore it in her company.

'Aww, is that one of your little pieces?' she asked, peering at the brooch. 'What is it? Some kind of bird?'

'It's an owl,' Lottie said, indignantly. 'Can't you see?'

'Lottie, don't be cheeky,' I said, biting back my smile. My four-year-old did not suffer fools gladly.

Chloe thrust her charm bracelet into my face and gave it a shake. 'Do you like my new Pandora?'

Mass-produced, impersonal, and ridiculously expensive. I couldn't have disliked it more.

'It's beautiful.' I smiled, sucking a speck of gravy from my thumb. 'Now who's for pudding? I fancy chocolate brownie. What about you, Lottie?'

Chloe spoke over my daughter as she enthused about the ice-cream sundae. 'Gareth doesn't mind spending money on *my* jewellery. Heaven knows what it would be like if I had to make my own. Have you ever tried making your own clothes?' She tittered. 'Maybe you could save on those too.'

'There's not much call for designer labels down at the surgery,' I said, still surveying the menu.

'And I don't know what I'd do without you,' Sean interjected, reaching across and squeezing my hand. 'I'm sure half of them old codgers only come to spend time in your company.'

Chloe's response was a dour smile. She had worked at the surgery when she and Sean were engaged, and all people did was complain about her bad attitude and requests for money. It must have stuck in her craw that I was liked by the people she grew up with, who barely gave her the time of day.

'More drinks?' Gareth interjected, rising from his chair. 'Chloe, why don't you help me?'

'I don't think you need . . .' Chloe began to say, before catching his stern look. 'Oh, all right then,' she huffed, tottering after him to the bar.

'Sorry, love,' Sean said. 'I don't know why she has to be so full on all the time.'

'Doesn't bother me,' I lied, knowing Sean felt as uncomfortable with her behaviour as I did. After spending ten minutes in deep conversation at the bar, Chloe turned on her heel and walked out. Red-faced, Gareth joined us at the table.

'Sorry about that,' he murmured, handing us our drinks. 'Chloe's not feeling well. She's gone home for a lie-down.'

I nodded sympathetically. I had other things to worry about than her temper tantrums. As if to prove my point, Solomon's phone beeped in my pocket. Another notification. I forgot all about Chloe as I prepared myself for his next demand.

CHAPTER THIRTY-SIX
SOLOMON

2016

There would be no Sunday roast waiting for Solomon when he got home. He watched from the distance, with the help of his powerful binoculars. No law against birdwatching – at least that was his excuse, should someone ask what he was up to. But his interest was focused solely on the Hare and Hounds pub. His stomach grumbled, and another stab of resentment pierced his soul. Like a poisoned arrow, it strengthened the bitterness fuelling his thirst for revenge. He should be the one with Rebecca, having a Sunday dinner with their child between them. He had planned the perfect life, but now he was here, fresh out of prison, watching other people have a good time. But they wouldn't be smiling for much longer. Any second now Rebecca would be reading his latest text. Lowering his binoculars, he cast his mind back, remembering the days that had seemed to hold so much promise.

He knew he had taken a risk, revisiting the hospital after their first date. Rebecca's mother dying so soon into their relationship could have put it in jeopardy. But what seemed like early days for Rebecca had felt like a lifetime of waiting for him, and he had not been able to wait another second for them to be together. Good looking, intelligent, and completely benevolent, she ticked all the boxes of his spousal requirements. 'Good breeding stock,' as his father used to say. The meticulous planning he had put into this project had all seemed worthwhile. He had found her in a local newspaper article and analysed her like a piece of computer data. Then he got to work on increasing the likelihood of a successful match, watching how she interacted with others, becoming the sort of man who would appeal to her needs.

He researched Rebecca's family too. Her father was such a flake; it was hardly any wonder that she had attracted losers too scared to commit. Solomon had taken it all into account as he worked out the perfect persona. Then he created imaginary scenarios and worked out how the most loving, attentive boyfriend would react. Holding her gaze, valuing her opinion, and unprompted acts of generosity and kindness. Such drivel was often to be found within the pages of women's romantic novels, and he would flirt with random strangers, spending time honing his craft.

He had purposely planned their first meeting to be fleeting, leaving Rebecca disappointed and desperate for more. The trick was to give her a little affection, then disappear into the crowd leaving her lost and alone. Solomon grinned as he recalled ducking out between the crowds of runners at the marathon. He didn't need a medal; he had his eyes on a much bigger prize. After training hard, he had made the race look effortless in order to appeal to her basest instincts when choosing a fit mate.

Rebecca's eyes had lit up like an excited puppy at the hospital, and it pleased him to see the effect he had on her when he stroked her hair. Such power over another was a powerful aphrodisiac but, back then, it had been far too soon to introduce her to his sexual tastes. The evening had gone much better than he expected, and his last-minute gesture of buying Estelle's favourite flowers was a stroke of genius. What a fool he had been. He truly believed she would never abandon him as the others had done.

He could still remember the stink of the hospital, and it had taken all of his willpower to shake the woman's cold, limp hand. But he masked his disgust well, in order to garner her approval. It was a kindness, saving Rebecca from the pain of watching her mother die. Their last moments had been perfect, a beautiful memory to help her recover from her loss. And this was how she had repaid him. His jaw clenched as the memory invoked fresh anger, and he eased the phone from his pocket, awaiting Rebecca's response. He had been patient. But now his patience was coming to an end. And time was running out for the Walker family.

CHAPTER
THIRTY-SEVEN
REBECCA

2016

The toilet cubicle door vibrated as I slammed it shut and wrenched the bolt across. Nothing would give Solomon greater pleasure than wrecking my day. But I had kept my emotions in check, allowing my mask to slip only behind the privacy of the door. On the other side of the cubicle a mother entered, scolding her young daughter for getting ice-cream on her clothes. A tiny sliver of resentment made itself known. It wasn't fair. I deserved a normal life, just like her. I glanced down at the latest text, wondering how far Solomon was going to push me this time.

```
Victim number four. Arson.

Gareth Walker or ?
```

```
Enter target here _____

This will default to: Gareth if incomplete.

You have thirty seconds to decide.

00:29
```

Arson? Once again, Solomon took me completely by surprise. My knowledge of the law had been gleaned by online searches, but I had expected him to up his game with increasingly violent offences. It was no coincidence that he had named the one person we were spending our afternoon with. Was he really out there, in the freezing cold, spending hours watching our movements? Hadn't he better things to do? There was no way I could put forward a homeless man for an arson offence. But I could not allow Gareth to lose his farm, either. If it were as easy as just naming a property, then there were loads of empty buildings in the area. But I knew this had to be specific to a person, and I couldn't mess around. It had to be a property in Pontyferry that someone I knew lived in. The clock ticked down, and I racked my brain for the names that had suddenly deserted me. I thought of another neglect case, an alcoholic who lived on his own had been fined for leaving the carcasses of dead animals on his land. He was a far cry from Gareth, who cared more for his animals than any profits. I typed in his name, hoping it wouldn't earn me a trip to hell. If I wasn't in hell already.

Now all I could do was stress about getting away to witness the fire. There was no way I was going to enter the house to watch. I'd panicked with the burglary, risking my neck by entering the house. Tentatively I had entered through the insecure back door, but my efforts at being discreet fell to pieces at the sight of Nigel holding a gun to what I thought was Solomon's head. It was such a stupid thing to do and yet . . . if I had to go back, I don't think I would do it any differently.

All my pondering made the moments until the response came through fly by, and I was washing my hands when the phone responded to my request. Snatching a wad of toilet paper from the cubicle, I hastily dried my hands and checked the screen.

```
Notification number four. Arson.

Adam Pritchard.

Tomorrow at 2am.

High Street, Pontyferry.

You are a Silent Witness.

Talk to police and you die.
```

I sighed. Another 2 a.m. incident. And on the High Street? Just how did he expect to get away with that? And arson. It was a serious crime. With the potential for a great deal of harm. How long a jail sentence would he get for that? I caught my thoughts as they raced around my head. What was the point? This was crazy. The best I could do was to get my family through it in one piece.

CHAPTER
THIRTY-EIGHT
REBECCA

2016

Bringing a bored Lottie home was the perfect excuse to leave Sean and Gareth watching rugby in the pub. Sean promised to follow me shortly, but I encouraged him to stay and get a lift back with Gareth when the game was over. It gave me enough time to look up the surgery client list on my battered laptop, and pull up Adam Pritchard's home address. Solomon must have got it wrong because, according to our client list, Mr Pritchard's address was a mile up the road, not in town.

I lifted the phone, my finger hovering over the buttons. Would it seem suspicious if I called him to check? And on a Sunday? Probably. Regardless, I dialled the number. He picked up after three rings. I cleared my throat, and tried to sound bright.

'Hello, this is Pontyferry Veterinary Practice. We're updating our systems and I just wanted to check that the address we have for you is correct. Are you still living in Slab Lane?'

'Hello. No, I haven't lived there in over a year. I'm in the town now, see. The council got me one of them adapted places.'

'Adapted?' I asked, my heart sinking.

'Yeah, for the wheelchair. So I won't be using the vet's anymore. I had to get rid of me dog. I couldn't manage him after the legs went. You may as well take me off the system, love.'

'Oh, I'm sorry to hear that. I'll remove your details from the database so we won't be bothering you again.'

I was ready to hang up the phone when a thought occurred. 'My um . . . my sister-in-law has MS. She might have to apply for an adapted house. How's it working out for you?'

'Oh, not too bad. It's not as lonesome here as it was on the farm. I couldn't manage it in the last few years, not since my boys left for America.'

'Do you mind me asking, do you have help at all? Or do you have to do it all on your own?'

'I get the meals on wheels but, after that, I'm on my own.'

'Oh, I see. I hear there's some good clubs in town, bingo and things, maybe you could enquire about getting out a bit. I might have the number, if you'd like me to look it up.' I really was grasping at straws, trying to get him out of the house, even just for a few hours. If Solomon knew I was tipping him off, he'd revert back to the original victim.

The man chuckled. 'No thanks, love, I'd rather stay in and watch *Corrie* of an evening, thanks all the same.'

'OK then,' I said, in my most light-hearted voice. 'Have a good day. Sorry to have troubled you.'

'Not at all, been nice talking to you.'

I rested my head in my hands and groaned. What had I done? Not only had I instigated a potential fire to a place in town, I'd brought it to the home of a wheelchair-bound victim. Mr Pritchard wasn't the cruel man I'd thought him to be. He was simply ill and unable to cope with his farm. Solomon must have been shocked to see me nominate such a vulnerable man. What if he couldn't get out on time? I threaded my fingers through my hair, clenching it tightly. How the hell was I going to witness this fire and walk away? But the game was clear. I couldn't call the police. I only hoped Solomon wasn't listening to me. But, to be fair, I never mentioned his name or address out loud. I called a few more numbers, updating their addresses on the system. I told myself I was just keeping busy, doing my job. But inside I was shaking. My fingers struggled to type as they hit all the wrong keys. The thought of sneaking out into town to witness it made me feel sick. But this was what Solomon wanted. Me to be faced with a moral dilemma, choosing the safety of my family over an innocent victim. How could I be so cold? And how the hell was I going to get through the rest of the day? I clicked into Google maps and was about to type in the address when I thought of the texts Solomon had sent, incriminating me in the offences. I couldn't afford to do anything online. And yet I'd just telephoned the home of the next victim. Shit. For the next hour I continued updating the old addresses on the database, hoping my call to Adam Pritchard would get buried somewhere. Could the police even look up phone calls? Of course they could. And it didn't matter how many calls I made at my end, because he was unlikely to have received any other calls that day. *Stupid*, I thought, smacking the heel of my palm against my forehead. *Stupid, stupid, stupid.* I had really messed up this time.

CHAPTER THIRTY-NINE

Diary Entry: 2nd September 2005

I've thought long and hard about finishing my last entry. It ended abruptly, not because Solomon came in, but because I just couldn't write anymore. The video footage has changed everything. Maybe one day I'll be able to write about it, but for now I'm overwhelmed with shame, and cannot bring myself to relive those moments again.

I must have passed out shortly after he showed me. When I woke, it was dark outside. Confused and disorientated, I realised I was still wearing the clothes I had dressed in that day. Rubbing my eyes, I tried to make out the time on my phone. It was 3 a.m., and I was alone. I pushed my feet into my slippers and crossed the room to find my bedroom door unlocked. It was then that it hit me. Solomon did not need to keep me prisoner, because his hold over me was so strong.

Perhaps he expected me to fall apart because of the footage of us together. But instead it fuelled my determination to leave. If I stepped out of line, he would make it public, for all the world to see. And I would never live down the shame. So I decided to stay, but only while I figured out what to do. I would be the perfect fiancée, and bend to his will. But Solomon didn't know me as well as he thought. I was weak when we met, consumed with an ever-growing anxiety. But I was not always that way. Wilful, stubborn, and quick to react; these were my usual traits, which had been quashed for too long. I just needed to plough through the fog and find my way back to myself. Solomon had crossed a line, and I would do whatever it took to get away.

I turned on the shower, standing stock-still as hot spikes of water reddened my skin. Despite my decision to stay, I fantasised about leaving; just packing my bags and walking out. But it was my house, one that held so many precious memories. And the minute I took a bus, or boarded a train, he would distribute the video for all to see. It was why he had me say those humiliating things. I soaped my skin, knowing no amount of lather would wash away the shame. I didn't know what to do. Everything I had was built up in the community where I lived. Solomon would find me, and if I tried to get another teaching job, he would send them the footage. I couldn't begin to imagine what had happened in his childhood to make him so twisted. I bit back my tears as I turned the water temperature down. Mum would want me to get out of this, and I would find a way. But I needed some advice first. Selina would know what to do.

I made breakfast early, hoping to catch Solomon before he went to work. I would have to tread carefully. I had not forgotten the feel of his hand on my clavicle as he bore down on me the day before. He had slept in my mother's room. Now all the pretence had left our relationship, he could sleep where he wanted.

He seemed surprised as he walked into the kitchen, inhaling the smell of pancakes, bacon and eggs. A pot of fresh coffee was laid on the table, and I smiled as he joined me at the cooker.

He slipped his hand around my waist, kissing me appreciatively on the cheek. My stomach lurched, but I leaned into him, covering his hand with mine as it rested on my stomach. I shifted to switch off the gas. 'It's my way of saying sorry,' I said, in my most convincing voice. 'I've had a lot of time to think about what I've done. I'm not going to pretend I agree with what you did.' I sighed, deciding not to plaster my remorse on too thickly. 'But I believe our relationship is worth fighting for.'

He nodded approvingly as he noticed the engagement ring was back on my finger, making encouraging comments about wiping the slate clean.

'Aren't you joining me?' he said, taking a seat.

I sat across from him, the smell of the food making me feel ill. 'I'd love to, but I won't.' I sighed, looking at the pancakes. 'I've also been thinking about what you said before. I *have* been letting myself go a bit.' I rubbed my head, which still hurt from where he had pulled my hair the day before. 'I was wondering if it would be OK for me to go into Colchester today, get my nails done? I've got some money set aside, I don't expect you to pay.'

Solomon's lips thinned. I knew he would not be that easy to fool, but I had prepared a back-up plan.

'I'll pop into the school on the way, and give in my notice. I don't think there's any point in me working there, not now.' My words trailed away as I caught his frown. 'That's what you want, isn't it?'

'Can I trust you, Rebecca?' Solomon said, regarding me over his coffee. 'Because you know what'll happen if you talk. I've got quite a collection of email addresses, and I'm sure your sixth-formers would be flattered to hear what you think about them.'

I nodded, deciding the safest thing would be to say nothing at all.

He waited for an answer, before commenting that sharing home movies wasn't against the law.

Given the fact that his father was a superintendent, I told him it was highly unlikely I'd call the police. I tried to curb the edge in my voice as he worked his way through the feast I had prepared.

He dabbed his mouth before dropping his napkin on the table. My benevolence must have turned him on, because he came up behind me as I bent over the dishwasher, and ground himself against my hips. My hand rested on the knife I had just inserted into the cutlery department and, for half a second, I frightened myself with the thoughts that ran through my head. I released the knife, and swivelled around to face him.

'We've got some time before I have to go to work,' he said, groping my skirt.

It was typical. All the times I yearned for him to want me, and now, when I could barely stand being in the same room as him, I suddenly turned him on. I untangled myself from his grip, offering a cramped smile. 'Please, Sol, not yet, eh? I need some time to get my head around things . . . what you did to my mum.' Silence fell between us, and I whispered the question that had been haunting me all morning. 'Did she suffer near the end? Please, I need to know,' I said, my heart aching for my mother.

His smile dropped, and he released his grip. 'You have to go spoiling things, don't you? Just when everything was going so well.' He picked up his suit jacket from the chair and pushed his hands through the sleeves. 'I'm going to work in a bad mood now, and it's all your fault.'

I blurted an apology, needing to keep him sweet. If he left now, he wouldn't let me go to Colchester, and breaking the rules would come with a price I could not afford. I rested my hand on his chest as I planted a kiss on his cheek. 'I promise I won't mention it again. Tonight. Let's make up when you come home. We can do whatever you like.'

'All right then,' Solomon said. 'After dinner. Cook something nice. Steak, with some home-made cheesecake for dessert. And don't forget to see Nora while you're in Colchester, and give in your notice. I'll pop into the estate agent's during my lunch hour, get the ball rolling on the sale of the house.'

'Perfect,' I said, waving him off. But it was far from perfect. Gaining financial control over me was another step towards total domination. I checked he had left, before taking my mobile from its hiding place and calling Selina. I had found Solomon dialling 1471 on the house phone too many times to think he wasn't checking up on my calls.

'It's me,' I said, my voice shaking as I contemplated what I was about to do. 'I need to get away, but I don't know what to do.'

'What's happened?' Selina said. 'Did you tell him to go?'

I told her I'd tried to end it but he just wouldn't leave.

'He hasn't got a choice, honey. Just change the locks, pack his bags, and leave them on the doorstep. If he refuses to leave, call the cops. They'll give him some strong advice, believe me.'

If only it were that simple. I muttered as much, and could hear Selina's voice harden as she asked if Solomon had hit me. I almost wished that was all it was.

I checked the window for the tenth time, half expecting him to pull up on the drive. I thought about how he had pulled my hair and slapped me hard on the face. It was nothing compared to what he claimed to have done to Mum. But, even now, I struggled to believe he had committed murder. And if I couldn't convince myself, what hope did I have of persuading my friend?

I cleared my throat, explaining that Solomon was blackmailing me, without going into too much detail about the video itself. I was unable to bring myself to say any more. But Selina didn't react the way I expected, instead questioning my medication and asking me if I had got it right.

I sighed with frustration. Why was it so hard to persuade everyone that I was OK?

'There's nothing wrong with me. He just tells everyone there is,' I replied, but she was too busy ranting to listen to what I had to say.

'God. I can't believe he'd do that. He always seemed so nice,' she said, and I wondered when they had met because, apart from passing us in the hospital, I could not remember them being introduced. She spoke about refuges, or coming to stay with her.

But my courage escaped me when the opportunity to leave arose. She might not have been so welcoming if she knew just how dangerous he was. I couldn't put Selina at risk for something I had inadvertently brought on myself.

'How about blackmailing him in return?' she said. 'I bet he hasn't thought about that. How would he feel if you went to the papers and said he made up having a disease?'

Selina's boyfriend was a journalist, and it was a story he would probably be only too keen to print. My heart thudded in my chest, and I wished I had kept my big mouth shut.

'Which will bring all the more attention to the video when it goes live. Please don't do anything. I *am* going to leave him, but I need to plan my escape.'

Seconds passed as Selina seemed to mull it over. 'Just pack a bag and come to mine. I'm worried about you.'

Like a light switch being flicked on, the answer came. She was right. I had to leave. I knew what I had to do.

'OK. I'll go. I've got to speak to Citizens Advice first. Can I meet you in Colchester after that? Say Starbucks, about three?'

I nodded into the phone as Selina agreed. My hands were shaking from my sudden decision. I knew it was the right one. But I would not pack a bag. Solomon had a habit of coming home at odd times of the day. I could give no indication that I was planning to leave. I removed my necklace, and fastened my mother's locket around my neck.

CHAPTER FORTY

REBECCA

2016

I had put Lottie to bed by the time Gareth rang our doorbell, accompanied by my sozzled husband. It did not take much to get him drunk, as he was usually too busy working to spend much time in the pub. I pulled back our heavy oak door to allow them inside, pushing my enthusiastic dog into the kitchen and dismissing Gareth's apologies as he deposited Sean onto the sofa in front of the TV.

Gareth was only a couple of years younger than Sean, although, with his sandy-blond hair, people assumed they were friends rather than brothers. A broken nose from a rugby injury had given Gareth's face a lived-in look, and he had the kind of personality that made everyone want to be his friend.

'I'd forgotten what a lightweight he is,' Gareth said, following me into the kitchen for a coffee. 'I guess it's my fault, for bending his ear for so long.'

I hopped onto a high stool at the breakfast bar. 'It does him good to let his hair down. I take it things aren't too good with you?'

Gareth shook his head. 'It's Chloe. Her behaviour today . . . well, it's embarrassing. Flirting with Sean like that. I don't know how you didn't lamp her one.'

I chuckled, lifting a crumb from the black granite with the pad of my finger. 'It doesn't bother me. Have you tried talking to her? Asking her what's wrong?'

Gareth sighed. 'I know what's wrong. I just don't know what to do about it.'

I raised my eyebrows in a *go on* gesture.

'We've been talking about starting a family. At least, I have. But Chloe wants me to sell the farm and use the money to go travelling.'

'And you don't?'

'You know me, Becky, I'm a farmer through and through. But she knew that when she met me. It's not as if I've changed.'

It was true. She left Sean at the altar because of her itchy feet. Yet she never took the plunge and left the town she grew up in.

'I'd have a chat with her, but I don't think she likes me very much,' I said, rising to close the blinds. A chill had descended, bringing with it a light frost, and I peered out through the window, wondering if Solomon was keeping watch.

'She's jealous. She sees you happy and contented, all the things she's not. But it's driving a wedge between us. To be honest, I don't know if we'll get through it.'

'Can't you compromise? Go on a two-week holiday or something like that? We could help out with the farm, keep it ticking over,' I said. It was not a bad idea. Getting Gareth out of the way would protect him from any involvement in Solomon's plans.

'With what?' Gareth snorted. 'She spends money as quick as I make it. That bracelet, it cost over five hundred pounds, with all those bloody charms. And for what? I don't begrudge her spending money on herself, but the clothes, the jewellery, it's got to stop.'

'What did Sean say?'

'Not much. She's still got a thing for him, you know. After they split up, Sean went travelling, did all the things she wanted to do. I think she regrets leaving him.'

'I'm sure that's not true,' I said, knowing it probably was. 'She's most likely trying to make you jealous, so you'll fight for her.'

'But that's the thing,' Gareth said, sadly. 'I don't know if our marriage is worth fighting for.'

I tried to advise Gareth, but if Chloe was that desperate to travel, I couldn't help but feel that she should. Or was it because of my own reasons, because I was not as at ease with her flirting as I was letting on?

That night, and with the help of several coffees, I managed to sober Sean up enough for me not to be scared to leave Lottie in his care. Later, as I sat up in bed, my husband snoring soundly beside me, my mind flitted between thoughts of Solomon and Chloe, the two people who threatened my world. I told myself I was being silly worrying about Chloe, and set my mind to focusing on my next task. But then I remembered occasionally hearing the lilt of Sean's laughter as he chatted with her on the phone, and I knew she would remain in the background, ready to resurface as my insecurities grew.

The thought of another night-time rendezvous was exhausting. I longed for the old days, before Solomon got in touch. But as I snuck out under the cover of darkness, I knew that things would never be the same again.

I parked my scooter down a side street in Pontyferry, grateful for the lack of CCTV. I had ridden the three miles amazed at just how desolate the village was. I felt like an actress in a Western film, riding into a ghost town, as I awaited a showdown. The only signs of life were a flashing neon takeaway sign in the kebab shop, which was clearly closed, and a couple of lights dotted in the flats over the small parade of shops. A light extinguished, and I was overcome by a sense of dread. I rubbed my arms as the night chill bit into my clothes, wondering how Solomon was going to get away with setting the property on fire. The text implicating me in the crimes weighed heavy in my mind. I couldn't allow myself to be seen, yet if Solomon didn't see me, then he'd do it all over again, and everything that had happened so far suggested that next time it would be far worse.

Mr Pritchard's property was on the corner, just as you entered the town. I peeped out from the side street across the road, hiding from the street lamps' orange glare. The front of the property was too well lit for the attacker to gain entry. I checked my watch. I had just five minutes to get to the back. I scuttled like a rat across the road.

I tiptoed past the high wooden fence, holding my breath as the gate creaked to announce my arrival. A security light was already beaming down, spotlighting my activity. I walked down the narrow garden, pushing through the dew-damp overgrown grass. I felt jittery inside, and it took all my resolve not to turn and run away. I was breaking the law, on someone else's property, and I was not there because of good intent. It was a good thing the police weren't out in force in the village: before Solomon, they never needed to be. I wondered how different things would be by the time he was finished. I finally reached the end of the long, narrow garden, just in time to see a figure in a balaclava bending over an object in his hand. My eyes widened as I realised what he was holding, and the flick of his lighter broke the silence as he tried to light the wad of cloth sticking out of the bottle in his hand. A clear liquid pooled in the bottom. I gasped. It was a home-made petrol bomb. Mr Pritchard wouldn't stand a chance. The words had left my mouth before I could stop myself.

'Don't,' I rasped, as the lighter finally ignited in flame. 'Please, he's in a wheelchair, he'll never get out.'

The whites of his teeth glinted under his balaclava, as his lips curled upwards into a smile. He touched the lighter to the cloth, and I watched with horror as it was engulfed in flame. The figure placed it at the back door, unable to hide his delight as his eyes met mine.

'No,' I whispered, ignoring the bark of a dog in the distance. I forgot all about Solomon's threats and the game I had agreed to play. All I could think of was Mr Pritchard, alone and unable to make his escape. I ran to extinguish the cloth before it reached the liquid, but I was deadened by a punch to the side of the head. I stared in disbelief at my assailant, stunned by the sudden act of violence. The brief pause gave him time to throw a second punch, and this time everything went black.

I woke up to the sounds of sirens in the distance. I was lying in the gutter on my back, watching the skyline glow in a hazy reddish hue. I jerked up, and was rewarded by searing pain in my temple.

Mr Pritchard, I whispered, wincing as the sharp blows of a headache rained down. I got to my feet, realising I was back where I started, down the side alley next to my scooter. Did they get him out in time? The bottle was too big to go through the letterbox, but it would have exploded at the door. I imagined it sending splinters of glass into the kitchen, searing the brittle nets on the kitchen window. My jeans were soaked and the side of my temple ached. I had to get away. I shuddered as I imagined being carried from the scene. But it was not in an effort to save me; the act of violence left me in no doubt of that. I had been stupid, and had acted on impulse. Each crime brought me further into his darkness, implicating me even more.

Shaking, I made my way home, praying that Sean was still asleep. I was meant to have left the house for only a few minutes, but I must have been unconscious for twenty. How on earth was I going to explain the rising bruise on the side of my head?

I sighed with relief as I crept in through our front door, frozen to the bone after riding home in wet clothes. Plunged in darkness, the house was the same as when I had left it. I shushed Bear as he came padding towards me, his ears pricked, as if to ask where I had been. I bent to accept his slobbery kisses, grateful he had too much common sense to bark. I had switched off the engine of my bike and pushed it into the yard. It paid to try to keep one step ahead. Right now I needed to get to bed before Sean noticed I was gone. Kicking off my boots, I reluctantly undid my jacket and left them both in the hall. I ached all over and even my feet were chilled, my socks wet from my time in the gutter. It was 3 a.m. and soon the sky would be brightening as sunrise crept in. But I kept thinking of Mr Pritchard, trapped in his house as the flames licked around him. Had he got away? The attacker's chilling smile flashed in my memory, like an evil Cheshire cat. Just who was he? Another one of Solomon's puppets? Or had he come to carry out the deed himself? Regardless of who he was – just how could he do that? There would be another tragedy in Pontyferry. I could feel it in my bones. And if Solomon could do that so easily to an innocent man, just what had he planned for me? My throat felt like it was lined with sandpaper, and I padded towards the kitchen for a drink of water before bed. But I was not prepared for the shock that awaited me, and gasped in horror as I opened the door to see a figure standing in wait.

CHAPTER FORTY-ONE

REBECCA

2016

I grasped my hand to my chest, feeling the reassuring cold metal of my mother's silver locket under my palm. 'You nearly gave me a heart attack,' I said breathily, as my husband's face came into view. He was bare-chested, with tousled hair, and I figured he must have pulled on his tracksuit bottoms to come and look for me downstairs. My head ached, I felt scared for my family and totally out of my depth. I wanted to cry, to tell him the truth, and find solace in his arms.

But his expression was cold as he turned to face me. '*I* gave *you* a fright? Do you know what time it is? Where have you been?'

'I was out,' I muttered, my mind racing as I tried to formulate a better excuse.

Pain seared through my left eye as he switched on the kitchen spotlights overhead. My head was still throbbing, and I instinctively touched the broken skin on my temple.

Sean approached, his anger dissipating. 'Your head . . . What happened to you?' He touched the skin, and I sucked in a sharp intake of breath as he prodded the bruise. 'This is nasty. What on earth happened?'

I pulled back my head and walked to the cupboard for a glass.

'I couldn't sleep, so I went out for a ride. But I hit a rock and fell off the scooter. Serves me right for not wearing my helmet.'

'What? But it's gone three in the morning.'

'I'm sorry,' I said, hating the sound of the apology as it left my lips. Saying sorry was something I had done far too often in my relationship with Solomon. I was not that woman anymore.

'I've not been sleeping. Sometimes I go out at night to clear my head.'

'Is this why you've been sleeping in the other room some nights?'

I tilted back my head, allowing the cool, clear water to glide down my throat. If only he knew: I was doing everything I could to preserve our family – with somebody else paying the price.

'It's just this business with Solomon—' I found myself saying.

'Solomon, of course,' Sean said, shaking his head. 'I should have known. The third person in this marriage. Has he been in touch, is that what it is?'

'No,' I said in a quiet voice.

'Well, what then?' Sean said, frowning as he searched my face for answers. 'Just what did he do to you?'

'Why are you getting annoyed with me?' I said. All I wanted to do was forget everything that had happened and go to bed.

'Because you won't talk to me. I've tried not to push you, but it's like . . .' His face contorted as he tried to find the words. 'It's like living with a ghost. Most of the time, you're not here at all.'

I was tired, mentally and physically. All I wanted was to curl up in the warmth of my bed and get some much-needed sleep. 'If I'm so paper thin, why did you marry me?' I said, tears welling behind my eyes.

'Because I love you. I've loved you from the minute we met. That's why I can't bear to see you in pain. But I can't go on like this. Marriage is meant to be a partnership. You don't hold back because you think the other person won't be there to support you. I thought you knew me better than that.'

'I want to tell you, but I can't.' My words came out as a whine, and I swallowed back the tears.

'Oh, darlin',' Sean said, lowering his voice, 'did he beat you? Is that what it is?'

'More than that,' I blurted, stepping back from his offer of an embrace.

'Well, what then?'

'He . . .' I covered my face with my hands. I wanted to tell him everything. To relay the whole sorry story, right up to the present day. The barstool exhaled a wheeze as I plopped down, the strength draining from my muscles. 'Sexual. The things we did . . . he talked me into. I look back now and it makes me feel sick.'

'OK,' Sean said, the heat leaving his voice. 'Did he force himself on you?'

'Please, I can't bear to talk about it,' I said, Sean's words making my skin crawl.

Sean's fist curled. 'Bastard.' He pulled me close. 'It's OK, sweetheart, he can't hurt you anymore. I won't let him.'

'You don't want to know any more?' I said, a sob catching in my throat as I leaned into the muscles of his chest.

'No. Not unless you want to tell me. What's important is that we can move on from this, live our lives without him.'

'I wish it was that easy,' I said. I had just traded off old and dirty secrets for the real ones I was so readily hiding. What did that make me, using my sordid past to squirm out of what was happening right now? Solomon was changing me, tarnishing our relationship. Just how much damage would he do before this was all over?

CHAPTER
FORTY-TWO
SOLOMON

2016

Solomon whistled as he trotted up the concrete steps to work. Last night had been a rush. Such experiences helped him get through the treadmill of life, and his probation officer was pleased with how he was settling back into the mainstream. He sat down at his desk, his mind wandering as he powered up his computer. The grin he had fallen asleep wearing had still been there when he awoke. He'd had a delicious dream about locking Rebecca's family in their home and setting it alight. Even the dog had howled and barked as the flames singed his fur. Not that he would do that to a dumb animal. That would be cruel. His smile widened. He had taken a big risk, carrying it out himself. But the closer he came to being caught, the bigger the kick as he recalled his escape. He had enjoyed testing Rebecca, pushing her to her limits. Standing there in her black jeans and sweater, her face all twisted with angst.

Felicity sashayed over, bending as she placed a fresh cup of coffee on his desk. Her blouse gaped open, offering him a view of her ample cleavage encased in a black lacy bra.

'You're looking like the cat that got the cream,' she purred. 'What have you been up to?'

'Wouldn't you like to know,' Solomon said, raising the cup to his lips. The smell of her perfume was intoxicating, and it was no secret that she hit on most of the men who came through the prison programme.

She crossed her ankles as she leaned against his desk, murmuring something about being available next weekend if he wanted to go for a drink. But she was an alley cat, too easy for Solomon's liking. And he was getting on too well with his job to make ripples with the staff.

'Some other time,' Solomon replied, supposing he might as well keep his options open.

'Your loss, jailbird,' she said, launching herself from his desk and sauntering down the corridor. That was fine, Solomon thought. He would deal with her another time.

He logged on to the system, bringing up his emails and getting to work. He was functioning on three hours' sleep, but had never felt better. Mother was still in bed when he checked the CCTV, having barely shifted from the night before. Having managed to dissuade her from getting the flu jab, he wondered if she was coming down with the virus. He made a mental note to telephone her later. The garden was looking shabby, and the house was not going to clean itself. He could have sworn he saw a rat in the kitchen the other day. He could do an online shop later, send her some value-brand tinned stew. It was similar enough to the slop they fed him at boarding school. He thought about a trick he had played once, how he'd bought some tins of dog food and switched the labels just for fun. But his heart wasn't in it anymore. He had bored of his mother. It was time to let her go.

He tapped a few keys on the keyboard, justifying his existence at work. He thought about Rebecca, and how he had carried her, unconscious, under the shadow of the night. Her head had lolled to one side and, if he'd had a car, he would have been tempted to bring her home. But he had to stick to the game, and hunt by the gentlemanly rules of fair play and good sportsmanship. Besides, he didn't want the game to end yet. He was having too much of a good time.

CHAPTER FORTY-THREE

Diary Entry: 2nd September 2005

My head is spinning as I write this, and I barely know where to begin. I never thought I'd come to rely on you so much, but you're my one constant, and my thoughts always seem clearer when I've spent time with you. It seems daft, speaking directly to a journal. But you've come to mean so much more.

My journey to Colchester went ahead as planned but, as I sat in Starbucks, my heart sank deeper with every minute that ticked past. It was four o'clock. Selina was not coming, and I had no credit left on my phone. I checked it for the tenth time, expecting a text. It didn't seem like her not to show and, at the very least, she would let me know where she was. The coffee shop was filling with students and I took the hint when the girl working behind the counter came and wiped my table for the second time. I nodded my thanks before heading out onto the cobbled pedestrian walkway. A sudden gust of wind howled around me, sending dust and empty crisp wrappers dancing along the pavement.

I buttoned my cardigan over my blouse, wondering how the weather had changed so quickly. But I had not expected to be outside this long, and panic began to set in as I realised Solomon would be home soon, expecting a slap-up meal, and the things I had promised afterwards. I shuddered. I could not go back there. Not now.

I leaned into the wind as I crossed the road to the cash machine. My mind was whirring as I shoved my debit card in the slot. The usual argument going back and forth: should I go or should I return and stand up for what was mine? I had a few hundred pounds in the bank, enough to keep me going for a couple of weeks, while I figured out what I was going to do. Mum's funeral had cleaned out what was left of her savings, but at least the house was paid for. I tried to see a way out. If I could get another job somewhere, then sell the house, I would have enough money to start again. I chewed my bottom lip as I typed in my pin number to make a withdrawal. But my heart froze as the balance flashed up. Ten pounds. That was all I had left. I jabbed the button to request a statement, and it seemed to take ages to spit out the results. I pulled the printout from the machine, as the wind threatened to snatch it away. It displayed three separate withdrawals, taken out on consecutive days. In Frinton-on-Sea. Solomon. My legs felt like jelly as I made my way to the nearest bench.

People milled about in Culver Square, clutching their shopping bags as they made the most of the sales. I sat watching as couples held hands, chatting animatedly between themselves. Envying their lifestyle, I wished that for once I could have a normal life of my own. I sat there for what seemed like forever, trying to work out the lesser of the two evils: wait for Selina to get in touch, or go home and try to find out what had happened to my money. I had been careful. There was no way Solomon could have known I was leaving.

I counted out the change in my purse, and got to a phone box to tell Solomon I was running late. My heart thumped in my chest as I told him I was on my way home. I tried to sound natural, telling him I couldn't get the shopping because the money was all gone. But Solomon simply came up with some story about me agreeing to the withdrawal to pay the estate agent's fees.

'Don't you remember?' he said, turning it back on me.

My silence relayed that I didn't.

'You said you wanted to contribute, because *I've* been paying for all the shopping. Anyway, don't worry about the food, I'll pick something up on the way.'

I bit back the tears as I hung up the phone, grateful for my return train ticket home. Solomon had never mentioned withdrawing money. Worse still, he had allowed me to go to Colchester, knowing he had emptied my account. Estate agents weren't paid up front. They took the proceeds from the sale of the house. But, as he had pointed out, he was paying towards our living costs and I was not in a position to complain.

Maybe if I talked to him, explained the situation, I thought, but I knew deep down that Solomon would not listen. I walked down the hill to catch my train, my footsteps heavy as they returned me to my persecutor. As the train chugged to Clacton, I could not shift the uneasiness creeping up my spine. I slipped off my mother's necklace and stowed it in my purse.

By the time I got home, Solomon had his feet up in front of the television. His empty plate was discarded on the coffee table in front of him, but there was no dinner waiting for me. I instinctively knew something was wrong.

'Ah, you're home,' he said, getting up to kiss me. But his mouth was rough as he pressed it against my cheek, and his grip tightened around my arms. He waited until I was inside, and locked the door behind me. Fear crawled over me. I could not leave now, even if I wanted to.

He smiled, apologising for the 'mishap' regarding the money. But all the while his eyes were cool.

'We'll have a joint account soon,' he said. 'If you need any money in the meantime, just ask.'

So that was it. He had cleaned me out, and now the sick pay from my job had dried up, all I had left was the change in my pocket. I stood silently before him, my breath ragged as I exhaled.

His words were light and airy, but his eyes carried an intensity that I had seen before. He was playing with me, like a cat cornering a mouse. I tried to brush past him, but he gripped my arms tighter.

It was then I noticed that the television was on a music channel loud enough to drown out our conversation. Our house was situated on a corner, about a quarter of a mile from the seafront. The house next door was vacant, so the only people who would hear us argue would be any holidaymakers who had veered off course. And Solomon was not taking any chances.

'What's wrong? Didn't your little friend show up today?' he said in a churlish voice.

I swallowed, my heart picking up pace so fast it felt like a bird was trapped in my chest.

'Well? I'm waiting for an answer,' he said, shaking me so hard my teeth rattled in my skull.

I tried to tell him I was upset, knowing there was no point in lying. It was hardly unreasonable, after all he had done.

'So you thought it would be a good idea to disobey my orders and go blabbing to your friend,' he said, his hands rising to the base of my throat. I flinched as he touched my face, closing my eyes as his cool fingertips caressed my skin.

'It was nothing,' I said. 'Just a chat, it didn't mean anything.'

'Liar,' he growled. 'I know all about your secret phone calls, and your appointment with Citizens Advice.' He pushed me back against the wall, his grip firm on my throat. I could feel my veins pulsate under his fingers. I grasped at his arms.

'Please,' I said. 'You've got it wrong. There's something I need to tell you.'

'More lies?' he said, drops of spittle landing on my cheek as he spoke between clenched teeth. 'You disloyal bitch. Did you really think I wouldn't find out? Selina told me all about your plans. How did you think I felt, hearing that from a third party?'

His fingers squeezed tighter and my words came in whistles as I struggled to breathe. I begged for release, gasping as my lungs burned for air.

Solomon dropped his hand, and I dragged in a clawing breath. I was shaking violently, and the look in his eye left me in no doubt that if I pushed him now he would kill me. I forced myself to swallow through the pain, my hands protectively nursing my vulnerable airways. But I couldn't stop thinking of Selina. Had she called him? Challenged him for his behaviour? But why? She barely knew him.

Solomon was still infuriated, his nostrils flaring from a rage that showed no sign of subsiding.

'If you ever think of leaving me, you end up the same as your mother, do you hear me? Nobody betrays me and gets away with it. Think on that, the next time you start plotting against me.'

'I'm sorry,' I said, stumbling over to the sofa, the infernal noise of drum and bass on the music channel reverberating through my brain.

The fact I had apologised brought a smile to his face. Now he could see the fear in my eyes, he had gained his objective. I expected him to hit me, but instead he smiled, tracing his hand down my tear-stained cheek and kissing me roughly on the mouth. Confusion swept over me. Just what was going on? I froze, wishing the key was in the door, but knowing I would not get very far on my own. Solomon kept kissing the tears off my face and throat, his hands roaming all over my shaking body. Then I realised what he was trying to do. It was my fear, my submission that turned him on. It was why he didn't enjoy our intimacy, but now he was more aroused than ever. If I fought him, I risked a beating. So I allowed him to kiss me and undo my blouse. My body trembled as he pushed me onto the sofa. But rather than stopping him, my weakness turned him on even more. So I let him have me, because it was too dangerous to say no.

Afterwards, he went into the bathroom, and I heard the bath being filled. He ran his fingers through his mop of hair and smiled as if nothing had happened. 'I ran a bath for you, darling. Why don't you have a soak while I make you some food?'

I wiped my tears with the back of my hand. My hair was dishevelled, my mascara running, and a sob still caught in the back of my throat. But Solomon was happy, because he had asserted his dominance. In his world, everything was back to how it should be. I nodded blindly, stumbling to the bathroom. There was no point in trying to leave now because his anger was still close at hand, and Solomon could change in the blink of an eye.

It wasn't until later when I was coming out of the bathroom that I heard him murmuring on the phone. 'No, she's not here,' Solomon said, glancing up at me. 'Rebecca came home ages ago. They were meant to meet for a coffee at three but she didn't show.'

I tightened my bathrobe as Solomon beckoned me over, and was aghast when he handed me the receiver.

'Sweetheart, it's Selina's boyfriend. She's not shown up at work today, and her phone's switched off. Here, talk to him. He's very worried.' He paused, before speaking down the phone. 'Sorry, Joe, can you hang on? Rebecca's not been very well since her mother died. She's on a lot of medication . . .' he mumbled, shaking the receiver as he urged me to take it.

My mouth gaped open as I stood frozen to the spot. Was this some kind of trick?

Solomon gently smiled. 'It's OK, Joe won't bite,' he said, as if he was talking to some terrified child.

I took the receiver, my hands shaking. I wanted to tell him everything, to call the police because something awful had surely happened to Selina. But I had no proof, and Solomon was in such close proximity that I had to protect myself. I could not risk any more violence. I had more than myself to think about now.

'Sorry. I waited an hour but she didn't show. Have you not heard from her today at all?' I said, swallowing through the soreness in my throat. I felt as if I'd been swallowing razor blades. I could still feel Solomon's fingers tightening around my windpipe, and I prayed that Selina had not fallen victim to the same treatment.

'No. If she doesn't come back soon, I'll have to call the police.'

I was at a loss as to what to say and Solomon took the phone from my grasp. He chatted to Joe, reassuring him in such a friendly manner that you would never believe he had been trying to throttle me half an hour before. I walked towards the mirror, noticing the red marks at the base of my throat. I couldn't believe that Solomon had handed me the phone. I could have told Joe everything and had the police banging on my door. But then what? It was one person's word against another's. Even with bruises on my skin, he would say he was acting in self-defence. And even if he was prosecuted, he would not serve time in prison for a common assault. I knew, because I had dealt with a similar case between sixth-formers in my school. Solomon disconnected the call and smiled. Handing me the phone was a test of my loyalty, and I passed with flying colours. But I would not be a victim. I would leave Solomon. But I would have to do it alone.

CHAPTER FORTY-FOUR

REBECCA

2016

'How did your Sunday dinner with the lovely Chloe go?' Rhian smirked, taking a stool at the breakfast bar. She had left her crutches in the hall, and it was good to see her a little steadier on her feet.

I shoved a plate of muffins under her nose. 'She stormed out.' I refrained from rolling my eyes. 'I think her marriage is going through a rough patch.'

'I'm not surprised. The last time I went over there, she introduced me to her friend as her poor disabled sister-in-law. Like I haven't got a fucking name.' She tore off a chunk of blueberry muffin and began to chew.

'Oh dear.' I giggled, imagining the reaction such an introduction would provoke. 'What did you say?'

Rhian swallowed. 'I told her friend that I wasn't ill, I was just exhausted from my shag session the night before.'

'You didn't.'

'What? She was lucky I didn't punch her lights out. Cheeky bitch.'

I snorted back a giggle, trying to scrape up some sympathy for the woman who had an uncanny knack for upsetting everyone I knew. 'I'm sure she meant well.'

'I'm sure she didn't.'

'How's things going with your new hunk? What's his name again?'

Rhian's eyes glittered mischievously. 'Luke. And things are going very well. He's talking about coming to meet you all, God help him.'

'What's he look like?' I asked, visions of Solomon rising in my thoughts.

'He's tall, stubbled, and has the most gorgeous blue eyes, really piercing. Oh, and he's *very* well equipped.'

'Rhian!' I said, snorting back another giggle of relief and astonishment. Blue eyes. Not grey. The information eased my paranoia.

'You're looking tired. Everything all right?' Rhian asked, her smile fading to an expression of concern.

Rhian was someone I had come to trust, and Solomon's presence weighed heavy on my mind. Could I burden her with the truth? And would she understand? I opened my mouth to speak, my fears on the tip of my tongue.

Lottie skipped into the room, still in her bunny-rabbit onesie. Bear plodded beside her, not seeming to mind that his head was decorated with a princess tiara.

'I'd best be off,' I said, giving my daughter a quick cuddle. 'You be good now for Auntie Rhian,' I added, kissing her softly on the cheek.

I admonished myself as I stepped outside. I could not believe how close I had been to blurting out the truth. How many people would get hurt before this was over? I owed it to my family to keep them out of my mess. At least Mr Pritchard had survived the fire. The barking dog in the alley had alerted a neighbour, who called the firefighters before the explosive could do any serious harm. But I could not afford to become complacent. I could just as easily have been hearing about a funeral, as the gossips spread the news. My head was too sore from the incident for me to wear my helmet, so I was forced to drive Sean's old banger of a car. We seldom went to work together in his Land Rover. He was always getting called away, and the surgery was five miles down the road, too far to walk. I had just shoved the key into the ignition when a text came through on Solomon's phone. Surely not already? The smile I was wearing died on my lips as I fumbled in my bag for my mobile.

Victim number five. Actual Bodily Harm.

Gareth Walker or ?

Enter target here _____

This will default to: Gareth if incomplete.

You have thirty seconds to decide.

00:29

I had been expecting an act of violence, and was surprised it had taken him this long to deliver it. Seeing Gareth's name on the text filled me with guilt. As if he needed anything else to worry about. The seconds counted down. Who was I going to pick? I could have inputted the name of a random person from the town but I knew, deep down, there was a better way. I sat motionless as the timer ran down. Five, four, three.

The idea of nominating Gareth had come to me some time ago. Like Sean, Gareth was strong and stocky, but he came with a hot-headed temper that had got him into trouble in his teens. Solomon would be committed to administering a low-level assault only, and unlike Geoffrey and the spitting incident, Gareth would not stand by and allow it to happen. Sean's brother was not some doddery old farmer, or an elderly person who could be bullied around. He was strong, fast, and a lot bigger than Solomon. I wanted Gareth to give Solomon the hiding of his life. The notification popped up to tell me that Gareth was my final choice. I pocketed the phone. What was Solomon thinking now? Was he angry? Or did he think that I was just some evil woman who did not care about the people around me?

I drove to the surgery, my mind on autopilot as I pulled down the dusty visor to blot out the morning sun. Now the fifth crime was dawning, things were going to get a whole lot more serious. Each time I tried to think ahead to what Solomon had planned, I found my mind going back to the old days, when I protected myself with a foggy haze. Each time, I pushed away the reality that a murderer was intent on ripping my life apart. I knew he was saving the best for last: Bear, Rhian, Sean, Lottie. Just who was next? Solomon would play dirty in order to get what he wanted. But I could play dirty too. I was not about to give up the life I had carved out for myself.

I threw myself into work at the surgery as I waited for the confirmation to come through. I had not made it easy for him this time. I would have loved to have seen his face as he realised the challenge that lay ahead. I was almost beginning to hope that he had given up, when my phone beeped.

CHAPTER FORTY-FIVE
REBECCA

2016

Notification number five. Actual Bodily Harm.

Gareth Walker.

Tomorrow at 11pm.

The rear cowsheds.

You are a Silent Witness.

Talk to police and you die.

I felt both guilty and pleased to see Gareth listed as the next victim. He was the best hope I had of finishing this once and for all. Like me, Gareth was not the sort of person to call the police, and would deal with it in his own way. I had to stop myself from searching the definition of actual bodily harm online. I was adept at deleting my Internet search history, but the police could dig up all sorts if our computer was seized. I looked across the surgery at Sean, who was gently cradling a terrier coming out of anaesthetic. My heart swelled with love as he whispered comforting words to the dazed dog. He was the very antithesis of Solomon. But if he knew what I was doing, he would never speak to me again.

I vowed to make our evening as normal as possible, cooking Sean's favourite meal of cottage pie in an attempt to make up for my recent odd behaviour. With our food eaten and Lottie finally in bed, I came out of her room, unable to stop myself surveying the pictures on the wall. Everything was as it should be, and I felt myself relax. That is, until I caught sight of the loft hatch, which was only partially closed. The trouble with our loft door was that you had to give it a good push to ensure it was aligned with the ceiling. Otherwise, one of the corners would jut out. I don't know what made me look upwards, but I instantly knew someone had been up there. I hesitated, conscious the space was just feet away from Lottie's room. Taking a deep breath, I opened my mouth to call for Sean. But what would I say? He knew nothing of Solomon's texts, and that was the way it had to stay. I had to go up there and check it out for myself.

My wide-handled scissors sticking out of my jeans pocket, I gathered all my courage and pulled down the retractable ladder. I was halfway up when I heard Sean's voice as he climbed the stairs.

'What are you doing?' he said, keeping his voice low.

'Just checking,' I said. 'The door, it wasn't shut properly, and I thought I heard noises in the loft.'

'It's probably just pigeons,' he said, looking uneasy as he stepped onto the landing. 'Leave it, come and have your dessert.'

I probably *would* have left it, had he spoken in his usual voice. But the gruffness of his tone made me stiffen. I did not like being told what to do. I gave him a deaf ear as I poked my head into the hatch, and activated the torch on my phone. 'You're right,' I said. 'There's nothing up here.' I was about to step back down when I saw it. The corner of my journal sticking out of the crate. That wasn't where I left it. Of that much, I was sure. Had Solomon been up here? Reading my innermost thoughts? But as I glared back down at my husband's guilty expression, I knew the person snooping was closer to home. I plucked the journal out of the crate, inspecting the broken silver clasp, and I felt my anger rise. Hugging it close to my chest, I didn't speak another word until I was well out of Lottie's earshot.

'I'm sorry,' Sean said, as he followed me downstairs into the kitchen. 'I wanted to find out what was wrong with you.'

'So you broke my final present from my mum?' The words were slow and deliberate, my anger simmering under the surface as I closed the blinds. Our argument didn't need an audience. 'It's a diary, Sean. How could you invade my privacy like that?'

'I hold my hands up,' Sean said, his physical gestures coordinating with his words. 'I was wrong. But you've been acting strange since Solomon was released. I had to know what he did to you to make you so scared.'

'He's a fucking murderer!' I screamed, unable to hold it in any longer. 'How many times do I have to tell you?'

'All right, babe, chill out, I was only—'

'Only what?' I said, taking two steps towards him. 'Trying to control me? To get inside my head? Well, here you go then, fill your boots!'

Pulling at the journal I began to shred the pages, ripping them from the delicate stitching and throwing them at Sean. Aghast, he tried to stop me, but my temper was too great, and I pulled away from his grip. I eyed the pages as I grabbed a fistful.

'April 2005, that was a good year, here you go, have a read of that.' I ripped out the page and balled it in my fist. Throwing it in his direction, I turned another page.

'Mum dying . . . Mmm, that's a bit boring. Oh, here we go, the first time Solomon beat me, that's more like it, or what about the pregnancy? I bet you feasted your eyes on that!'

I was raving now, my emotions spilling out of my body like lava, hot tears coursing down my cheek. Bear nervously paced the floor, a deep whine rumbling in his chest.

'Stop it,' Sean said, pulling me close to him and enveloping me in his arms. The journal fell between us, and I tried to fight him off. But he was too strong, and drained of energy, I succumbed to his grip, burying my head in the curve of his chest as I allowed the tears to flow.

My anger evaporated as I reasoned with his actions, because I would have done the same thing myself. And if I thought that much of my journal, then I wouldn't have hidden it away in the loft. I closed my eyes, my words punctuated by sobs.

'You won't want me now,' I said. 'N—now you know the truth.'

'Oh, babe, how could you think that of me? I felt terrible after reading it. I tried to talk to you about it, but you kept pushing me away.'

'There's one thing I couldn't bear to write,' I said, taking a deep shuddering breath.

'The video?'

I nodded, holding him close so I did not need to meet his gaze. 'Yes. It's time you knew the truth.'

CHAPTER FORTY-SIX

REBECCA

2016

I allowed him to guide me to the table, but I still could not meet his gaze. Wiping my tears with the back of my sleeve, I talked about the events that had led up to that day.

'You've got to understand that I was a different person then,' I sniffled, my hands buried inside the sleeves of my jumper. 'He had a way of controlling people. He wasn't someone you said no to.'

Sean shook his head. 'You don't have to tell me if you don't want to.'

But I kept talking, afraid that if I stopped the words would never come. 'That night, he blindfolded me. I felt spaced out – he'd given me something to drink beforehand. My hands were tied, and he made me say all this stuff . . . it was rough. Rougher than he'd ever been before.'

My tears returned as I recalled the scene. 'It wasn't until he showed me the footage that I realised he was recording us all along.'

'Us?' Sean said. 'You mean, you and Solomon?'

I shook my head, my cheeks flushed with shame. 'There was another man, someone I didn't recognise. He had sex with me, and I didn't even know until he made me watch it back.'

Sean pulled me in for a second time, whispering soothing syllables in my ear. 'Hush now, he can't hurt you anymore, I won't let him.'

'But I'm not finished,' I said, ignoring the voice in my brain warning me that I'd said enough. But my confession was interrupted by Lottie calling out for a drink. Sean drew me back, rubbing my tears with his thumb.

'You've told me now. Let's leave it in the past, where it belongs.' He hugged me one more time before rising to get Lottie a drink. It wasn't in the past. That was the trouble. But it seemed my husband had heard all he could take. I knelt to pick up the pages of my journal, my ugly secrets, scattered across the floor. This wasn't the person who Sean married. What did he think of me now?

Getting away at eleven proved more difficult than slipping away in the dead of night. Sean was in the kitchen, poring over some research papers as he sat at the kitchen table. He had a veterinary conference coming up soon, and I wondered how I would fare while he was away. I'd been forcing myself to take just one day at a time. It was the only way I could see myself getting through it. The hallway clock ticked to 10.45 as I came downstairs in my black jacket and boots.

'Where are you off to?' Sean said, his head rising from his paperwork. It was only then that I noticed he'd had a haircut. He must have called into the barber's before he came home.

'Just for some air, I won't be long.'

'At this hour of the night? Come to bed, why don't you? I'm just finishing up here.'

'Do I question you when you're roaming around the hills at all hours?' I had not meant my remark to be so snippy, but I had to get away, even if it meant invoking a row.

'That's when I'm on call-out, you can't compare that to—'

'To what? Gallivanting around the hills because I'm messed up in the head? I'm just getting some air. I'll be back in half an hour. Stop fussing.' I couldn't help but snap. The stress of the last few days was getting to me, and the last thing I wanted to do was leave the sanctuary of my home.

'At least take the dog,' Sean said, as Bear came padding out after me, his ears pricked at the mention of a walk.

'Sorry, boy, not today,' I whispered, conscious of the time ticking away. I quietly pushed on my helmet, the bruise on my temple reminding me of the seriousness of the task. I comforted myself that at least Sean couldn't follow me, not with Lottie tucked up in bed. He had not said much since our row. Sean was not a man of many words, and I don't think he knew how to cope with what I'd said.

As much as I loved riding my scooter, it wasn't really cut out for the Welsh valleys after dark. I was able to gain access by driving through the fields, and every inch of me shook as my scooter rattled down over the freeze-dried mud. I was used to the farm, having helped out each lambing season, when it was a case of all hands on deck. A mile from the house, it was dotted with sheds old and new, and I was able to park the scooter in a vacant galvanised hut.

By the time I got to the cowsheds at the back of Gareth's farm, it was almost eleven o'clock. I blew into my fingers and stamped my feet, trying to ease the numbness growing under my skin. The strong, musky odour of goats assailed my nostrils. I was so used to animals; I could differentiate them by smell. I jammed my frozen fingers under my armpits in an effort to warm them up. Gareth was not a creature of habit, and I prayed it would all be over with soon. I was drained, emotionally and physically, and longed for a decent night's sleep. I poked my head out to look for Solomon. But all I could see was the bare dirt track I drove in on, and the cowsheds further down. A broad full moon afforded me a clear view, and in the distance I could hear the lowing of the cows. But the eleven o'clock deadline came and went. I guessed it was driving Solomon mad.

I inhaled the cool night air, hoping he would not call things off. Then a darker thought entered my mind. Had I been lured into a trap? Was Solomon visiting my home while I was miles away? I checked my phone, then remembered the backlight and quickly extinguished it. The cattle were all at the end of the field, and Gareth would give them a quick headcount to make sure none had broken out. A rustling noise echoed in the distance. It had to be Solomon, or one of his minions, perhaps the bearded man from before. The thought bloomed a shiver of regret. Why hadn't I thought of that? Solomon would never face Gareth head-on, he would just send someone bigger to do the job. It was too late to back out now. The sound of a motorbike speared through the night. I poked out my head to see a quad bike tearing up the hill. I had forgotten Gareth no longer came up here on foot. I prayed he was wearing a helmet. But what then? I had no idea what the attacker was going to do. Would he pull out a knife and try and stab him? How on earth was he going to hit him when he was driving at bike speed? This was Sean's brother. What the hell had I got him into? I clenched my fists as panic overtook me, fighting the urge to stop Gareth and make him turn around. My heart thundered, and the wind whistled through the cracks in the shed as I fought a battle in my head. The bike drew nearer and I pulled my head back from between the doors. Just where was Solomon? The hairs prickled at the back of my neck. He could be standing right behind me. I peered to look around, but could see nothing apart from some rotting hay bales and unused tools. The bike motored past, and I craned my neck as I caught sight of Gareth driving away.

No, I whispered into the darkness. *Why aren't you wearing a helmet?* My fingernails pushed into the palms of my hands as I searched the moonlit path for whoever was carrying out the attack. A plank of wood flashed from behind a tree, hitting Gareth squarely in the face. Losing control of the handlebars, he came off his quad bike, landing with a grunt on the soil. The bike lurched forward, roaring up on two wheels, before falling into a pothole and cutting out. I clasped my hands over my mouth, knowing the best way I could protect him was to keep my silence. In the distance, someone flitted between the trees. I stood out, flashing the backlight on my phone. All the while my mind was thinking, *What are you doing, waving at that monster?* The tinted black helmet glanced in my direction, and the driver revved the throttle of his motorbike before darting away. It was my turn to do the same. But, as Gareth lay soundless on the earth, every fibre in my being screamed to check if he was OK.

CHAPTER
FORTY-SEVEN

Diary Entry: 3rd September 2005

As with all my entries, this one has been eventful. It's not that long ago that I was an English teacher, living with my mum. Now my life has been turned on its head. I've got to cling to the hope that I can get back to that normality one day, with nobody to answer to but myself. But at least I know now what happened to Selina.

I knew he was setting me up when he went out on the pretence of buying milk, because he never leaves his phone behind. On the coffee table in the living room, it seemed to glare at me as I paused, daring me to pick it up. I almost jumped out of my skin when it rang, and tentatively I approached it, as if it were a stick of dynamite about to explode. Selina had not been far from my mind, and any minute I expected to receive news that something awful had befallen her. So when I saw her name flash up on Solomon's phone, I could not have been more surprised.

Snatching it from the coffee table, I pressed the accept button, barely daring to speak. Selina sounded so scared that I barely recognised her voice.

'Hello, Solomon?' she said. 'Are you there?'

'No, he's not,' I said, flatly. 'It's me.'

Selina paused, and for a second I thought she was going to hang up. I listened to the sound of passing traffic in the background, and imagined her standing outside the hospital, in the car park she visited for cigarette breaks. It was a spot she had called me from many times before, but the voice on the other end of the line sounded far from her normal cheery self.

'Rebecca,' she finally spoke. 'Are you OK?'

'No thanks to you. Why did you warn Solomon I was leaving? You barely know him.' I stared through the net curtains, watching out for his return.

'It's not what you think.' Her words dragged, sounding heavy with remorse. 'Sometimes, we'd meet for a coffee after work. He seemed like such a nice guy, and when he said you were having problems—'

'You decided to believe him over me.'

'Now hang on,' Selina said. 'Anyone could see you were struggling. When we met, it was out of concern for you.'

The thought of my friend having secret meetings with my tormentor enforced the sense of betrayal further. 'Even when you found out he was lying about his illness? You still took his side over mine?'

'No,' Selina gasped, the strength in her voice returning. 'You mustn't believe that, not for a second.' She spoke quickly as she relayed her disgust at his actions, and how she rang to confront him for what he did. She was angry, she said, but he wouldn't listen, because by then it was too late.

'Too late for what?' I said, trying to second-guess what she was going to say.

'I can't say. But you're right. He's a psycho. You need to get out of there.'

'Your boyfriend rang looking for you last night. I was so worried. I thought he'd done something to hurt you.'

'It wasn't like that. I went to my mum's yesterday, that's all.'

'Because you were scared. He's got to you, hasn't he? That's why you're calling him, because you're worried by what he might do.'

Her silence was answer enough. I didn't know how Solomon was manipulating her, but it must have been serious for her to betray my trust. I sighed. 'Listen, it's OK. I know what he's like. Let's just leave it at that. I think it's best if we stay away from each other from now on.'

Selina did not try to argue. As I hung up the phone, I wondered if Solomon had set up the call all along. Getting Selina to ring, then leaving his phone at home. It was another way of telling me that he could infiltrate my contacts. Just what had he done to her, to make her so scared?

Solomon returned empty-handed, not even disguising the fact his departure had been a ploy all along.

My requests to go for a walk were turned down. 'Trust has to be earned,' he said, reminding me just how hurt he was by my attempt to leave. Besides, my bruises were clearly visible from the night before, and we could not have anyone seeing those. They might get the wrong idea.

I've stopped taking the tablets completely now, hiding them under my tongue and storing them in my shoes. But he's always watching, and sometimes I look up from my book to see him glaring at me with that cold-eyed stare. *How many girlfriends did he have before me?* I think. *And where are they now?*

I wonder how I've allowed myself to virtually hand my life over to someone I barely know. Solomon knows everything about me. But what do I actually know about him? He has a good job, developing computer programs that will make him a lot of money. His mum and dad live in Frinton, and his relationship with them is strained at best. I know what he likes to eat, how exact he is about everything, and how he's a stickler for timekeeping. But I'm yet to meet any of his friends, or find out what happened to him to make him the fractured person that he is. It's my fault for letting him in. My head stuffed full of ideals, I placed him so high on a pedestal that I could not hear the alarm bells sounding in the back of my fuddled brain. I clung to him after Mother died, like a raft bobbing about in the storm. And it's only now that I can see just how dependent I've become. To me, being alone was the most terrifying thing in the world. As she lay dying, every night I prayed that I would find someone so I wouldn't be lost in the abyss of having to fend for myself. But now I can see that being alone is not so bad after all. It was the fear of it that paralysed me, and not knowing how I would manage. But nothing could be worse than living under the same roof as a murderer. Solomon will tire of me one day, and what will happen to me then?

I know too much, and I have the potential to turn his life upside down. He made it quite clear that he will kill me if I try to leave again. And now that violence is being introduced into our relationship, I don't doubt the authenticity of his words. I could run to the ends of the earth to try to escape him, and I would find him there, waiting for me, with that self-satisfied sneer. But I have so much more to consider than just me. I lied when I said I was visiting Citizens Advice, because the truth was too hard to bear. My visit was with the doctor, who confirmed what I suspected. I'm pregnant. And I don't know where to turn.

CHAPTER
FORTY-EIGHT
SOLOMON

2016

Solomon could not help but grin as he ended the call with his probation officer. She was pleased with him, *oh whoopee doo*. Silly bitch. She had no idea what he was up to, not a single clue. Her call had been well timed. He had been tempted to look up Selina, to see if she was still in the relationship she gave up her friend to protect. Amazing really, when the shit hits the fan, you find out who your true friends are. He recalled the time they spent together, when Selina had been quick to dump Rebecca for something that was all her own fault.

It was only down to his powers of observation that he had picked up on the friendship between them at the hospital. It was something he had kept a very close eye on. After all, he didn't want Rebecca blabbing about their relationship. As a schoolteacher, she was too prim and proper to admit her sexual tastes to her colleagues. But, as a nurse,

Selina would have seen and heard it all before. She was the perfect choice when it came to a confidante. And that was a risk he could not take. So he wormed his way into her life. Just like he had with Rebecca, he used his charm to reel Selina in, being kind, generous, and caring. She was OK-looking, but nothing like Rebecca. Besides, she was not his type. Too feisty for starters. But when she went to the pub after a row with her boyfriend, Solomon was there to offer a shoulder to cry on.

She spoke about her row, and Solomon confided how tough life had been, living with Rebecca since her mother died. Most of the time she was spaced out on medication, he said, and he had to work hard to get her to take the correct dose, or she flew into a rage. His voice was thick with rehearsed emotion. Sometimes she would be angry and out of control, while other days were like living with a zombie. Selina offered to help, but he said he was finding his way through it. But some days were just so dark. They consoled each other as they drank. Shots for Selina, and lager tops for him. Being the gentleman that he was, he insisted he take the train with her, just so he could see her safely to the door. Giving that tenner to the homeless guy begging at the station was worth it, to see the admiration on her face. She lived alone, which Solomon already knew, as he had previously checked out her flat.

By the time she got to the door it was raining hard, and she had only just noticed that Solomon had left his coat on the train. In reality, it was back at the bar, and he had already texted the barman to keep it safe until his return. Wobbling on her feet, she swung open the front door and he followed her inside. He was soaked through, his slim-fitting white shirt outlining the definition of his chest. She handed him a towel but, as he took it, he touched her face, and they ended up in an embrace. They barely made it up the stairs to her room. Selina insisted on taking control, stripping off as she straddled him on the landing carpet. He allowed himself to be dominated, knowing her guilt would rise more quickly if she was the one who had been in control. Afterwards, they agreed never to speak about it again – she would go back to her boyfriend, and he would be with Rebecca. It was not like he had been unfaithful, because he was protecting their relationship after all. And it was not as if he got a huge amount of enjoyment out of it. But it served his purpose, and he was the first person she rang when Rebecca contacted her to confide about her mistreatment.

Solomon smiled as he recalled the conversation. Even now, it was clear in his mind. Lying about an illness was nothing to him, but clearly a big deal to her. On and on she had ranted, about how she felt betrayed because she had thought he was a decent guy. Solomon had taken pleasure in proving her wrong. It was amazing how quickly she had backed down when he threatened to tell her boyfriend about their fling. It compounded his belief that he was the only one for Rebecca, and she was better off without her friends.

He sighed at the missed opportunity. How he would love to telephone Selina now, just to hear the uncertainty in her voice. But his probation officer had made him think again. It was best to leave Selina in the past, and focus all his attention on Rebecca. She was his, to do with as he pleased, and he would squeeze the life from her body rather than let her go.

CHAPTER
FORTY-NINE
REBECCA

2016

I had watched from my vantage point, an argument going back and forth in my mind. It was as if Sean had inhabited my brain, and was pleading with me to go to his brother's aid. I stepped out in the moonlight, and froze at the sound of a moan, followed by a soft scuffle in the earth as Gareth rose to his feet. I jerked back into cover and exhaled in relief, hiding long enough for him to pass me as he shuffled back to the farm.

I had not expected to sleep, and the next morning I was woken by Sean as he gently shook me by the shoulder. I must have been dreaming about Solomon, because I shrieked in response, clawing the blankets, ready to run from the room. I slowly came to, sobered by the worried expression on Sean's face. This was not just about me. Other people were suffering, and I reminded myself to act surprised as news of his brother filtered through.

'I've got to go,' Sean said. 'Gareth's in hospital.'

I peered at the clock. It was 4 a.m. and the light of the moon was casting streaks through the bedroom blinds. 'What's going on?' I said, doing my best to act confused.

'Gareth disturbed an intruder on the farm last night, trying to steal the stock. Chloe's only just managed to persuade him to go to the hospital. She's really upset. I'll call you when I get there.'

'Wait,' I said, pulling my dressing gown from the bedpost. 'How serious is it?'

'She thinks he's got a broken nose, concussion. I'll call you later, yeah?'

'Again?' I said, wondering how his face would look, with a nose broken for the second time. And it was all my fault. I waited for Sean's customary peck on the cheek. But he was gone, with nothing but the jingle of car keys in his wake as he left through the front door.

I was on my third cup of coffee in the surgery when he rang to update us that Gareth was OK. His face had taken a battering, and he was staying overnight due to his concussion, but there would be no long-term damage. Sean was down for call-outs most of the day, and I relied on Geoffrey's banter to keep my mind off what had happened the night before. But Solomon was going at the pace of a steam train, and my heart plummeted as the phone buzzed in my pocket. I held my breath as I checked the phone. Rather than another notification, I had been sent a file. I frowned. Just what game was he playing with me now?

'That's a big sigh,' Geoffrey said, leaning over the reception counter.

'I'm just tired,' I said, concealing the phone in my tunic pocket. 'Do you mind if I get five minutes' fresh air?'

'Of course, my dear, take as long as you like. I'll man the phones in your absence, use my sexy phone voice if anyone calls.'

'Be still my beating heart,' I said with a wink, grabbing my jacket from the rack. It was turning out to be a beautiful day, but I could not escape the chill I had carried since last night.

I walked out of range of the surgery, following the road down the hill until I came to a turnstile on the left. There were lots of walkways in Pontyferry, and this one carried through the fields to a hiking trail. I perched myself on the wooden step, crossing my legs as I rested the phone on my lap. The file was named 'Betrayal', and I assumed it would be about me.

'What now?' I sighed as I downloaded the attachment. It was a video clip, complete with sound. It took me a few seconds to realise that it was not me featured in the footage, but Chloe and my husband.

Sean was pacing the oak floor of Gareth and Chloe's living room, while Chloe was on the sofa, pleading with him to sit down. But there was something about their exchange that made me think that Gareth was not on the scene.

'Sweetheart, please, sit down,' Chloe said, patting the space beside her.

But Sean was biting his thumbnail, his forehead furrowed. 'This is wrong, all wrong,' he said, before doing as she said.

Immediately I knew this was something I did not want to see. Yet I could not tear my eyes away. My anxieties rose as I watched them interact. For a woman who was meant to be upset, she was immaculately turned out, in her designer clothes and perfectly applied make-up. I felt a lump rise to my throat. What chance did I have, next to someone like her?

'We can't deny our feelings any longer,' Chloe said, sliding her hand onto his thigh. 'Please. Come to bed with me.'

Sean shook his head, but did not move away. 'I've told you before. I've got too much to lose. Lottie, my marriage.'

'Which is a sham,' Chloe said. 'When's the last time she made you feel really alive? You saw how she reacted when I felt your knee. She wasn't even bothered. If that was me, I'd tear the eyes out of anyone making a move on you.'

Sean shook his head. 'Chloe. Please don't do this.'

'What do you even know about her? Nothing.' She took Sean's hand and placed it on her left breast. 'But you know me, what's in here. Childhood sweethearts. We should never have split up.'

'Don't,' Sean said, pulling his hand away. 'You're married to my brother, for God's sake.'

Chloe moved in. 'Only because I couldn't have you. Don't you remember the fun we used to have? We can go travelling, see the world, or just stay in bed all day. I've saved some money. Please say you'll come away with me.'

Sean rose, his hands resting on his hips. 'It's all water under the bridge. I'm with Becky now.' Yet his eyes were locked on Chloe's, caught in her trance.

'Becky.' She said it like it was a dirty word. 'Can Becky give you this?' She rose from the sofa, and snaked her hand around the back of his neck.

Tears pricked my eyes, and I whispered into the valley air, *Don't do it, Sean, please don't*, knowing that whatever happened had already taken place – and that there was nothing I could do about it.

Sean lowered his head to meet her lips, locking himself in her embrace. The video blurred as I blinked away the tears, sick to the stomach at what I had just witnessed. Abruptly, the footage cut off, and the phone fell from my fingers to the ground. But just as it did, another text came through, and I stared in disbelief as the next message came up, ready to play straight into Solomon's hands.

CHAPTER FIFTY
REBECCA

2016

Victim number six. Poisoning.

Chloe Walker or ?

Enter target here _____

This will default to: Chloe Walker if incomplete.

You have twenty seconds to decide.

00:19

An involuntary laugh escaped my lips. It sounded bitter and hard, like it was coming from someone else. I imagined Solomon chuckling at my expense. Yet, as the clock counted backwards, I could not think of a more fitting candidate. Like with Gareth, I allowed the clock to run down. I would never have allowed her to be a victim had I not watched her seduce my husband. Yet Solomon was not to blame for Sean's behaviour. He had had ample opportunities to walk away. But in the heat of anger, what had I done? Chloe getting poisoned had wider implications than just for her. This affected us all. What would Sean think of me now? Did I still care? Like pieces on a chessboard, each of Solomon's offences was strategically placed, and I had been a willing pawn. I had implicated myself in yet another crime.

The response came an hour later, when I was cleaning out the animal cages. I had pulled myself together enough to return to the surgery, telling Geoffrey I had a headache, but was OK to stay. Rhian hated cleaning up, because bending played havoc with her knees, so I always made sure it was completed by the end of the day. It was almost therapeutic, scrubbing the steel cages as my mind tried to make sense of my husband's betrayal. I told myself that they just kissed, because Solomon would have revelled in showing me if it went any further. But why hadn't Sean just walked away? And how many times had they met up before? I thought he loved me, but I must have been wrong. I jerked upwards as the phone beeped in my pocket, hitting my head on the cage ceiling. I winced, dragging myself away from the antiseptic smell. Was it the second instalment of their video? A wave of nausea rose at the thought. I was unsure if I could bear to watch. With shaking hands, I opened the notification. A response to my nomination earlier in the day.

```
Notification number six. Poisoning.

Chloe Walker.
```

Tonight at 9pm.

The Belvedere Hotel.

You are a Silent Witness.

Talk to police and you die.

The Belvedere. One of the few hotels in town. Sean had always been reluctant to go there, saying the food was not to his taste. But Rhian had long since let it slip that it was the place where he proposed to Chloe. Well, the food won't be to Chloe's taste either, I thought, biting back a smile.

CHAPTER
FIFTY-ONE

Diary Entry: 10th September 2005

I've barely dared to think about my pregnancy since my last entry, and I haven't allowed it to alter my resolve to get away. I was too scared to go back to work after he threatened to blackmail me. The knowledge that I could walk into a class of sniggering students, who had been made privy to the video of me with Solomon, was too much to bear. Not that you could see his face. The shame was mine alone. So I handed in my notice, relinquishing my last strand of independence. And Solomon became his calm, loving self again. But, after a few days of being nice to me, he seemed to get bored. He began spending longer at work, as if purposely trying to catch me out. He rang home every thirty minutes, knowing I could not go too far. I thought about walking out, but any attempt would come with a beating, and I could not risk him hurting the baby I had yet to tell him about. So I waited until the perfect moment presented itself.

It was lunchtime, and the estate agent had a viewing for my home. I cleaned it within an inch of its life, as per Solomon's instruction, and it broke my heart to imagine other people moving in. But little by little I detached myself from sentimental objects, and stored my precious memories away in my head. I remembered Selina's offer of finding me a women's refuge. At least dealing with impartial people meant they would not be put at risk. So I waited until the estate agent was busy, and asked if I could use his phone to report that my landline was broken. Slowly he handed it over, and it was like being passed a key to a locked door. I hid myself away in the bathroom, my hands shaking as I dialled the refuge's number.

'Hello,' I said, aware that time was precious. 'I'm in an abusive relationship and I need to get away. Can you help me?'

They did not ask for too many details – they must have guessed from my hushed words that I did not have the luxury of time to explain. I gave only my first name, saying that I desperately needed their help. The woman on the phone was lovely, and told me I was lucky because a girl was leaving today, and my case needed priority attention, so I would most likely get the room. All I had to do was get on the train and she would meet me at the other end. They did not give out their address over the phone, but we could go to a coffee shop and talk things through. Then she could bring me back to the refuge. I hung up the phone, feeling real relief for the first time in months. I had my baby to think about now, and I had to get us both somewhere safe. I returned the phone to the estate agent and waited for him to leave with the prospective buyer. My heart pounded as I gathered together the loose change I had managed to collect from Solomon's pockets over the last week. As he left cash lying around, I sometimes wondered if he was testing me to see what I would do.

I ran all the way to the train station, knowing Solomon would call the house soon. But when I got to Clacton station, I could have cried. I had missed my train by minutes, and had to wait half an hour for the next one to come. It felt like forever, and I knew that Solomon would be hunting me down. Standing on the platform, with the sun's rays beating down on me, I had never felt so alone. I sat on the metal bench, my arms wrapped around my stomach as I tried to focus on the positives. Starting a new life had seemed like a pipe dream, but this time I would have support from people who understood. They had the power to move me anywhere in the country, somewhere I could start again. I wished I was safe within the walls of the refuge, instead of making the journey to Chelmsford alone. I realised I was crying, and wiped the tears away. It was so tantalisingly close, I could almost touch it, and I wrung my fingers as I willed the train to hurry up. I imagined Solomon calling home, swearing as the tone came back engaged. I had left the phone off the hook, but he would know something was up. My heart lifted as the train came into view. I stood, shielding my face from the glare of the sun, daring to hope I was safe. But my optimism did not last long, as footsteps behind me made me catch my breath.

CHAPTER
FIFTY-TWO
REBECCA

2016

Sean had proposed in a setting far more beautiful than the Belvedere
Hotel. At least it seemed so to me. Like a child, I viewed parts of Wales
with magical wonderment, so when he brought me to the southern tip
of Snowdonia, I knew he had something special planned. Llyn Barfog,
known as the Bearded Lake, was a couple of miles east of Aberdovey,
and we lay in the heather as Sean recounted the myths attached to the
lands. The legend of King Arthur and his battle with the monstrous
Afanc was one he had recounted to our daughter a hundred times since.
But back then, after my experience with Solomon, I had to work hard
to build trust in a future with another man. It was a gentle chat, rather
than a full-on proposal, and as we decided to choose a ring together, I
accepted a hula hoop instead.

I put aside my reminiscing, having decided that my marriage was worth fighting for. A whole host of butterflies fluttered in my stomach, as I entered the scene of the next proposed crime. I tried to blend in with my surroundings, ordering a drink at the bar. I was wearing a long black coat over my clothes, trying to be as inconspicuous as possible as I told the waiter I was waiting for a friend. I managed to find a yucca plant to hide behind, with a good view of any patrons coming into the restaurant. For once, I was devoid of fear, and my contempt for Chloe was laced with an ugly thirst for revenge. But, deep down, I knew it was wrong. And the cloak of anger I chose to wear had become paper thin. I could allow hatred to consume me, and become as bitter and twisted as Solomon. But the truth was I didn't want any more people to get hurt. I didn't want any of this.

My thoughts were cut short as Chloe's shrill laughter filled the air. I kept my head down until she was seated, wearing a red dress that suggested she had not come to dine alone. Gareth was still recovering from his injuries, and I had left Sean at home with Lottie, so who was she with? Her dinner date joined her, and all hope within me died. The dark hair, his hazy blue eyes. It was not her husband sitting across from her – it was mine. For a few seconds, time stopped as I tried to comprehend the situation. This was more than a one-off kiss. Sean lied to me, in order to meet his ex-love. A quick text to Rhian revealed she had been asked to babysit Lottie, because Sean had been called away to a sick animal. *Sick animal indeed*, I thought, as I watched Chloe reach out to touch his hand. My fists clenched. How dare she? But my seething gaze did not catch their attention. They were too wrapped up in conversation to see me at the bar.

A waiter breezed past, and I did a double take as I realised who it was. Solomon. My heart dropped like a stone in my chest. All those other times I had not been entirely sure. But now – there was no denying the identity of the source of my pain. And the look on his face revealed he was enjoying every single second. This was the man who had taken my mother's life. And yet here he was, brazenly sauntering around with a tray in his hand. He hadn't changed much since I last saw him, a decade ago. He was a little thinner, his skin paler than before. But still the same handsome man, more than capable of charming his intended prey.

The restaurant was filling up fast, and the staff did not seem to notice him approach Chloe's table with a tray. I sat back and watched the show, hoping he had put a dose of laxatives in her drink. He was wearing the same waistcoat as the waiters, with a white shirt and black trousers; the uniform wasn't difficult to imitate. On a busy night the staff didn't have time to check who was milling around and, judging by Chloe's surprised expression, she must have been told the drinks were on the house. Sean began to shake his head, but Chloe stopped him, taking the glass of fizz and knocking it back. Greedy cow. Serves her right. The words streaked through my mind before I could stop them. I watched her hand fall under the table and reach for my husband's knee. Sean jerked, admonishing her as she pulled it back. Solomon seemed to disappear into thin air, but not before he caught my eye and gave me a triumphant wink. He thought he had it all sewn up. I sidled out the back entrance without being seen. Chloe would get her comeuppance soon enough. I just had to worry about my husband.

Endless scenarios ran through my brain as I awaited Sean's return home. What if Solomon ended up killing her? What if Sean got the blame? He owned a surgery, and had plenty of access to drugs. I bit my nails as I paced the kitchen. Having thanked Rhian, I paid for her taxi, batting off her expression of concern. She wasn't stupid. She knew something was wrong. But that would be a conversation for another day. I told myself to calm down. I had not planned any confrontations. It was better to say nothing and see how things went. But as Sean entered the kitchen, the expression on his face told me things were serious.

'Becky,' he said, dropping his car keys on the kitchen table. 'We need to talk.'

CHAPTER FIFTY-THREE

REBECCA

2016

We need to talk. Those four words rooted me to the spot, and I clung to the back of the chair as I tried to maintain some normality in my voice. Because, despite what had gone on between Sean and Chloe, I still loved my husband, and was willing to forgive any mistakes he had made. But what if he said he was leaving me for her? I took a deep breath as the stirrings of deep-rooted anxiety made themselves known. I had foolishly believed I was strong, independent, and capable of facing anything that was thrown at me. But seeing him in that video with Chloe made me realise just how much I needed him in my life.

'Sounds serious,' I murmured, pulling out the chair and sitting down. Bear ambled over, picking up on my sadness. He rested his chin on my lap, and I scratched his soft brown fur.

Sean approached the kitchen table, but did not sit down. 'I need to be honest with you. I wasn't on call-out tonight. I'm sorry, but I lied to Rhian.'

'You're scaring me, Sean,' I said, as a ball of anxiety lodged in my throat. 'Where were you?'

He raked his fingers through his hair, looking pained as the words passed his lips. 'With Chloe,' he said, exhaling. 'She's been pressuring me to get back with her. I'm sorry. I should have told you sooner.'

I felt the blood leave my face. I told myself that this is where my husband packs a bag and turns his back on the stranger he married. That this is where the dream ends. 'Don't go,' I said, softly.

'What?' Sean pulled out a chair, and reached for my hand as he sat. His flesh was warm, and I curled my fingers through his.

'Sweetheart, I'm not going anywhere. I just thought you should know. The last thing I want is to keep secrets from you.'

I thought of all *my* secrets. The burden had never felt heavier.

'Remember the other evening when Gareth was bending my ear? Well, I've been getting the same from Chloe for the last couple of weeks too. Their marriage is in serious trouble, and they've both come to me for advice.'

She came to you for more than advice, I thought, but stayed silent to allow him to speak.

'Sometimes she'd come to the surgery at closing time to talk. I never bothered mentioning it, because I didn't want Gareth to think I was taking sides. But I've known her since we were kids. I didn't have the heart to turn her away.'

'Go on,' I said, praying he would tell me the whole truth. I needed to trust Sean, if we had any hope of staying together, and if he lied about his kiss with Chloe, then it meant he was lying about other stuff too.

'I've been stupid, I can see that now, reminiscing about old times instead of telling her to talk to her husband. I think I might have given her some ideas.' He rubbed the back of his neck, forcing the words.

'She, well . . . she made a pass at me. I told her she was being silly, but she kept saying that she loved me, and all that stuff.' He searched my face for a reaction, but in truth there was nothing there. I was reliving that moment, just as he was, praying he would be consistent with the truth.

'I told her it wasn't right, talking like that. She was my brother's wife and me a married man. But she didn't seem to think of it as cheating, because we've been engaged before.'

'She's got a very warped sense of what a relationship is about,' I said, wondering what she was doing right now. Had the drugs Solomon administered taken effect? Was she going to be OK? I drew my attention back to Sean, who was staring at our hands, naturally intertwined. But for how long?

'I told her I'd never leave you, much less Lottie. But she was very insistent. She got all touchy feely, and I got up to leave, and then . . .' He swallowed, his throat producing a dry clicking sound. 'Then she kissed me.'

I was waiting for more. Because everything he had said was exactly what had played out on video.

'I don't want to hurt you, darlin', but you need to know the truth.'

I cleared my throat. 'And?'

Sean looked at me, puzzled. 'What?'

'What. Happened. Next?' My tone was loud and clear this time, and a look of fleeting horror crossed Sean's face.

'Nothing. I pushed her away.'

I nodded, not entirely convinced. 'Have you slept together? Tell me the truth.'

Sean shook his head vehemently. 'No, of course not. How could you think that?'

'How could *I*?' My eyes widened in disbelief. Here was my husband, after lying about where he was and snogging the face off his ex-love. And he looks at me like it's all my fault? I would not allow any man to treat me as if I was at fault again. Releasing my fingers from his grip, I narrowed my eyes in disbelief.

'Come on, Sean, don't give me that crap. There's obviously still some chemistry between you. She wouldn't have kissed you otherwise. Tell me the truth. You must have enjoyed it, wanted more.'

Sean raked his hair with his fingers. 'I never would have slept with her. Not for anything.'

'But you enjoyed the kiss?'

'Maybe, just for a second, I was reminded of old times. But then I thought of you and Lottie and I felt terrible, listening to her, when I should have been talking to you. Becky, I know we're having problems, but it's nothing that can't be fixed. Any feelings I had for her are dead. That kiss, well, it made me realise that.'

The fact we were still having problems was news to me, and reminded me of how distant I had been. My emotional outbursts, the nights I came to bed late, Sean must have taken them as signs that I was unhappy with him.

'I wanted to tell you straight away, but you were just so detached, and I'm not blaming it on you, honestly I'm not. If I had been honest with Chloe from the start, she would never have got the idea of us getting back together.'

I nodded, my flare of anger returning to its box. It was wrong to tar Sean with the same brush as Solomon. Because he was ten times the man that manipulative murdering bastard would ever be.

'I've seen the way she looks at you, but she's the sort of person that only wants something that's out of reach. That's why she dumped you to go travelling, then decided to stay. It's why she got with your brother, and now it's why she wants to be with you. But the fact is you've been honest, and I can't fault you for that.'

Sean took my hands and kissed them. I ran my palm over the stubble on his cheek. There was one more question I had to ask. 'So where were you tonight?'

'She wouldn't leave me alone. I thought it would be safer to meet up in public, so I could tell her how I felt – that I loved you and Lottie, and she'd got it wrong.'

'And how did she take it?'

'She rushed off, said she wasn't feeling well. I think she's got the message this time. Am I forgiven?'

I rose from my chair and walked to the kitchen window, feeling hurt and betrayed. It took a long time for me to communicate the words stuck in my throat. 'Of course I forgive you. And Sean?'

'Yes?' he said, casting me an unsure glance.

'Just because I don't jump up and down and start screaming doesn't mean that I don't care. I respect you as my husband, and I do love you. Up until today, I didn't think that needed to be said. I'll tell you every day if I have to. But if you let her come between us again, we're finished.'

I silently checked on Lottie, my little star, the centre of my universe. I could not allow anything to disrupt her happy home. Both Solomon and Chloe had caused cracks in our relationship, and I told myself that this was the last time. Whatever Solomon had planned next, I was not having any part in it. Tomorrow I would go for a walk, and throw away Solomon's phone.

CHAPTER
FIFTY-FOUR

Diary Entry: 12th September 2005

My diary entries have become snatched moments but, without them, I think I'd go mad. Sometimes, my inner voice tries to justify Solomon's behaviour, telling me it would be easier to stay. It's easier to believe he was lying about my mum, and that things will be better when we're married. Then I read back my outpourings of despair, and remember what he's put me through. But there's no going back now, and I'm not making excuses for him anymore.

My last update was of my escape, standing on the train platform as footsteps approached from behind. The sound made me almost jump out of my skin and, as the stranger passed, I realised I had been holding my breath. How had I become so fearful of one man? But I knew why, and I could not allow myself to contemplate what Solomon had done. Staying strong was the only way I would get out of this, and I would not be beaten anymore. By the time the train pulled into Kelvedon I began to relax. Chelmsford was just minutes away. Sitting in the empty carriage, lulled by the comforting rock, I fantasised about starting again. But, as the carriage door opened, my blood ran cold. I raised my eyes to see the face of my tormentor. It was Solomon. And he had just boarded the train. I inched my body against the window, as if somehow I could jump through the glass to freedom. A feeble smile was all I could offer, as he assessed me with his icy cool eyes.

'Out shopping then?' Solomon was sweating as he looked me up and down. He sat beside me and put his arm over my shoulder, his fingers digging into my flesh.

My breath quickened. 'Yes,' I squeaked, trying to keep my voice steady as I made up some feeble excuse about buying him a surprise. I dared to ask what he was doing here. There was no reason for Solomon to be boarding the train other than to find me. He worked in Chelmsford, which meant he would have had to have driven from there to Kelvedon to catch my train. I felt my heart sink in my chest. Getting a present was a poor excuse. Could I get away with it?

Solomon bared his teeth in an ugly smile, suggesting we go home instead. 'Leave the shopping for another day,' he said, and his comment about having something better in mind broke me out in a cold sweat. I thought about the last time Solomon punished me for running away, and the things he was capable of. My stomach clenched in anticipation, and I began to cry for the unborn child I was yet to come to terms with.

'Please don't make me go back there.'

Solomon's head swivelled as the ticket inspector's voice echoed from the next carriage. 'Shush now, stop that crying,' he said, his anger evaporating as the conductor drew near. 'I'm not going to hurt you. But I know where your dithery old aunt lives. If you don't pull yourself together, you'll be going to her funeral soon.'

I was not close to Aunt Betty, but she had always seemed like a sweet old soul, even if she was a bit eccentric. I remembered her at my mother's funeral, and how Solomon had chatted to her for ages. He handed me a tissue, and I wiped my tears and blew my nose. The inspector came and checked our tickets, oblivious to my distress. I wanted to ask for help, but the words were lodged in my throat. Solomon's hand had snaked down to my waist and pinched hard. Besides, what would a ticket inspector do? Only call the police, which would end up with them all being given front-row seats to watch my home video. My only hope was to go home and get to the refuge on another day. At least he didn't know about that. The refuge was my only hope.

So we exited the train at Chelmsford, and I fooled myself that it was not so bad because, as far as Solomon was concerned, I had left the house to buy him a gift with some money I had scraped together. It wasn't as if he knew I was conspiring against him. I had made sure of that. We must have looked like any other happy couple as we walked down the steps to catch the train back to Kelvedon so he could pick up his car. My eyes picked through the crowd, and I saw a dark-haired woman scanning the carriages. I knew it was the lady from the refuge, and I felt a piece of me die as I walked away. I thought of my eccentric Aunt Betty, cosy in her bungalow in York. I had visited her twice in my lifetime, but I could not have another death on my hands. I told myself there would be other chances, that the worst I could expect from Solomon was a telling off for not making him aware of my plans. It was safer not to tell him about the pregnancy, because he would never let me leave.

'You know I worry about you when you're on your own. You really should wait until we can go together,' Solomon whispered in my ear. 'You just don't think, do you?'

I was used to his barbed comments. 'Sorry, I'm not with it today.'

Solomon laughed. 'Darling, you've not been with it for a very long time.'

We were talking about dinner when we walked through the front door of my house. I had planned to make a curry, and home-made ice-cream for afters, to make up for upsetting him. I had almost convinced myself that he believed me, and everything would be all right. Solomon said that I had misunderstood him. He had never said that I wasn't allowed out. It was the thought of me leaving him that drove him to the edge. I nodded in agreement, wondering how he had found me so quickly.

But as soon as the door was closed everything changed. Solomon dropped the bags of shopping he was holding and whispered my name. I turned around, to feel the full force of his fist as he punched me in the stomach. My eyes watered as a fiery burst of pain consumed me. I was winded, and I lay on the ground, gasping for a breath that would not come. He stood over me, fists clenched, and I curled into a ball. All I could think of was our baby, but I was unable to speak as my lungs heaved for air.

'Do you really think you could have got away with it?' he said, spitting the words through clenched teeth. 'You stupid bitch. As if I'd ever let you leave me.'

CHAPTER
FIFTY-FIVE
REBECCA

2016

There weren't as many offences involving violence in criminal law as I thought. Common assault, actual bodily harm, grievous bodily harm, as well as the attempted offences, then murder. I knew exactly where this was heading. It had been his goal all along: to see if I could witness a murder without reporting it to the police. To sacrifice an innocent person so I could be free. But who would he nominate? Those nearest and dearest, of course, or maybe even me. But how could I witness my own murder? No, he would nominate Sean, Rhian, or Lottie. Did Solomon really have it in him to kill a child? I thought of all the hatred he had stored up inside him, and the answer was yes.

These were the thoughts that occupied my mind as I walked the well-worn grassy path from our house through the fields and beyond. Bear's deep bark echoed ahead of me, ears flopping, tail wagging. It was good to have a day off, where we didn't have to worry about work or Sean being called out. *That's if he had been on call-out all those times.* The words cut through me like a razor, and I pushed them to the back of my mind. Maybe, when this was all over, we could go for some couple's therapy, or whatever they were calling it these days. But for now I was content with putting a plaster over our troubles. Sean had cancelled the few appointments in the diary and decided to spend the day with me and Lottie. I left him cooking breakfast as I brought Bear out for a jaunt. Nobody, not even Solomon, was going to get in the way.

A quick call to Rhian had updated me that Chloe was ill, but already on the mend. I'm sure Solomon meant her far worse harm, but whatever drugs he had given her had quickly evacuated her system during a particularly nasty overnight case of diarrhoea and vomiting. Gareth had put it down to some dodgy seafood and I, for one, was relieved it had not warranted a visit to the doctor. But I put all thoughts of Chloe behind me, mildly pleased that karma had taught her a lesson. A flock of starlings flew overhead, delighting in the light breeze. I envied them their freedom, and wondered if my mum was up there somewhere, free of all earthly ties.

Perhaps I had been delusional, thinking I could throw away the phone and walk away. I could have smashed it against a rock, or discarded the sim card. Instead, I simply threw it in a tuft of grass and called Bear to heel as I turned for home. I had barely taken a step when I thought I heard it vibrate. I was imagining it, I told myself. How would I hear it out here, with the sound of the wind rustling in the trees? Shaking my head, I walked away. But each step I took was like walking in cement shoes, and I was filled with a sense of dread.

You've come so far, a voice argued in my head. *If you don't answer the text, it'll default to whoever's next on the list. You need to know what he's going to do.* I stiffened, thinking of my mother's words: *keep your enemies close, darling, you can get through this.* That was my mother's voice. I might have been imagining it, but it was enough to make me turn back and rescue the phone.

I dropped onto my knees as I scrabbled in the grass, with Bear's big wet snout in my ear. 'Geroff,' I said, pushing him backwards.

The action made him dance on his front paws, thinking I was playing a game. I wrapped my fingers around the cold black metal, vaguely remembering a scene from a horror movie I'd watched once, about a man who couldn't throw some haunted object away. As I stared at the screen, I saw I had not been imagining things. It *was* another text, confirming the last mission as complete. My earlier optimism drained away. Solomon was just getting into his stride.

CHAPTER
FIFTY-SIX
SOLOMON

2016

Solomon palmed the small box of contact lenses in his pocket. Luke's blue eyes had been the first thing Rhian had commented on, and it wouldn't do to forget them now. He had someone important to meet, and he could not wait to make their acquaintance.

Rhian's black jeans accentuated the curve of her hips. Without her crutches, she looked as healthy as anyone else in the park that day. Her red silk blouse could have passed for conservative, had a black leather jacket not completed her ensemble. The sight of her red heels gave his heart a little jolt. They were only an inch high, but enough to make his old friend paranoia pay him a little visit. For a fleeting moment he wondered if she was toying with him, because of something Rebecca had said. He told himself he was being silly, because if she had known his identity, she would never have left her precious daughter in Rhian's care.

He shoved his hands deep in his trouser pockets as he approached them, rattling his loose change.

'You must be Lottie,' he said, his voice drowned out by the sound of an approaching ice-cream van.

Only in Wales would an ice-cream van arrive in the winter, Solomon thought. But they had been lucky with the weather, and the sun shone as brightly as a spring day. The little girl smiled shyly, clinging to Rhian's trousers. She looked like something out of a photo shoot for a children's catalogue; her wavy blond hair was tied in two perfect bunches, and she was wearing a cute lemon cardigan over a flowery pink dress. Solomon bent down to meet her gaze. 'Would you like an ice-cream?'

'Mummy said I shouldn't talk to strangers,' she said shyly, eyeing up the children running to the ice-cream van.

'And Mummy's right,' Solomon said. 'My name is Luke. I'm your Auntie Rhian's friend. So I'm not a stranger at all. Now what flavour would you like? Strawberry? Chocolate?'

'Chocolate, please,' Lottie smiled, showing off a gap in her teeth.

'And what good manners you have,' he said, rising. 'That's going to earn you a double scoop. And what can I get you, gorgeous lady?' Solomon asked as he straightened to address Rhian.

'Ooh, same for me, thanks,' she replied with a smile. 'We were just about to go on the swings, while they're empty.'

'Well, don't let me stop you. I'll join you in a minute.' He watched them walk away, his mind focused on his future plans. Everything was coming together perfectly, and he could not wait to bring them to fruition.

CHAPTER
FIFTY-SEVEN
REBECCA

2016

In all the years Sean has known me, I've been to the spa three times. But I needed an excuse to get away by myself, in a last-ditch effort to put a stop to Solomon's plans. The idea of visiting Solomon's mother had come to me in the night, and Sean was too plagued with guilt about Chloe to say no. I felt bad, using his behaviour as an excuse to get away, but I told myself that I was doing it for us. Returning to Essex was daunting, and I half expected Sean's old estate car to break down. It felt surreal, as I parked up in town and took a breath of sea air. Apart from a couple of businesses that had closed down and reopened as something else, Frinton hadn't changed much over the years. I stretched my legs as I took in the pretty seaside resort.

Frinton was a place for the affluent and retired, with a stunning golden beach that stretched for miles. With its hanging baskets and traditional British shops, I wondered how such a place could have produced a monster like Solomon. I hoped that by visiting his mother I could unlock some of Solomon's past, find a way to make him understand. After all, none of the communications said anything about approaching his family, and his mother had always been an amenable sort.

I knew I was taking a chance, visiting without making arrangements, but from what I remembered of Anna Kemp, it seemed like she rarely left the house. I walked down the avenues, trying to deny the memories forcing their way through my thoughts. The sun was shining on this cold November day, but inside I felt hopeless and alone.

The house was as imposing as ever, but had lost a lot of its grandeur. The garden that once flourished with clipped hedges and rose bushes was now gravelled over in a blanket of grey. I stared up at the turrets I once found so charming, but which now seemed to represent the prison cells where Solomon would have kept me, if he'd had his way. I pressed the doorbell, and my muscles tensed as the door drew back. If Solomon answered, I would confront him. But the face that answered the door was one I barely recognised. Not only had the colour left Anna's hair, but she had shrunk several inches. Pallid and withered, she looked at me blankly, and I wondered if she still was in possession of her mind.

'Anna, it's me, Beck . . . Rebecca,' I corrected myself. 'Can I have a word?'

She stepped aside, like a woman who had spent her whole life being told what to do. I stepped into the hall, and glanced at the piles of junk mail spread on the floor. 'Do you want me to pick these up?' I said, already crouching to gather them. 'You could slip on them if you're not careful.'

'*Danke*,' Anna said, having still retained her German after all these years. 'I mean, thank you. It hurts to bend. My knees aren't so good these days. It's the arthritis.'

I gathered them up, separating them into two piles, bills and junk. 'Some of these look important,' I said, laying what looked like demands on the kitchen table as she showed me inside.

'Solomon takes care of the bills,' she said. 'But I don't know when he's coming back.'

But she wasn't looking at me. She was looking at the burglar alarm fixed to the corner of the ceiling. At least she had some form of security in the big old building, although I couldn't help but feel she would be better off in sheltered accommodation.

'Do you remember me?' I checked, taking a seat at the table. It seemed a silly question, given I was the one who sent her son to prison. But it had been years, and the faraway look in her eyes made me wonder if Solomon had been controlling her through medication, as he had with me. Or perhaps she had succumbed to dementia. I glanced around the kitchen as I waited for an answer, a mixture of disappointment and sadness washing over me.

Anna busied herself putting on the kettle, although, looking at the piles of tea-stained cups, I didn't want to trouble her for a brew. She glanced back, her eyes searching my face for a memory long buried. 'I don't know, you look familiar. Are you the girl in the newsagent's?'

'No,' I said, wondering if I had just wasted the day driving to see her. My fingers crept to the nape of my neck, and I realised my physical appearance had thrown her off. 'I used to have long blond hair. I—' The words stuck in my throat. 'I gave evidence against him . . . before he went to prison. I'm sorry, Anna, I know it's a lot to take in.'

'Rebecca . . .' The words were just a whisper on her lips as she took a seat at the table. 'Yes. I remember you. You said he killed that young man.'

'It's been a long time,' I said, desperate to move on. 'Have you heard from Solomon lately?'

'He used to live here. But he's moved away.' Her eyes followed the burglar alarm. 'Come home, son. I don't like being on my own.'

In some ways it was better if her mind was fading. It made my presence more bearable. I doubt I would have been as understanding in her shoes. After all, what mother doesn't side with her child? My gaze wandered over the kitchen. A saucepan was stained with porridge, and used teabags lay littered next to a kettle. I couldn't help but feel sorry for her, rattling around in this big old house. What a waste. Then I remembered a promise Solomon had made, that one day it would have been ours. I wasn't so envious after all. I took a deep breath as I offloaded my concerns.

'He's been contacting me since he's come out of prison. He's not meant to, you see, and, well, I'm scared.' I waited for a reaction but she stared ahead, her eyes a blank canvas.

'He's always been hot-tempered,' she said, keeping her voice low. 'Ever since he came back from boarding school. I said to my husband we never should have sent him there. But he paid a lot of money for them to take him so young. He said it would make a man of him. I had no choice.'

'Oh,' I said. 'He never really spoke about it to me.'

Anna leaned forward and whispered conspiratorially. 'He didn't like to talk about it. He used to plead with us to stay at home, but when he was ten, he stopped asking. He never mentioned it after that.'

'I thought if we could speak, that maybe I could persuade him to leave us alone. I just want to forget about what happened, get on with our lives,' I said, but Anna was still talking, lost in the past.

'No phone calls to home, they said. It would just upset him. But he was upset anyway.'

I could see it was pointless talking about the present, so I joined her. 'Why did you send him away so young?'

'I didn't want to. It was James. The truth is, he was jealous. He said Solomon took up all my time. But I was here, in this big house all alone. I had lots of time. But James wouldn't listen. He said if I left him, he'd make sure I never saw our son again.'

'But you were his mum,' I said, unable to comprehend how she had given up her son. 'You could have left, taken him away.'

'And go where? I had no money, no home. I couldn't give Solomon everything he needed. My mother, she was very ill in Germany. James paid for her care.'

I nodded. So this is where Solomon picked up the art of manipulation. And what a cruel teacher he'd had. 'What was Solomon like, as a child?' I asked.

'I only had him for a few weeks in the summer. He used to spend all his time in his tree house, reading books. James believed that children should be seen and not heard.' She sighed, her head bowed, like someone who had given up the fight.

From what I had seen of Solomon's father, I had no difficulty believing that. It was hardly any wonder I had met his parents only once, and our trip to Frinton was just to show me the house, rather than the relatives he had kept such a closely guarded secret.

Anna was still deep in thought, her tightly bound memories finding release. 'His father wanted him to join the police and climb the ranks like him. But Solomon was only ever interested in his computers. His tutors said he had an analytical mind. Liked to work things out.'

'Yes,' I said, painfully aware. 'Have you got a phone number for him? An address? I was hoping to get in touch, try to sort things out.'

'No,' she said. 'I'm sorry, you have to go. I shouldn't have let you in. I—' she stuttered, looking back up at the wall, then hanging her head like a naughty child. 'I thought you were someone else. Please leave.'

'Please, Mrs Kemp, I've driven for the whole day to get here. Can I see his room? See if he's left any sign?'

'Nobody's allowed in his room, not even me,' she said, her voice dropping to a harsh whisper.

I changed tack, trying to buy some time. If I could just get into his room, then I might find some clues. 'Do you have anyone coming to pop in on you? Help with the shopping? It can't be easy now you're all alone.'

'He orders what I need online and has it sent to me. All I have to do is ask.'

I glanced over her shoulder to the pile of empty cans, the gravy-stained lids bent upwards in a jagged yawn. 'But I thought you said you don't have a phone number?' I said.

'Please leave.' She stood, her hands buried in her apron pockets. 'If you don't leave, I'll have to call the police.'

'OK, I'm sorry, I'm going now.'

She followed me into the hall but, as I got to the door, she extended her hand. 'Thank you for coming. I'm sorry I couldn't help.'

I shook her hand. Her flesh felt cold and clammy, and I wondered when she had last turned on the heat. She pressed a note into my palm and I looked up to see her closing the door. Holding the note tightly in my grasp, I walked back down the avenue to my car. The light was beginning to fade, and I had a long journey home. As soon as I turned the corner, I opened the paper, which had been torn from what looked like an address book. Three words were scrawled over the page, written by an arthritic hand: HE WATCHES EVERYTHING. The words sent a chill down my flesh. What did she mean? That I was being watched? That she was? She had been happy to talk of the past, but ignored my questions about the present. She wasn't senile, though; she was scared. Pretending she didn't know me so she could allow me inside. But my snooping would land her in trouble, and that was when she urged me to leave. But how was he watching? A sea breeze freshened my thoughts, the shrill cry of a seagull bringing clarity. *Of course*, I thought, as it all became clear. That's why she kept looking up to the ceiling when she spoke. He ordered the food online because she told him what she needed. He was watching her on camera. I recalled the burglar-alarm box. The same one we had recently installed in our home. He was watching all of us.

CHAPTER
FIFTY-EIGHT

Diary Entry: 17th September 2005

Violence is not something I've encountered before Solomon and, here in my hotel room, I'm still shell-shocked from the last few days. The police have been amazing, so much better than I gave them credit for. But as soon as they find out about you, I know they'll take you from me, and I cannot hand you over without updating what happened first. I look in the mirror and still see the bruises of his attack, but the mental images frighten me more. I wonder if I'll ever truly be free.

That day, when Solomon confronted me, I'd never felt so alone in my life. Here was the man who purported to love me, cupping his hand around my throat and pinning me down against the floor. All because I had tried to leave. I watched in horror as he drew back his right fist, and I shielded my face with my hands. Whimpering through my shaking fingers, I waited for the blow to hit home. Relief flooded over me as he paused, distracted by the ring of his mobile phone. He released his grip and walked away, clearing his throat to answer it.

My stomach was still aching from his punch, and with the front door locked, my only escape was the stairs. If I could lock myself in the bathroom, it might give him enough time to calm down. But I had barely made it up the stairs when Solomon was swiping at my heels.

'I'm going to teach you a lesson you'll never forget,' he raged, before dragging me into the upstairs bedroom. I had been shocked by his sudden advances before, but this time I knew what was coming.

'No,' I shouted, slapping him across the face.

His eyes flashed in disbelief, but his smile only widened. He grabbed my wrist, pinning me against the bedroom wall as he kissed me hard on the lips. Screaming at him to get off me, I drew my knee up sharply against his groin. He gasped in pain as the blood left his face, and I took the opportunity to squirm free, running out onto the landing. But he clawed at me on the top of the stairs, pulling me back by my ponytail.

'I'm pregnant, you bastard!' I screamed, jerking away from him. I took a step back, and in that split second the world seemed to turn in slow motion. I could tell by his face that he was scared as I lost my footing and fell backwards from the top stair. My skull thumped against the step on the way down, and everything went dark.

When I awoke, Solomon was leaning over me, with a cool damp cloth on my forehead. Concern was etched on his face, the shock of my fall taking the heat from his temper. I wondered how long I had been lying there. He did not seem in any hurry to bring me to the hospital.

Telling me not to move, he pressed the cloth against my face. His voice was soft, almost comforting. 'You've had a nasty tumble, falling down the stairs like that. You gave me quite a fright.'

My head was throbbing. I felt like I had been run over by a steamroller. But I was more concerned about getting out of the house. My mouth was dry and the words came slowly as I asked him to get me to the hospital. Solomon bit his bottom lip as he decided my fate. I could see he was in turmoil about what to do with me.

'No,' he replied. 'Not after what happened today. I just can't trust you anymore,' he added, crocodile tears filling his eyes. 'Is it true? Are you really pregnant?'

'Yes.' I nodded, his image blurring as tears welled in my eyes. Or at least I was. How could a baby survive my fall?

But Solomon was too busy shifting blame to think about getting help. 'Why do you have to ruin everything by making me so angry? You're pregnant. You could have broken your neck falling down those stairs. What would people have thought? And the worst of it all is that I can't even bring you to the hospital, because I'm too scared of the lies you'll tell.'

There was no point in arguing. Solomon genuinely could not see how he was at fault.

'I'm sorry,' I croaked, not wanting to anger him. I was too vulnerable in my present state. I tried to move, and a slice of pain on my left side made me wince. 'I think I might have broken something.'

But my complaint fell on deaf ears, and Solomon heaved me to the sofa instead. A doctor was called, on the condition that I tell him it was an accident. The man seemed partially deaf, which was not surprising, given the growths of hair spurting from his ears. I wondered if he was still practicing, or another one of Solomon's father's old friends. He said I did not appear to have any broken bones, although he advised getting my ribs X-rayed to be on the safe side – that's if they would give me an X-ray, given my condition. I knew that while I was in the confines of my home I could not just blurt out what had happened. Solomon was unbalanced, and I would not have put it beyond him to hurt the doctor and cover it up too. The pregnancy test he gave me came up positive, but he informed us that pregnancy hormones can last for days after a loss, and I needed to have a scan. The exchange of money between them made me think his visit might not be noted on any records.

Solomon told anyone that called that I had fallen down the stairs after taking an overdose. I could not believe he managed to convince my old colleagues that I was suicidal. He then rang his workplace and said he needed to work from home for some time, because I could not be left alone. I thought about what Solomon had been going to do before I managed to get away, and shuddered. For now, he would be the doting boyfriend, buying me flowers and tending to my every need. We agreed not to mention the baby until I had the three-month scan. It gave enough time for my bruises to go down, and if I miscarried before that, then we would have our answer. That was Solomon's way of thinking, anyway. At least I was safe from his violence. That is, until his demons grew restless, and I angered him again. They were buried deep inside him, and each time they made an appearance, he went that little bit further. It was only a matter of time before he ended up killing me. It turned out that Solomon had found out about my phone call to the refuge, because he had set up hidden cameras in the house. His half-hourly calls were just a mind trick, he told me, because he had been monitoring me all along. It was stupid of me not to have realised, particularly given his technological expertise. He was able to watch me from his desktop, and on the day I'd made the phone call, he had been listening with his headphones as he worked. Lots of people in his office listened to music, although it must have come as quite a shock when he heard my phone call to the refuge. He had rushed out with an excuse, and boarded the train at Kelvedon.

He didn't apologise for what he'd done. He simply put it down to me winding him up, when all he wanted to do was love me and make me happy. I was ungrateful and stupid, getting in the way of our happiness, and risking our baby's life. It was like living with two different people. Most of the time he was loving and attentive. We even made love a couple of times, and I know that if I tried to explain that, nobody would understand. I had to make Solomon believe that I was sorry for his perceived betrayals, and that I was trying to change. But I never stopped believing that I could get away.

Solomon finally returned to work, reminding me that the cameras were in place and leaving me with no money. A couple had placed an offer on my house, and he seemed to feel more secure, now that he knew his plans were coming to fruition. Soon I would be living in Frinton with his parents, and he talked about setting up his own business so he could work at home full-time. I decided to make the most of my time in Mum's house, and threw my energies into making Solomon happy, at least until another opportunity to leave arose. I clung on to the hope that it would, although I tried hard not to think of the baby. I had to convince him that I was totally submissive. We even planned our wedding for the following spring. Maybe he wanted to believe the dream so badly he was willing to set aside any reservations for his perceived fantasy of a normal family life.

I was peeling potatoes when the doorbell rang, preparing roast dinner with all the trimmings. I seemed to spend half my life in Marigolds. I knew what was coming, as he had asked me to paint my nails red before he left for work that morning. I hated it. I hated the sex that was easier to agree to than being beaten for kicking up a fuss. I hated the precision with which our lives were timed, and most of all I hated him for turning me into the pathetic worthless shell of a person I had become. The loss of my mother had brought me to my lowest point, and Solomon enjoyed grinding me down even further, using me as nothing but a plaything to satisfy his needs. He told me he loved me ten times a day. But it was a love I would be glad to do without.

The doorbell rang a second time. I knew he would be watching me on the CCTV, so I glanced over to the camera and shrugged as if to say that I was not expecting any visitors. There were three cameras in the house that I knew of, disguised as portable air fresheners so they could be moved around. Daring to touch one would result in a punishment too severe to contemplate, so I left them be, painfully aware of my silent watcher.

'Jake,' I exclaimed, as I pulled back the door. 'I wasn't expecting to see you. Everything all right?' I said, surprised to see my teaching colleague wiping his feet on my welcome rug. He had been to my address just once before, when I had offered him my sofa after a work drinks night out.

'I was passing, so I thought I'd drop by,' he said, a hint of beer on his breath. He was dressed casually, wearing jeans and a sweater, and I patted down the creases in my linen trousers, realising I must have looked a state.

'Would you like to come in?' I asked, hoping he would say no.

'I'd love to,' he smiled, eyeing my rubber Marigolds and asking if I was doing the washing-up.

I covertly glanced up at the camera as he followed me into the kitchen. 'I'm peeling potatoes for dinner. You don't mind if I carry on, do you? I'm expecting my fiancé home in an hour and he likes to have it on the table when he comes in.' I hoped Solomon would be pleased at the mention of his status in our relationship. But I never imagined how a simple visit from a colleague would end. In twenty minutes, Jake would be dead.

CHAPTER
FIFTY-NINE
REBECCA

2016

I pored over my notebook as I sat at the table. I could not believe I had come this far. Six horrible crimes and four more left to witness. Thinking of some of the innocent victims made me want to cry. And then there was Mrs Kemp, living in squalor. But the Kemps hadn't been badly off. Was Solomon controlling their finances? Forcing her to live in poverty? The empty cans, her tattered clothes. I vowed to help her when this was all over. But I had to tread carefully, focus all my attention on getting to the end, without my family paying the price. I had a feeling that murder would feature as the tenth crime, and it made sense that grievous bodily harm would come into play. But I did not know what the other crimes could be. There was always the possibility of rape, or serious sexual offences. The thought of nominating a victim made my stomach churn. That was how Solomon liked it, being one step ahead and all thoughts focused on him. But his attendance at the hotel had come as a surprise. Was he growing in confidence because I had not called the police? Each crime put him at greater risk of being caught, which explained why he was rushing towards the final act of revenge. Would he kill himself after he had killed me? Is that what he had planned? No. He was more likely to go on living, if only to find some new conquests to satisfy his warped cravings.

I was exhausted from the emotional rollercoaster of the last few weeks. Sean and I were slowly getting back to ourselves, and all mention of Chloe had ceased. I could not take her on, as well as everything else going on in my life. The notifications were relentless, and I had barely recovered from my drive home from Frinton before the phone buzzed in my pocket again. Sean made a quip about asking for my money back, and it had taken me several seconds to realise he was talking about the spa. I had come home looking more frayed and stressed than when I left. Having found some privacy, I swiped the phone screen, holding my breath as I read the next text.

```
Victim  number  seven.  Grievous  Bodily
Harm.

Sean Walker or ?

Enter target here  _____

This  will  default  to:  Sean  Walker  if
incomplete.

You have twenty seconds to decide.

00:19
```

It was almost a relief when the text came. As scared as I was, I just wanted it over with. And it was no surprise to see Sean nominated. As if I would witness that. Grievous bodily harm could be anything short of murder. But it physically pained me to type in my nomination. GEORGE FAIRSHAW. HOMELESS MAN. My reserve name. I told myself that he would be numbed by the alcohol, incapable of feeling pain. Going to hospital would probably do him some good. They would wash him, provide him with a bed and a warm meal, perhaps even call his relatives, who could help him turn his life around.

But who did I think I was kidding? I was serving this poor man up on a plate. Tears welled in my eyes as I pressed send. The sick feelings of disgust and revulsion swept over me like a wave. I was still getting flashbacks to my past, and the terrible things Solomon had made me do when we were an item. I took a deep breath as I tried to pull myself together. I'd got this far, and after this there were just three more to go. But I couldn't see how he could do it without being caught. There were too many witnesses in town, which could end up with him, or a hired hand, back in prison. But Solomon had a way of getting what he wanted. Just how did he get footage of Sean and Chloe? Had he installed cameras in Chloe's house? Was he watching me too? Such a possibility had played on my mind since visiting his mother in Frinton. But I had inspected every inch of my home, unable to find any such technology. And the idea of Solomon fiddling with our burglar alarms seemed silly, now I was home. They were dotted throughout the house. Fitting a camera in each one would take considerable time. How could anyone spend that long under our roof without being discovered? Unless . . . Standing with my arms folded, I glared up at the white plastic box that was meant to keep us safe. A small green light peered like an unblinking eye from its casing, and my hand silently rose to my mouth. Of course. Why hadn't I thought of it before? The visit from XLR Security. The offer that had conveniently arrived just as the nightmare began.

I imagined Solomon on the other side, his gloating smile, daring me to smash each one. But I couldn't, because Sean would ask too many questions. All the times I'd thought Solomon was watching from the outside, and he had been in our home all along. Anger bloomed from within. I grabbed the broom as my outrage rose, digging my fingers into the wooden handle. Raising it above my head, I prepared to swipe. Then I heard the footsteps behind me.

'Mummy? What are you doing?'

It was Lottie. And she took the momentum out of my sails. 'Just getting rid of a cobweb.'

'Don't hurt the spiders, Mummy, they might have babies.'

'I think they've moved on, sweetie,' I said, warmed by her love of animals, big and small. Like a little doll, she looked so vulnerable, screwing up her face as she looked for creatures that weren't there. Satisfied with my explanation, she trotted off with Bear to play another game. I sighed. I wanted to scoop her up and drive away, somewhere Solomon would never find us. But I had run away once already. This time I had to stand up and fight. I riffled in the drawer, pulling out a roll of masking tape. Then, balancing on a chair, I tore off a strip with my teeth and covered it over the hole in the alarm. Were our burglar alarms really being used to secretly record us? Maybe not. But I would not rest until they were all covered up.

Twenty minutes later Lottie ran in alongside a disgruntled Bear, who was tripping over a princess cape neatly Velcroed around his neck. Long strings of dog drool hung from his jaws, and I quickly caught them with a tissue, untying the cape.

'He won't play. Tell him he has to play, Mummy.'

'Darling, you need to be gentle with him, treat him nicely,' I said, brushing the dog hairs from the pink velour.

'But I *am* kind, Mummy, I let him be Princess Anna,' she said, having bestowed the greatest honour of all.

'Yes, but you're a little girl and he's a doggie. They don't like playing dress-up. Did you have a nice time down the park today?'

It was one of the few occasions I was happy for her to go out with Rhian. She was going stir crazy inside, and I had consoled myself that if I was tied up with Solomon, then at least he could not hurt my family.

'I had ice-cream,' she said, skipping around the kitchen in her stocking feet.

'Yes, I know,' I said flatly. The evidence had been sorely apparent down the front of her new dress. 'Come on, bath and bed.'

I surveyed each room as I made my way upstairs, looking for hidden cameras, checking the locks on the doors and windows for the tenth time that day. Bear seemed to sense my unease as he waited outside the bathroom door for Lottie to finish her bath. Sean had offered not to leave, but I knew it was silly, getting suspicious each time he did his job. Besides, I had taken the call myself. Tanya McGuire was an experienced horsewoman, and would not have requested his presence unless her mare was in trouble.

I was sitting on the sofa, with Bear warming my feet, when the return notification came through. I wondered if Solomon varied the response times just to wind me up. I swiped the phone, then lay it face down on my lap, needing a few seconds to gather my strength before taking it in.

CHAPTER SIXTY
REBECCA

2016

```
Notification number seven. Grievous Bodily
Harm.

George Fairshaw

Tomorrow at 9am.

The precinct.

You are a Silent Witness.

Talk to police and you die.
```

I frowned. Nine in the morning? In town? Was that some kind of mistake? Sean's keys rattled in my front lock, and I jumped up to answer, remembering I had pushed the bolt across. 'Sorry,' I said. 'I forgot I locked the door.'

'You gave me a fright,' he said with a sheepish grin. 'I thought you'd changed the locks and kicked me out.'

I drew my husband in for a kiss, allaying his fears. I could smell the sweet tang of horseflesh and antiseptic on his skin. 'Successful delivery?' I said, when we came up for air.

'Yes, a gorgeous little filly. Gave us quite a fright she did, but she's doing just fine now.'

'Good. How about you get a nice hot bath, and I'll make you a late-night snack.'

'Thanks, love,' he said, a depth of emotion behind his eyes. I knew he was talking about more than the food.

I endured another bone-rattling ride as I drove to the precinct the next morning. My scooter had developed a debilitating rattle, a consequence of my late-night excursions in the Welsh hills. I promised myself I would buy a new one when all of this was over, then felt a pang as I realised there were no guarantees I would still be alive.

Lottie was with Rhian at the surgery, and I left under the guise of needing a few things in town. The morning chill crept under my clothes, and I braced myself for what was to come. Solomon was set to surprise me again, and I had no idea how he was going to get away with carrying out such a serious assault in front of the morning shoppers in town. We were heading for a showdown, and within the next few days, it would surely all be over. I switched off the ignition before dismounting my bike. It was time to witness a man being beaten for something that was not his fault, but mine.

I peered in Oxfam's window as I pretended to window-shop. But, in reality, I was checking the reflection for any signs of Solomon across the street. As usual, he was nowhere to be seen. Was his heart hammering in his chest like mine? Or was he excited at the thought of inflicting more pain? Taking a few more steps, I caught sight of George on the other side of the road. He was lying in his customary position: sprawled on the pavement with an empty bottle of whisky under his arm. My pulse quickened as I checked my phone. It was almost time. A smattering of people ambled down the street, too engaged in conversation to notice George. Should I cross the road? And where was Solomon? George siphoned off the last of his booze, then lifted his head as he was approached by a member of the Salvation Army. I faltered as I stepped off the kerb. The Salvation Army man crouched down beside him, offering him a small box of food. I squinted. It couldn't be. But the tall bearded man appeared familiar. He was a person I had met before. An image flashed in my mind: me standing outside Nigel Evans's home as a bearded man growled at me to leave. I nibbled my lip, putting it down to paranoia. The intruder was wearing a balaclava then. There was no way I could identify him by his stature and the colouring of his facial hair alone. Yet there was something about his presence that was darkly foreboding. Cars drove by and shoppers chatted, oblivious to the fact that a potential crime might be about to play out before them. I needed to get closer. To hear the sound of his voice. I watched with horror as the pair of them spoke, George nodding his head, seemingly pleased at the offering. Then I noticed the man's black leather gloves, and the quick darting movement as his hand jerked from underneath his coat, shielded by the box of food. He was holding something, but I was too far away to see. I waited for a break in the traffic before crossing the road. But I was too late. Their interaction was coming to an end. But where was the crime? I had expected punching and kicking. Violence capable of inflicting real harm.

I watched the bearded man walk away after bidding George a cheery goodbye. Was that it? I checked my watch. It was five minutes past the deadline. I licked my lips, barely daring to hope. Perhaps he had thought better of it, and called the whole thing off. Maybe I had got things wrong and, just this once, everything was going to be all right. Relief washed over me, but it was quickly followed by another thought. Where did that leave Sean? It was only as I walked past that I heard the wheeze escaping George's lips. A small pool of blood trickled down the pavement, and I quickened my pace as I pretended not to notice. The bearded man was just feet in front of me, and threw a glance over his shoulder to check I had not stopped to help. The tone of his voice and darkness of his eyes left me in no doubt. It was the same man from the burglary. But Solomon must be watching the scene play out. It made the hairs prickle on the back of my neck as I sensed his presence nearby. My heart thundered in my chest as the seriousness of the situation struck home. Glancing at the flats above the shops, I crossed the road for a second time, trying to contain the scream building up in my throat. Was he up there, watching from behind a net curtain? And what about George, leaking blood on the pavement? I could not be the one to call the emergency services. There, in the full view of shoppers, help was bound to come soon. But George had been sickly to begin with, and there were no guarantees he would come out of this alive.

CHAPTER
SIXTY-ONE
REBECCA

2016

It was torture, trying to carry on as normal as I waited to hear what had happened to George. The local news was yet to report any incident, and I wondered if it was due to his status in the community. But Pontyferry was a small town, and it was only a matter of time before the jungle drums started beating. I even convinced myself that I imagined the blood, until I popped into our nearest newsagent's for the evening paper.

The owner of the small narrow shop had made use of every inch of floor space, and a sweet tang of confectionery hung in the air like a fine mist. On one side were newspapers and magazines of every variation. To the right were bags of crisps, fizzy drinks, and boxes of chocolates. Paying for the paper, I flicked through the first couple of pages, my frustration mounting as I tried to find news. I wondered if I dared walk to George's old spot, when the newsagent called me back to give me my change. He was a short, dour-looking man, but his eyes lit up at the mention of gossip.

'Have you heard about what happened in town?' he asked. 'Nasty business that.'

'What happened?' I said, scoping the shop for CCTV. I reminded myself it was not against the law to gossip, and I should calm the hell down.

'The homeless fella on the precinct. Somebody stabbed him this morning. In broad daylight. And do you know what they used? A meat thermometer. What would possess anyone to do that?'

'God, that's awful,' I said, imagining the short metal spike. The perfect instrument for causing damage to internal organs.

'Pierced his lungs, so he couldn't cry out for help. It wasn't until the blood started seeping down the path that someone called for an ambulance. I don't know what the world's coming to.'

I peered at the paper, which mentioned nothing but a wounding. 'How do you know all this?'

The newsagent tapped a finger beside his nose and leaned over the counter, speaking in a whisper. 'My sister's one of the nurses treating him. It's very serious. He was living on borrowed time as it was, with all his health problems. You'd never think that he served his country, would you?'

'He did?' I asked, thinking that I was unable to feel any worse than I already did.

'Oh yeah, he was a war hero, won medals for gallantry. And now look at him, getting stabbed on the street. Very strange indeed.'

'I gave him some money once.' It was all I could think of to say. To imagine George being used as a pawn in a game that I started made me sick with remorse. 'Has he got any family?' I said, hoping that perhaps something could be rescued from this awful situation.

'A wife, but she left him a long time ago,' he replied. 'I should ring the newspaper up and fill them in,' he added, forgetting his earlier signal for discretion. 'Maybe I could make a collection for him, to help him through.'

I riffled in my purse. 'That sounds like a lovely idea. Here, this can start you off.'

Pushing ten pounds into his hand, I said goodbye before leaving his shop. Squeezing through a gaggle of students, I walked outside, filling my lungs with fresh air. George had been lying there as I stood by and watched. He was a war hero who had been reduced to a piece of gossip. And I was a vulture, hovering over his carcass.

I was grateful to see that Sean had cooked supper for us. I guessed he'd had enough of my recent burnt offerings. With so much going on, I just could not concentrate on anything for very long. Thoughts of the next notification made my head spin. As much as I had vowed to stay strong, Solomon had regained full control. But the game was not over yet. I would spend the rest of my life making it up to the victims if I had to: Margaret, George, Gareth, and the rest of them. I would be a better person when all of this was over. I had to be.

'Did you hear about that homeless man getting stabbed in the precinct?' Sean said, carving the lamb at dinner. It smelt delicious, and Lottie sat with her plastic knife and fork in hand as she awaited a helping.

'Yes,' I said, unable to meet his eye. 'It must have happened just after I left. He's a war hero, apparently.' I wondered if it was wrong to speak about this in front of our four-year-old child, but she seemed too preoccupied with her food to notice our conversation.

'They're putting together a collection in his memory, giving the proceeds to Help for Heroes.'

A cold chill ran down my spine. 'Memory? He's in hospital, isn't he?'

'He died,' Sean said, shaking his head. 'I don't know what this place is coming to, I really don't. Hand us your plate, love. I'll dish up your lamb.'

Home-made Yorkshire puddings, honey-glazed carrots, and crispy roast potatoes. Any other time I would have wolfed the lot. But my mind was on the death of an innocent man. One I had offered up.

'Thanks,' I said, my world collapsing around me as I passed over my plate.

'Are you OK?' Sean said. 'You've gone very pale.'

I forced a smile onto my lips, taking back my meat-laden plate. 'It's just a headache, nothing to worry about.'

'Do you want me to cancel the conference?' he asked. 'You're not worried about Chloe turning up, are you? It's just that I've spoken to Gareth and apparently they're making another go of their marriage.'

I responded with an involuntary snort. Chloe was the least of my worries, although at some point in the future we would be having words. One day, when this was all over, Sean and I would go away for a weekend, put our marriage back together, and I would make things right.

The thought gave me comfort, and I placed my hand over his, drawing strength from the warmth of his skin. I wanted him to go to the conference. Far away from Pontyferry, surrounded by people and cameras, the London Vet Show seemed like a safe place, and Sean's absence would give me the freedom to finish off what Solomon started here.

'No, I want you to go,' I said, truthfully. 'You've been looking forward to this for ages. I'm fine, honestly. It's just a headache. It'll clear soon. Now, what's for pudding?'

'Pudding,' Lottie piped up, and I leaned over to wipe a dribble of gravy from her chin.

CHAPTER SIXTY-TWO

Diary Entry: 12th December 2006

You come into this world alone, and you go out of it alone. As soon as you make peace with that, the sooner you learn there's no point being afraid. These are the things I told myself as I gathered my strength to start my life again. Giving evidence at the murder trial was one of the toughest things I've ever had to do. Solomon fought all the way, but I rejected the offer of screens and video interviews, choosing to stand tall and face him in court instead. I wanted to tell him that all this time he had been wrong, because he didn't know me at all. I was stronger than him and would not allow him ownership over my life anymore. Thankfully, I was in the capable hands of Bronwyn Maddox, the police detective investigating the case. We spent a lot of time together in those early days, and she was not in the least bit put off by the fact that Solomon's father was a superintendent in the police. The fact Solomon's parents did not attend the trial came as a shock to us all. And although Solomon had terrified me during our time together, I could not help but feel pity when his family refused to support him. I guess a little bit of me still cared about the man I met on marathon day. And as for Jake – it was all so tragic, the senseless waste of a life.

I used to torture myself with *if only* thoughts as I lay in bed at night. If only Jake had not come to my house that day, if only I had never met Solomon. Mum, Selina, Jake, they all suffered because of our toxic relationship and my bad life choices. I surprised myself by being able to return home once the police were finished with the house. Bronwyn helped me organise some deep cleaners, who scrubbed away the blood. But it was still there in my mind's eye, and at night the flashbacks would come, with sounds, smells, and emotions rich in colourful imagery. I tried filing it away in my brain, along with all the other ugly memories, too scared to return to my lowest ebb. How I got through those early days I do not know. I suppose I was a lot stronger than I give myself credit for. Bronwyn had told me that the jury were swayed by seeing me in the dock, scared and confused, my sobs echoing around the chambers.

Solomon had stared unblinkingly, his eyes full of hatred and blame. But he had no power over me now, and all I wanted to do was to start my life again. I would always carry guilt for my part in things, but I knew that if it had not been me, then Solomon would have met somebody else and made their life a misery too. He had to be stopped, one way or another, and I was the only person to do it. I remember holding my breath as the jury came back with their decision. After being battered in the witness box, I had wondered if perhaps he would be freed. If he was, I was as good as dead.

When the verdict came in, I was overwhelmed with relief. He was found guilty for murder, and I was finally free. On the evening of the verdict I cropped my hair and dyed it back to its natural brown. Then I packed up my belongings and left. I did not give any thought to what Solomon would do when or if he got out of prison. Sometimes you hear about people turning to God and finding the error of their ways, but I was not so naive that I thought this would be the case. So I started again, shortening my name and changing my appearance. I had no intention of starting another relationship, but as my mother used to say, 'How do you make God laugh? You tell him your plans.'

CHAPTER
SIXTY-THREE
REBECCA

2016

I did not make a big fuss of waving Sean away the next day. The last thing I wanted to do was to draw attention to the fact he was leaving. We kissed in the hall, and I looked over his shoulder as he opened the door, waiting expectantly for Rhian to return with Lottie. Their trip to the riding school in Shrewsbury had become a regular event and, as much as I tried to dissuade it, Sean had insisted that they go.

'She's not due back yet, relax,' Sean said. 'I was thinking, we could buy her a little pony if this all works out, give her a sense of responsibility.'

'We already have a little pony,' I said dryly, casting my glance down at our oversized dog. 'Besides, I'd prefer to spend the money on a new scooter.'

'We'll see,' Sean said. 'I'll ring you when I get there. Tell Lottie I'll bring home something nice.'

'Make sure you do,' I said, closing the door behind him.

At least Rhian had been kind enough to agree to stay with Lottie for the hour, then bring her straight home. Sean's old banger had given up the ghost after my trip to Essex, and he needed his Land Rover for the journey. I checked Solomon's phone for the tenth time. There were three crimes left, and one of them was bound to be murder. The more I thought about it, the more I realised I had made a mistake, giving in to Sean's wishes to let Lottie go. I would barricade us in if I had to. She was not leaving the house again until this whole sorry mess was over. I picked up my phone and dialled Rhian's number. Straight to voicemail. But then it would, if she was driving. I placed both phones on the table, side by side. The one on the left lit up as it buzzed. It was Solomon's phone.

```
Victims number eight & nine. Kidnapping.

Lottie & Rhian Walker or ?

Enter targets here _____

This will default to: Lottie & Rhian
Walker if incomplete.

You have ten seconds to decide.

00:09
```

My hand flew to my mouth. This was not meant to happen. How was it even possible? And how was I meant to choose a replacement? I didn't know of any double targets to nominate and, even if I did, I couldn't type their names . . . could I? The strength left my legs and I fell back onto the kitchen chair, watching horrified as the clock counted down. I jabbed in my own name as a last-ditch attempt, but had only got to REBEC— when the clock expired.

'Bastard!' I screamed, making Bear raise his head. With ten seconds on the clock, Solomon had set me up to fail. It couldn't happen. I wouldn't let it. As if I was going to witness my own child and sister-in-law being kidnapped. I'd kill him if I had to, but he wasn't hurting my family.

I waited for the notification to come through with a time and place. I would barricade Lottie and Rhian in if it came to it. We'd come to the end of the line. I was not playing his games anymore. But I should have known that Solomon had pre-empted my reaction. The phone beeped, sending me into a tailspin. I blinked away anxious tears, focusing on the words. My mind galloped ahead, imagining Solomon coming to steal my daughter in the dead of night. I read the words, and emitted a howl of despair.

```
Notification number eight & nine. Kidnapping.

Lottie & Rhian Walker.

Complete.

You are a Silent Witness.

Talk to police and they die.
```

Complete? What did he mean, *complete?* How was that possible? Where were they? My head spun as I took in the possibilities. Talk to police and *they* die. But of course I was going to call the police. Their safety took precedence over everything. I had to warn Rhian. Tell her to go to the nearest police station and wait. My hands shook as I dialled her number. No answer. Where the hell was she? Had he really taken them both? But how? My finger hovered over the dial pad. I was calling the police. What choice did I have? I had pressed the number nine just as his phone buzzed, making me jump out of my skin. I took in the words, and everything became clear.

CHAPTER
SIXTY-FOUR
REBECCA

2016

Final Victim number ten. Murder.

Sean Walker or ?

Enter target here _____

This will default to: Sean Walker if incomplete.

You have thirty seconds to decide.

00:29

He had proposed my husband, but the time had been extended, meaning he had a bigger target in his sights. *Why nominate Sean when he was away in London?* I thought. Perhaps he knew I would never allow it. Deep down, I had known it would always come to this. I typed in the name and awaited further notification.

The response was quick, and no doubt he was pleased. This was all my fault, and it was up to me to sort it out. I could scream and wail later. Right now, I had to keep a clear head. I had the biggest fight of my life ahead. Not for me, but for the lives of those I held most dear.

```
Notification number ten. Murder.

Rebecca Walker.

Today at 5pm.

Clacton on Sea.

Remember, I'm watching.

Talk to police and Lottie & Rhian die.
```

Clacton? Where we used to live? Of course. Cold fear gripped me as I realised he was taking me back to the scene of the murder, when everything changed. At least for now, Lottie and Rhian were safe. He would not harm them until he saw me first. Despite her disability, Rhian would have fought back. Just how could he take them both in broad daylight? Unless he was bluffing. I reread the message. *Remember, I'm watching.* I stood, gathering all of my strength, dealing with a ghost I could not see. I tried Rhian's phone again, but still no response. My hands itched as I tried to figure out what to do. The urge to call the police was uncontrollable.

I jumped up on the chair, and ripped the tape off the nearest alarm.

'Watching, are you?' I shouted to thin air. 'Well, fuck you!' I drove my middle fingers through the air. 'How about that, Solomon? Fuck you. I'm not going anywhere until I hear from my daughter. Do you hear me? Put her on the phone. I want to speak to her now.'

I took a deep breath as I awaited a response. Solomon couldn't really be watching me. How could he do both – monitor me *and* drive to Clacton with my daughter? Besides, she would never go with him in the first place. The idea was ridiculous. He was playing with my mind, just as he had when I met him. Any minute now Lottie and Rhian would walk in the door and—

The phone buzzed against the table, and I spun around to answer the call.

'Hello?' I gasped, hoping it wasn't a call about PPI or some other nonsense.

'Hello, Rebecca, or should I call you Becky?' Solomon's voice made my breath stop, and I grabbed the chair for support. I spun around the room, staring up at the four walls, feeling like a rat in a cage.

'Where's my daughter, Solomon? What have you done with her?'

I heard the rush of traffic in the background, and prayed he was just bluffing. 'All in good time. Oh, and my name's Luke. I'm Rhian's boyfriend. Good to meet you at last. You have a beautiful daughter, quite the chatterbox.'

Luke? But Rhian had said her boyfriend had blue eyes, and Solomon's were grey. I bit down hard on my bottom lip, cursing my complacency. I should have known. Solomon could overcome anything when he set his mind to it. My mind fell into confusion as I tried to understand. Luke was Solomon. He had dated her to get to me.

'Look. You've taught me a lesson. Please . . . just let them go. Lottie's only a child.'

Solomon replied in a cheerful voice. 'I'd love to stay and chat but I believe you have somewhere to be. Now I'll just let Lottie have a quick word.' He lowered his tone to a menacing whisper. 'If you say one word to upset her, you'll be sorry.'

'OK' was all I could say.

'Hello, Mummy,' Lottie said, excitedly. 'We're going to the beach! Luke's going to buy me some more ice-cream.'

'That's wonderful, darling,' I replied, as I fought back the tears. 'Are you OK? Where's Auntie Rhian?'

'Rhian's asleep. She's tired.'

'Where are you now, darling?' But all I heard was movement as the phone was taken from her hand.

'Say bye-bye to Mummy, Lottie. You're gonna see her real soon. Why don't you have a sleep next to Auntie Rhian? That's a good girl.'

'Bye, Mummy,' I heard her say, her words stretched in a yawn.

'Oh dear,' Solomon said. 'Time's running out. Best get yourself over here.'

'Listen to me, you bastard,' I said, my voice trembling as I gripped the phone. 'If you hurt one hair on her head, I'll kill you. Understand?'

Solomon laughed, a chilling sound. I heard a scuffle, and what sounded like a car door opening and closing. I gripped the phone tightly to my ear as the background noise of traffic grew louder.

'Listen to me, you slut. The only reason her and that red-haired bitch are still alive is because I chose to keep them that way. So I don't think you're in any position to be doling out threats, do you?'

Tears were falling freely down my face now, and I gripped the phone as if my life depended on it. 'Please don't hurt my baby. It's me you want.'

'As long as you stay in line, then she'll be returned to her father in one piece. I'm afraid I can't say the same for you. But, then again, you're very good at putting yourself first. If I don't see you at the allocated time – alone – they're both as good as dead.'

'All right,' I said, my voice shaking. 'Please, let me speak to her again.' But our conversation ended abruptly as the call was cut dead.

CHAPTER
SIXTY-FIVE

Diary Entry: 1st September 2010

My dearest journal, this is to be my last entry. I'm sitting here, in my little flat above the newsagent's, packing up my belongings and sorting out my junk. To be honest, I wasn't going to bring you. But I couldn't let you go. Perhaps one day I'll find the strength to destroy my old memories, but for now you serve as a warning and a reminder never to allow anyone to exercise such a level of control over me again.

I feel it fitting to end with a positive note, the new beginnings Mum intended you for. I've met someone, you see, and I feel hope for the future for the first time in years. All the times I dreamt about getting away, I never imagined that I would trust anyone enough to live with them again. Yet here I am, packing up my things to move in with the sweetest man, who presents only one personality, and carries no hidden agendas. As for me, I cannot say the same. Since coming to Wales, I've undergone a reinvention. I'm Becky now, with a whole new life. A scab has grown over the memories of my past, and I have no desire to pick at it and watch it bleed.

My first task when I moved here was to gain financial independence, and not fritter away the money from the sale of my house. Nobody had been more surprised than me at the speed of the sale. I knew little about the new owner, and wondered if it was someone with an interest in the macabre, or someone looking for a holiday home. I told myself it no longer mattered, because I was never returning there again. I first met Sean on my way to a job interview, bumbling around the Welsh valleys on my little Vespa, driving too fast for my own good. The air was thick with summer sun and the smell of the lush green foliage that bordered the winding roads. Such eruptions often come after a sudden shower of rain. It's an alien smell, but a welcome one, a complete contrast to the salt-infused air of Clacton-on-Sea.

Pressing my brakes as I took the bend, I realised too late that the road was slick with rain. I clung to my bike as it skidded into the gravel, grazing my knee as my scooter came down hard. I swore at my own stupidity, and the sting of my injury distracted me from the Land Rover that pulled up behind me. The soft tones of a Welsh accent asked me if I was all right. I wanted to reply that I was far from all right, as the trousers I had bought for my interview were ruined. But I was too suspicious of any man to make small talk, and looked up at him, tongue-tied. Thinking back now, I wonder what he made of it all. I was well known in the village, with my conspicuous polka-dot motorcycle helmet and neck scarf to match. A young Audrey Hepburn, Sean had called me, although I was feeling far from glamorous as he helped me get to my feet. Sucking his teeth, he pointed out the blood running down my shredded trousers. He could have told me off for my bad driving but, instead, he asked if he could check the wound.

He was not a doctor, he said, but a vet. And, I soon discovered, the person interviewing me for the job. He did not raise an eyebrow when I declined to sit in his vehicle. So there, on the side of the road, he dressed my wound. I spoke about my newly found love of Wales, and he talked about his aspirations for his practice. By the time we parted, I had been offered the position. I don't know what the other candidates made of my impromptu recruitment, but falling from my bike was a blessing in disguise. Our time spent working together sparked the beginning of a warm, comfortable relationship, a total contrast to what I'd had with Solomon.

I try not to think about what will happen when he eventually gets released. I don't feel any bitterness towards him anymore, and I hope we can *both* put this behind us. All I can do is to stay strong. Because even killers deserve a second chance at life.

CHAPTER
SIXTY-SIX
SOLOMON

2016

Taking Lottie had been child's play. In fact, Solomon was almost disappointed at how easy it had been. He had surprised Rhian by turning up at the equestrian centre before her. It was somewhere they had visited before, so the staff were not surprised to see him. It was all about trust, and Lottie had begun to feel comfortable in his presence.

'What are you doing here?' Rhian said, walking towards him. She was using her stick today, and the look of discomfort on her face as it wobbled suggested she should be using both crutches instead. Lottie was wearing a pair of jodhpurs and little riding boots. She swung her riding hat from its chin strap as she trotted to the stable.

'Luuuke,' she said, dragging out the vowels. 'Are you here to watch me?' she asked, apparently pleased to see him.

'I am,' Solomon said, tweaking her nose. 'But first I'm going to take your Auntie Rhian for a picnic. You don't mind, do you? We're only going around the corner.'

It did not take long to find a suitable spot in the fields. He spread the chequered blanket on the grass, and opened up the well-stocked wicker basket. There were no crappy Tesco bags and soggy sandwiches from him. Everything had to be perfect if he wanted to lure Rhian in. And besides, she made it so easy, updating all her favourite foods on social media with mind-numbing regularity.

'You shouldn't have gone to all this trouble,' Rhian said, biting into a strawberry as they sat back and admired the views of the hills. 'How did you know I'd be here?'

'You told me,' Solomon said, convincingly. 'Don't you remember?'

Rhian's shrug of her shoulders suggested she didn't.

Solomon handed her a plastic wine glass, and uncorked a small bottle of rosé. 'I thought I'd come over and surprise you. Am I moving too fast?' He began to top up her drink.

'Thanks,' she said, taking a sip of the fizzy pink wine. 'Although it's a bit early for bubbles, and I've got to drive back. Becky will go ape if she smells booze on my breath.'

'Don't worry about that,' Solomon grinned, his artificially blue eyes regarding her coolly. 'I can drive you both back, maybe even pop in to say hello. I thought I could stay overnight at yours, and we could arrange to pick up your car in the morning.' He leaned forward and lightly rubbed his thumb over her jawbone. 'That's if you want me to stay. I'm still waiting for you to answer my question.'

Rhian laughed, knocking back her wine. 'Honey, I can't even remember what you asked me, but you're welcome at mine any time.'

Solomon topped up her glass. 'In that case, let's get this party started.'

By the time they got back to the stables, Rhian was complaining of feeling tired. The drugs he had given her were designed to work within the hour, and he steadied her as he placed a hand around the waist of her dress. They watched Lottie finish her class, Solomon cheering enthusiastically as she rode around the indoor arena.

The beauty of it was that Solomon was able to listen to Rebecca while he was with Rhian. All he needed was his iPhone, the app connected to the CCTV he had installed, and an earphone in one ear.

By the end of the lesson, he knew all about Sean's trip to the London conference, although he wondered how he had missed it in the first place. Probably because he had been watching Mother. The silly old bag had caught the flu, and returned to bed after Rebecca called round. Now she was showing no signs of improvement, and he would have to call in on her when this was all over. She had barely eaten, just rising for the toilet and to replenish her water. He wanted to punish her for letting Rebecca in, but he had taken some pleasure from watching their discomfort as they spoke. He lowered his phone, quickly checking the app before Rhian noticed – not that she would, she was spaced out already. The grainy grey image of his mother's room came into view. The lazy cow was still in bed and had not even opened the blinds. In fact, she hadn't moved all day. A dark grin touched his lips. This day was getting better and better.

The riding instructor grasped Rhian's arm as she handed Lottie over. 'Are you OK, Rhian? You don't look very well.'

'She's not,' Solomon said, steering her away. 'She's been overdoing it lately, you know, with her MS and everything. I'm going to take her home, keep a close eye on her.'

'Home . . . take me home.' Rhian's voice trailed away. Satisfied the stable staff were out of view, he dumped Rhian in the back of the car, throwing her walking stick on top of her.

Lottie waited expectantly outside the car, still buzzing after her lesson. Placing his hands under her armpits, Solomon hoisted her up into his arms. A small gasp escaped her lips, and she looked unsurely at him.

'Do you know what we're going to do now?' Solomon said, cocking his head to one side.

'Go home to Mummy?' Lottie said, shyly.

'No, your mum and I have something much more fun planned. But it's a secret. Are you good at keeping secrets?'

Lottie's eyes sparkled at the prospect of some excitement. She nodded, her riding hat tilting onto her forehead.

Solomon placed her on the ground, and opened the passenger door of the car. 'We're going on an adventure, to the beach. Mummy's going to meet us there.'

'Oh!' she piped up, scooting onto the back seat. 'I love the beach.'

Solomon pulled across the seatbelt and clicked it into place. 'So do I. We can have ice-cream and go on the pier, even play on the sand if you want to. Does that sound like fun?'

'Yes, yes,' she said, wriggling with excitement.

'Auntie Rhian is very tired and needs a sleep. So when we get there, we'll wake her up, and it'll be a big surprise. Would you like that?'

Lottie seemed to mull it over for a few seconds, and then nodded her head.

'Good,' Solomon said, handing her a cushion. 'This is for you to rest your head. You might like to have a little sleep too, because it's a long way away.' He leaned across Rhian, who was babbling some nonsense about getting back to Rebecca. After strapping her in, he placed a pillow behind her head; not for any concern for her welfare, but in case he was stopped by police. He hoped Lottie would sleep too. The last thing he wanted was to listen to her chatter for the next four hours. He hated every inch of her being, and had often fantasised about snapping her little neck. But not before he caught up with Rebecca.

CHAPTER
SIXTY-SEVEN
REBECCA

2016

Salt air filtered through the vents of Gareth's car, and I surrendered to the smell, inhaling it deep into my lungs. Since what happened with Solomon, I hated the scent of the sea. But today I was taking my life back. Solomon was not going to terrorise me anymore. I was early. Twenty minutes early, in fact, and as I found a parking space, I pondered the best course of action.

It had hit me like a sledgehammer when I realised I had no car to drive. It had not even occurred to me that Sean's old estate had refused to start since my previous excursion to Essex. Panicking, I drove to Gareth and Chloe's on my scooter. By then I was so upset, I barely managed to garble the words. Gareth knew I had family in Essex, although I had never spoken openly about my past. Spinning a tale about a sick family member, I pleaded to borrow their car. There must have been something wild in my expression, because Chloe handed me the keys without a single snide comment. And now I was here, sitting parked around the corner from my old house, trying to build up the courage to face the man from my nightmares, the man who had taken my child.

'Sod it,' I said to myself, deciding not to wait another second. My legs felt like jelly as I walked up the path to the house I once called home. It was never what you would call a palace but, as with Solomon's house in Frinton, I was taken aback to see how shabby it had become. Little had changed since the day I moved out. The front garden where Mum used to grow her flowers had now been paved. But the same lace curtains hung from the windows, holes eaten through the pattern Mum had once chosen with care. Tufts of green moss cloaked the roof tiles, and the once-whitewashed walls had now taken on a slushy-green hue. It was sad to see my old home so dilapidated, but I had long since said my goodbyes, and was more concerned with what was within its walls.

Taking some deep breaths, I stood before the door. What was I meant to do? Politely ring the doorbell? And who was going to answer? I would start as I meant to go on, and I rapped my knuckles against the frosted glass, my heart pounding as a tall, dark shadow approached.

'Well, well, so you made it,' Solomon said, grasping my wrist tightly as he stood at the open door. 'Now I suggest you turn around and call your little helpers off. They won't find her here.'

Having Solomon's face in such close proximity to mine made me want to turn and run. I checked his clothes for signs of blood. His chinos and shirt were neatly pressed and, thankfully, blood-free. I guessed he was trying to bluff me, but I snatched away my wrist and pushed past him in the hall.

'I'm alone,' I said, feeling a sense of finality as he locked the door behind me. 'And if you were watching me, you'd know that.'

'In that case, come in . . . make yourself at home. Do you like what I've done with the place?' he said, grinning as he held his arms wide. The drooping wallpaper, the smell of damp plaster – this had stopped being a home a long time ago.

My eyes darted around the hall as I walked into the belly of the house. 'You own this house?' I said, willing my heart rate to slow down.

'Of course. I instructed my solicitor to buy it on my behalf. It's been lying idle all this time. But now you're here, we can fix that, can't we?'

He led me into the living room. It was just as I had left it but, after so many years of neglect, the walls and ceiling bloomed with damp. I cast my eyes to the floor, where the murder had taken place. It was like walking back into the set of a horror movie that I had played a part in many years ago.

'Take off your jacket,' Solomon said, the smile dropping from his face.

I folded my arms over my chest. 'If you think for a second I—'

Solomon snorted. 'Don't flatter yourself. I need to check you for weapons. Arms up.'

I stood with my arms raised as Solomon patted me down. I had been tempted to bring a knife, but that brought a risk in itself, and I would not have put it past Solomon to turn it on my daughter.

'Where are they?' I asked. I was shaking in Solomon's presence. He occupied so many of my nightmares, a part of me struggled to believe he was real.

'All in good time. I would say we're due a catch-up first, wouldn't you?' he replied, the sly smile returning to his face. It was one I had seen many times, when he was gaining pleasure from others' discomfort.

'If you think I'm going to stand here while you play games, you've got another thing coming. I'll rip this house apart to find them, if I have to.'

'Very well,' Solomon said, sliding out his phone. 'But she's not here. She's fast asleep somewhere else, curled up with her Auntie Rhian. Look.' He waved the phone in front of my face. A grey image of their sleeping figures appeared on the screen.

'You've drugged her,' I said, knowing it was the only way of keeping them sedated.

'It was that or tie her up. She'll be returned safely to your husband as soon as we're through.'

'What do you want from me, Solomon?' I said, my fingers curling into fists by my side.

'To finish the game, of course,' he said. 'Isn't that what this has all been about?'

'You've had your murder. That man died. Not exactly playing by the rules, are you?'

'Oh, a spark of defiance. I like it,' Solomon said, reaching out to touch me. 'Remember what used to happen when you defied me? Ah, precious memories.'

His fingers were icy cold as he caressed my throat, invoking chilling memories of the past. I swallowed beneath the strength of his touch, forcing myself to stand my ground. He was pale and drawn, the hardship of his years in prison evident on his face.

I flinched as he caressed the nape of my neck. 'You've cut off all your lovely blond hair. That's a shame. We used to have a lot of fun with it, didn't we, Rebecca?'

Hearing Solomon use my full name in such a context made my skin crawl. Like a predator circling his prey, he was sizing me up, planning his next move. But I stood firm, narrowing my eyes as I glared in response.

'So what's it like sleeping with farm boy?' he said. 'Does he know about your colourful history? Something tells me not.'

'You're pathetic.' I stared up at him, my eyes alight with defiance. 'Don't you think that threat is getting just a little bit old?' I swiped away his hand. 'I'm not afraid of you anymore, Solomon. I'm not the frightened little girl I used to be.'

But my attempts at being strong backfired and Solomon threw back his head and laughed. 'Bravo, what a stalwart performance! But you forget I've been watching your every move. I've seen how scared you've been, running around your house, like a spider in the bath when the tap's turned on. It brought me great joy to see the amount of times you checked the locks on your windows and doors, scratching your head as you wondered just how I was getting in. Would you like to know how?'

He paused for effect, revelling in being the centre of my attention. 'I never imagined you'd fall for the offer of a free security upgrade. And when I came knocking, your husband opened the door and welcomed me inside. He even watched as I installed the cameras in your alarm system, because you told him I was enhancing your security. Just how stupid can you get?' He gave a dry, humourless chuckle.

'Well, you must have been working off sound only, because I covered them up after I figured out what you were up to.'

Solomon laughed. 'Not all of them. But let's not talk about that. You're here now. Back in our home, where you belong. Do you remember that night? That perfect night we spent with your mother? Who would have thought that just hours later she would be dead?'

'I don't want to hear it,' I said, although there was a part of me that felt I should. Who was I to turn my back on my mother's last moments, when I was the one responsible for what had happened to her?

'It's amazing how easy it is to slip in and out of places, if you're wearing the right clothes. Of course, it had helped, being able to go into her room and scope it out. That was so nice of you to let me in, because I might not have been successful had I not been able to check it out beforehand.' Solomon gave me a contemptuous smile. 'I told her that I'd take care of you, as soon as she was out of the way. It's nice to know that she died in the knowledge I'd be here to take over. Don't you think?'

I swiped away my tears, as I envisaged his words. 'You're evil,' I whispered, bitterness and anger rising within. *Death by natural causes*, that's what her death certificate said. But we both knew different. And Solomon was more than happy to point that out. I could see what he was doing, exposing my weaknesses, reeling me into the past. But I was not that person anymore, and I would not give him the power. Whatever had happened to my mother, she would want me to stand up to Solomon and put an end to him once and for all.

I wanted to slap him in the face, to demand he stop this. I took a step back and called Lottie's name, but only silence was returned.

'You've had your fun with me. Now give me my daughter back, so I can take her and Rhian home.'

Solomon lashed out with a backhander, stinging me hard on the jaw and sending me sprawling on the floor. A trickle of blood poured down my chin from my lip.

'I haven't even started with you yet. I think it's about time you were taught a lesson.'

The words chilled me, because I knew exactly what they meant. I scooted back on the floor, picking myself up as quickly as I could.

Solomon stood over me, a salacious smile spreading across his lips.

I tried one more time to appeal to what was left of his better nature.

'Please, Sol, I'm sorry for everything, really I am. But isn't it time just to put all that behind us? You're still young enough to start again. I won't tell a soul. All I want is to get my daughter and go home.'

'But you are home,' Solomon said. 'This is *our* home, full of happy memories.' He tilted his head, and his words frightened me to the core. 'We began our days here, and we will end our days here, together. We could have been so happy, had you not destroyed every ounce of love that we shared.'

'Love?' I blurted out the word in an incredulous laugh. 'You have no idea what love is. You're incapable of feeling it. When you first met me, it was all a lie. You conned me, pretending to be something you're not. All because of this master plan of yours. Trying to fix something that was broken in your life – by breaking me in return. And now look at you, picking on a disabled woman and a four-year-old. Makes you feel like the big man, does it?' I finished, getting to my feet. 'What have they ever done to you?'

A choked scream left my lips as Solomon seized me by the throat. Tilting my jawbone upwards, he forced my gaze on his. 'I'll tell you what your daughter did. She took the place of our child, the child you were carrying when we were together. The child you killed. An eye for an eye, isn't that what the Bible says? You didn't really think I was going to allow you to nominate yourself as murder victim, did you? How can you witness your own murder?'

'No—' I said, gasping for breath as I clawed at his shirt sleeves. 'I won't . . . stand by and watch.'

'Oh, I think you will, because that's the sort of selfish bitch you are. You think nothing of killing a child to preserve your own skin. I spent some time researching abortion,' Solomon said. 'It's quite a brutal process, you know, so I think it's only fair that I afford your daughter the same treatment.'

'It's not true,' I said, heaving for air as he released his grip. I was sweating, despite the chill in the air. The prolonged argument with Solomon was wasting precious time. If only I had called for help. How could I have been so stupid? But there was one small chance for redemption, if not for me, for Lottie and Rhian. It was time to tell the truth. I didn't end the pregnancy – he did.

'I didn't have an abortion. It was *you* who ended it, that night when you punched me in the stomach and I fell down the stairs. When I went to the doctor for my twelve-week scan, they told me the baby inside me had already died. It never progressed past eight weeks, and that was all your fault. I had every intention of keeping it, and starting my life again.'

Solomon frowned, dropping his guard for just seconds as confusion crossed his face.

'I don't believe you,' he said. But the look on his face told me he did. Silence passed between us, and he turned to face the window.

'I lied. They're both in your bedroom. Just take them and go.'

I stared at the back of his head, barely daring to believe the words. It was over. He was setting us free. Even while I was racing up to the bedroom I knew it could be a trap. My bedroom door was a tantalising sight. Nearly there. Just another couple of steps . . . But what if the image he had shown me was old, and Lottie and Rhian were already dead? I burst open the door, filled with trepidation. My heart racing, I stared at the bed in disbelief. Behind me, Solomon's shadow filled the doorway.

CHAPTER
SIXTY-EIGHT
REBECCA

2016

'No!' I cried, my words echoing in the hollow room as I stared at the vacant bed. Strewn across the mouldy duvet was a cheap blond wig, a pair of black lace-top stockings and, on the floor, a pair of red stilettos. I spun on my heel, intent on checking the other rooms.

'Ah ah ah, not yet,' Solomon said, pointing to the stockings. 'If you want to see your daughter, you've got to earn your reward.'

A moan erupted from the other side of the wall. Lottie and Rhian were in the next room.

Solomon checked his watch and tutted. 'We've run way over time, and now it looks like she's waking up. Best you get a move on.'

His voice was devoid of emotion.

I threw him a look of disgust, preparing to push past him. 'So you want sex? Is that what this has all been about? You really think I'm going to allow that, after everything you've done?'

He dipped his hand into the waistband of his trousers, and I stepped back into the room. For in his hand was an old-fashioned revolver.

'I don't think you've got a choice. You see, first I'm going to screw you, so when the police find your dead body, they'll know you came here for sex. Remember that text you sent, excitedly planning this day?' Solomon smiled, as all his scheming came to fruition. 'Then, when we're done, I'm going to shoot the cripple out there and, lastly, your little girl. And then your husband can be like me, wishing he never set eyes on your face.'

My mind swam in fear and confusion. Solomon had lied about his intentions so many times, I could no longer anticipate his next move. He raised the gun and took three steps towards me.

I squeezed my eyes shut, raking in a sudden breath, as cold steel touched my temple.

'Of course, I might just be fucking with your mind. If you're good, real good, I may just let you live. So do as you're told and we'll find out either way.'

I slowly walked towards the bed. Solomon made my flesh crawl, yet one false move and he would pull the trigger. I picked up the stockings, mulling it over. I remembered how lost he got during sex. If I allowed him to feed from my fear, perhaps I could distract him long enough to wrestle the gun away. It looked like an old revolver, probably something he rescued from his parents' loft. I considered the fact that it might not even be loaded. But with Lottie and Rhian next door, I was not willing to take the chance.

'Please, Solomon, don't make me do this,' I said, allowing tears to fall down my face. A shaky voice, a trembling hand, I put them all into action to give off the illusion I was at his mercy. But, inside, I summoned all my anger to the forefront, ready for the fight of my life.

Solomon smiled. 'You've got two minutes. Then I go in there and shoot them both.'

I picked up the stiletto, feeling the weight of the shoe in my hand. It was the nearest thing I had to a weapon, but I couldn't cross the room quickly enough to hurt him. I knew what I had to do. But the thought of being with Solomon made my insides shrivel. I slipped off my pumps and pushed my feet into the stilettos. They were a perfect fit.

Solomon seemed entranced as he watched me put them on. 'The head in my old school used to watch porn, you know,' he said, walking to the window and pushing back the net with the barrel of his gun.

'Every night he watched the same movies, featuring this blond bit wearing nothing but stockings and red stilettos. I guess that's where it all started,' he said, returning his gaze to me. 'You reminded me of those times, both good and bad in equal measure.'

I slipped on the wig and turned to face him, allowing my fingers to fumble with the buttons of my blouse. 'I can't undo the buttons,' I said. 'My hands – they're shaking too much.'

'Oh, for fuck's sake, just pull the damned thing off.' Solomon lunged forward and ripped the front of my blouse.

The letterbox flapped open downstairs, and Solomon froze.

'Becky? Are you in there?' A man's voice shouted from below, and instinctively I opened my mouth to reply. It was Sean. How did he know I was here? And was he alone?

Solomon gripped my mouth, shoving the cold metal of the gun against my cheek. 'Make a sound and I'll shoot you.'

'Becky?' he called again. This was the best chance I had of escape. I lifted my leg and stamped on Solomon's foot, stabbing him with the point of the heel.

'He's got a gun,' I shouted, although the words came out in a garble over the sound of Solomon's scream. He was hopping on one foot, beads of sweat rising on his forehead, which was now flushed red. I had seconds to react, and I grabbed the weapon.

Solomon swivelled from left to right as we both grappled with the barrel of the gun. Trying to get away, he staggered towards the door, and I knew he was heading for the landing to carry out his threat against Lottie and Rhian.

'You stupid bitch,' he said between clenched teeth as I kicked and bit with all my might. 'I was going to spare them. But now you can watch them die.'

'No, I won't,' I said, my heart feeling like it was going to burst as he fought to shake me off. A loud crashing noise filled the air as the front door caved in. Grappling with the gun, I shouted a warning, still clinging to Solomon as I tried to prise his fingers away. Footsteps thundered up the stairs as my husband rushed to find us. My courage faltered. Any second now, he would burst in through the door, and Solomon would shoot without warning. Pushing Solomon against the wall, I sealed the gap between our bodies, winding my finger tightly around the trigger.

'What the fuck?' Solomon whispered, his eyes bulging as they met mine. Our bodies pressed together, the gun jammed under our ribs. My finger wound tighter as I prepared to pull the trigger.

CHAPTER
SIXTY-NINE
REBECCA

2016

'Rebecca, don't do this,' Solomon said, as panic flooded his face. One of us was going to get shot. I was willing to take the chance, as long as it bought Sean some time to save Lottie and Rhian. They were innocent – unlike me – and, as he entered the room, I shouted to him to get Lottie out, praying the sirens I could hear in the distance were coming for us.

But Sean fixed his glare on Solomon, his boots heavy on the carpet as he ran towards us, taking us both down in a rugby tackle. The full force of my husband's weight hit me from the side, knocking the air from my lungs. I gritted my teeth. Solomon's breath was hot on my face as we fought for control of the gun. Sean's insistent hands wriggled between us, trying to take the weapon that could rip my life apart. Perhaps Sean could have stopped him without anyone getting hurt.

But, with the police drawing near, my mind raced ahead to everything that Solomon knew.

I could not allow my husband and daughter to know that I was a murderer. Because it was not Solomon who killed Jake all those years ago. It was me. And if Sean found out I blamed Solomon just to get away, he would leave me, and I would have to start over again. I needed him, Lottie needed him and, after all he had done, Solomon deserved to die. Sean tried to break Solomon and me apart while we rolled around on the damp pink carpet, the gun jammed between our bodies as we fought. I felt his fingers wriggle further in the space between us, and I knew that time was running out.

Everything seemed to stop in that moment, as an alternate future flashed before me. I would never be free while Solomon was still alive. Tilting the gun, I squeezed the trigger, closing my eyes tight. The blast of the shot jerked our bodies backwards. The dull thud of a weapon hit the carpet, followed by a slow pool of fresh blood. But it was trickling from Solomon's body, not mine, and I cried out in relief as I realised I was still alive.

'Becky, oh my God, Becky, are you all right?' Sean said, still on his knees as he pulled me up from the floor. 'Gareth rang. He said you were in a state.'

Sean's words trailed away as he mentioned calling the police. I scrambled from his grip, forcing myself upright. 'The police?' I gasped, remembering the sirens as I raced over to the window. 'They're here.' I shied away from Solomon's body. I knew he was dead.

Sean reached forward to pick up the gun. I should have stopped him, told him to leave it be. But my mind was racing as I thought about my daughter growing up with her mother in jail. I had killed someone for the second time, and I knew what I had to do.

'You shot him,' I gasped. 'You've got to say it was self-defence.'

Sean dropped the gun in horror, his face masked in confusion. 'But I thought . . . I was just trying to get it off him.'

The fog in my mind cleared as Lottie's muffled voice echoed from the next room. 'Mummy? I want my mummy.'

Numerous feet hit the stairwell, bellowing instructions for us to get to our knees. Sean raised his hands in the air, to show he wasn't armed.

I stumbled towards them, forcing fresh tears from my eyes. 'It was self-defence,' I cried, just like before. 'I witnessed everything.'

CHAPTER SEVENTY

Diary Entry: 18th September 2005

I thought I could finish my last entry by leaving it there. Jake's murder was so horrific, and I'm loath to relive it again. Yet I know that I have to rid myself of the truth if I am to find closure. It was only a few days ago, but it feels like a lifetime has passed.

I was at my weakest point. I had been forced to push back the grief I felt for Mum, because Solomon was jealous of any thought that was not focused on him. He would have infiltrated my dreams if he could, and every word from my mouth was measured, so as not to anger him. Repressed anger bubbled beneath the mire of my anxiety. Sometimes it took my breath, surfacing without warning. Lack of sleep caused by incessant worrying made me jittery and nervous. I had lost more weight than was good for me, and the drugs Solomon insisted I take made me light-headed and woozy.

Had I been thinking with a clear head, I would have told Jake I was not up to visitors, instead of asking him inside. It was too much of a risk having another man in the house, even with Solomon watching from a distance. He would not be pleased by this new-found friendship. Jake was young, hot-tempered, a bit of a loose cannon. I often wondered how he had got into teaching, because he was not what you'd call a good influence on the students. He was too fond of alcohol, and would buy booze for the kids hanging around the supermarkets at night. I was sure I could smell beer on his breath as he called at the door. But I was at a low ebb, and found it easier just to let him in. I glanced at the camera, foolishly hoping that Solomon would accept the gesture as an acknowledgement of his presence.

I was certainly aware of the time. Jake remarked that the curtains were closed, and made some comment about a romantic night in. I was used to living in artificial light. I forced a chuckle in response, unable to impart the truth. It was another ploy by Solomon to put off any visitors. Except today it didn't work. Jake followed me into the kitchen, watching me peel the potatoes. He wasn't really registering anything I had to say. He seemed annoyed over something, an incident that had happened at school. I listened to his ramblings as I peeled, nodding and responding in all the right places.

'Listen to me, talking all about myself, when we should be talking about you,' he said, taking a step towards me. 'You know, I've always fancied you, Rebecca. But I imagined you to be prim and proper in the bedroom.'

I blurted a nervous laugh. 'Did you now? Just as well I'm engaged to someone else then, isn't it?'

Jake's eyes roamed over my body. 'So I was quite surprised to see your home movie online. Dirty little minx, aren't you?'

The potato I was peeling bounced into the sink. 'What are you talking about?'

'You know,' he said, his smile broadening as he lay his hands on my hips. 'The clip on the sex site of you having a threesome. I recognised you straight away. Quite the kinky pair, you and your boyfriend, him bringing home a bloke, then watching on. So how many times have you done it? Not up to the job, is he?'

A wave of revulsion passed over me. Had Solomon really shared what happened online? 'How dare you,' I said, jerking back from his touch. 'I don't know what you saw, but you've got it wrong. I want you to leave.'

'Oh, c'mon, it's too late to start acting coy now. Even with the blindfold I could tell it was you,' he said, pinning me up against the kitchen counter. 'So how about it? No one needs to know. I'm good at keeping secrets.'

'Get off me,' I cried, as I tried to wriggle free. But I was no match for his strength, and his grip tightened on my hips. All of the hurt and frustration of the last few months rose inside me. I reached up to the counter and grabbed the knife I had been using just minutes before. 'Out!' I screamed, holding it up. 'Get the hell out of my house.'

Jake stepped back, pausing when we reached the living room. 'Oh, c'mon, Rebecca, you don't want me to go, not really.'

I lowered the knife, my limbs trembling. I was emotionally and mentally exhausted. All I wanted was to be left alone. 'Please, Jake. Just go.'

Jake smiled. But it was a cold smile, and his fingers bit into my flesh as he grasped me tightly by the wrist. He jerked me forward and kissed me hard on the lips. His unshaven face was rough on my skin, and I could taste the alcohol that I had smelt on his breath. But as he wrapped his hands around my waist, fresh anger emerged. He didn't think I had the guts to do it. To him, I was an object, there for his satisfaction. He was just like Solomon. His hands were under my blouse, fiddling with the clasp of my bra as he pressed himself against me. In that second he *was* Solomon, and I had had enough.

A dark mist descended, bringing with it white-hot fury. Pushing him back, I raised the knife and plunged it into his chest with both hands. I felt it tear through the layers of his flesh, and I felt nothing but satisfaction. He was the abuse and pain I had suffered. I had to stop him. I could not take any more.

His eyes grew wide as he staggered back, the knife still embedded in his chest.

Solomon burst through the door just as Jake heaved for breath.

'What have you done?' Solomon said, taking in the scene.

I stepped back, and kept stepping back, until I bumped against the frame of the kitchen door. Solomon rushed to Jake, pulling at the knife, almost falling backwards as he released it from the cavity. Blood spurted out from the wound, hitting Solomon's face and clothes. And all the while my mind was whirring, like the cogs of a tightly wound clock. I hadn't killed Solomon. Because he was still here. What had just happened?

Jake clawed the air, the life leaving his legs as he crumpled to the floor. Flat on his back, he stared up at the ceiling, blood seeping into the mat below. I stared at my shaking hands, but my gloves were devoid of blood. Unable to scream, horror grasped my heart in a cold vice-like grip.

'Call an ambulance,' Solomon said, putting two fingers to the arteries in Jake's neck as the life left his face.

But I was frozen to the spot. It was too late for an ambulance. Jake was dead. 'He . . . he tried to rape me.' The words tumbled from my mouth.

Solomon gasped, surveying the scene for a second time. 'We can fix this,' he said, edging away from the river of blood as it found an exit from Jake's body. Springing up, he ran to the kitchen. 'First, we need to get rid of this.' He grabbed a carrier bag from the kitchen drawer and dropped the knife inside. Numbly, I watched Solomon wash his hands and face in the sink. Drying them on a tea towel, he joined me in the living room, beads of perspiration gathering on his forehead.

'We've got to act quick. I'll hide the knife and get some cleaning stuff, bin bags, stuff like that. We'll get rid of the body and we won't tell a soul.'

I nodded. He rushed into the bedroom and quickly got changed into clean clothes, stowing the knife away in his jacket before heading for the door. 'I'll be back soon. Whatever you do, don't answer the door to anyone.'

But dark thoughts were creeping into my mind, and I knew what I had to do. Solomon had even more power over me now, and it was only a matter of time before I ended up as a problem that needed to be sorted. I had just killed a man. But why should I go to prison for something Solomon made me do? I removed my gloves and shoved them into the drawer. The sound of his car revved outside. I had just minutes to act. I kicked off the heels that Solomon liked me to wear, shoving my feet into my slippers. A small act of defiance to the man I had come to hate, but there was a much bigger one to come.

Pleading self-defence could earn me a reprieve, but Solomon would never let me go. I remembered him saying that the cameras did not record my actions, but streamed them live to his computer. All the cameras would show was what a controlling partner he had been. And there would be other evidence to back that up, as well as the diary I kept hidden away. My call to the refuge, borrowing the estate agent's phone, and details of the doctor who saw me at our home. All diarised in my journal. This was my only chance of freedom. Jake was dead, it was too late for him now, but I still had a chance to be free. I thought of my mother, and how Solomon had ended her life without remorse. There was no proof of that, but she deserved justice. And Solomon deserved to rot in prison. I had my plan. I would tell the police that Solomon had attacked Jake in a fit of jealousy. I would hint that Jake and I had been more than close. My bruises were testament to Solomon's violence, and at the very least I had a cracked rib, which would show up on X-rays. So I smashed my Tiffany lamp to show a disagreement had taken place. Sitting in the darkness, I dialled treble nine and kneeled on the floor beside Jake's body, waiting for the police to show.

I've been writing this on a scrap piece of A4 paper, because my journal is now evidence. It has served its purpose, documenting the intricate details of Solomon's abuse. I've been told that it'll be returned after the court case. But this particular entry will never see the light of day. Only Solomon and I know the truth, and nobody believes him, because of the things he did. But a deeply ingrained habit has driven me to finish what I started. I've changed history, and this is the only true written account. Now I'm going to watch it burn. I might be a murderer, but only because Solomon made me that way, and I deserve the chance to begin again.

CHAPTER
SEVENTY-ONE
REBECCA

2017

The house I shared with my mum remains unsold since Solomon's death. Sometimes I check the website of the estate agent to see if anybody has bought it yet. But two murders in one house is more than bad luck: it hints at evil. Not that I ever want to set foot in it again. My home and heart is firmly in Wales with my family.

I close my laptop shut as Lottie comes running in. Her cheeks are flushed pink, and Bear trots behind her, tongue lolling, looking perfectly happy to have three strings of tinsel around his neck. Sean and I are on a new footing. He has a better understanding of me now. And I understand that I did not need to be ashamed for the things Solomon made me do.

'Is she here yet?' Lottie says, throwing her arms around my torso in a hug. I kiss the top of her soft blond head.

'Soon. You do know those decorations are going in the loft, don't you?'

Despite it being January, Lottie is struggling to let Christmas go.

But, before she can answer, Bear runs to the hall to greet the driver of the car pulling into our yard. They're here. I automatically switch on the kettle and start pulling cups from the dresser.

'They're here, they're here!' Lottie shouts, her voice trailing into the hall. I hear the scratch of Sean's key in the lock, but this time my heart does not pound. I'm safe. And I always will be, because Solomon is gone.

'Have you got me a present?'

I roll my eyes at Lottie's request, but our guest seems happy to hear it.

'Indeed I have, *Mäuschen*, and one for Mummy too.'

'You shouldn't have,' I say to Anna, as she joins me in the kitchen.

It might seem like an odd set-up, Solomon's mother living nearby, but I recognise so much of her in me, and Lottie is enthralled to have a grandmother figure in her life. When the police found Solomon's phone, they also found the app he used to record her movements. Anna was fighting a bad case of the flu, and for a while it seemed like she would be next on the list of Solomon's casualties. Sean never questioned my compulsion to see her through her illness, and it's a delight to have her renting a cottage near our home. Anna has grieved for her son, without laying blame at my door.

The doorbell rings, and I hear the familiar sound of crutches echo through the hall.

'Please tell me that's stollen cake,' she says, as she watches me open the tin Anna has just handed over.

'It might be,' I say, my mouth watering as I inhale the rich scent of cinnamon, raisins, and rum. It's one aspect of Christmas I'm not ready to let go.

Thankfully, Lottie and Rhian are none the worse for their experience with Solomon, although it has made them wary of strangers. But at least I know my daughter will not have to look over her shoulder every time she goes out.

Pictures of my mother grace the mantelpiece in the living room. I can think of her and draw on our happy memories, now justice has been served. I find comfort in the hope that she is all around me. Sometimes, as a gentle breeze floats past, it feels like her fingers touching my hair.

Sean wants us to have more children, but I need to figure out what's right for me. It frightened me, how easily I turned on him when the police arrived. It was not self-preservation that drove me on, but Lottie's voice, calling from the room next door. What if she meets someone like Solomon one day? What if she's too scared to open up and tell people the truth? I vowed that I would always be there for my daughter, but sometimes I frighten myself. Just how far will I go to protect her? I know the answer to that question, and it chills me to the bone.

LETTER FROM THE AUTHOR

Thank you for reading *Witness*. I hope you enjoyed it. The subject of domestic abuse is close to my heart, having spent several years of my career safeguarding high-risk victims and their families. While most victims may not experience such a dramatic turn of events as Rebecca, I hope I have portrayed the strength it takes to escape an abusive relationship, which can be as much about coercive control as physical violence. I would urge anyone in such circumstances to seek help, whether it be through a women's refuge, the police or an outside agency.

If you have enjoyed my writing, I would be immensely grateful if you could write a review. I'd love to hear what you think, and it can also help other readers discover one of my books for the first time. Or perhaps you could recommend it to friends, family or your book club.

I do hope you can join me for my next offering. Until next time.

ACKNOWLEDGEMENTS

Thanks to:

The team at Thomas and Mercer, particularly my editors Jane Snelgrove and Sophie Missing, who have helped bring this book to fruition. It has been a pleasure working with you from day one.

Madeleine Milburn, for being a fantastic agent; also to the lovely Mel Sherratt and Angela Marsons for taking the time to read my first draft and provide encouraging words. Cyllene Griffiths for giving me an insight into the beautiful Welsh landscape.

Friends and family. Thank you for being there every step of the way.

Lastly, to readers, book reviewers and book clubs who have championed my books and enabled me to pursue my dream job of writing full-time. Thank you a million times over. Your support means the world to me.